The Argentine Kidnapping

The Argentine Kidnapping

Bill Sheehy

ROBERT HALE · LONDON

© Bill Sheehy 2010
First published in Great Britain 2010

ISBN 978-0-7090-8994-0

Robert Hale Limited
Clerkenwell House
Clerkenwell Green
London EC1R 0HT

www.halebooks.com

The right of Bill Sheehy to be identified as
author of this work has been asserted by him
in accordance with the Copyright, Designs and
Patents Act 1988

2 4 6 8 10 9 7 5 3 1

Typeset in 11/13¾pt Classical Garamond
by Derek Doyle & Associates, Shaw Heath
Printed in Great Britain by the MPG Books Group,
Bodmin and King's Lynn

PROLOGUE

The bottom line was that Frank Gorman was a small-town banker and kidnapping of any kind was something for the police, not a banker. His first thought when the man sitting across the desk from him said what he wanted was the cliché, 'why me, God?' That caused the banker to frown. People who worked in financial institutions just didn't think that way. No, sir, it just wouldn't do.

When his secretary, Mildred, announced Mr Gussling she had had to remind him who the man was.

'You met with him a few weeks ago, Mr Gorman. Remember, when he came in to open an account. Theodore Gussling. He's some kind of vice-president with Havershack Industries. He and his wife – I can't recall her name – had just returned to San Francisco after having run the company's Buenos Aires office.'

Havershack Industries. Yes, he knew that company, one of the bank's major customers, an international business with offices in the City.

'Ah, yes, now I remember. A self-important sort of man. Somewhat arrogant, I thought.' The secretary's head moved slightly in agreement.

'Hmm.' Gorman frowned. 'Yes, as I recall he and his wife wanted to transfer funds and take out a remodelling construction loan. Did he say what he wanted to see me about? I do hope there isn't any trouble. As I recollect the construction loan was a ninety-day arrangement for the remodelling of their home.'

'That's correct, sir. But no, he didn't say what he wanted to talk to you about.'

'Well, show the man in. Havershack brings a lot of business to the bank. Invite him in, Mildred, and see if he'll have coffee.'

Theodore Gussling didn't want coffee, thank you. He was in a hurry.

'Thank you for seeing me, Mr Gorman,' he said, taking the client's chair and, Gorman saw, sitting on the very edge of the seat. 'I didn't know who else to turn to about this problem and thought of you. When we talked a few weeks ago, you mentioned someone, a man I believe is the kind of man I'm looking for.'

Gorman's welcoming smile faded, being replaced with frown-lines furrowing his forehead.

'I'm afraid I don't understand, Mr Gussling. Does this have to do with the construction loan you took out?'

'No, no, no. It has nothing to do with the bank. No, nothing like that. Let me explain. My wife's been kidnapped. Before, when we were talking, you mentioned something about one aspect of your business. It was a little story about one of your contract employees, the one who is so successful with repossessing cars for the bank.'

'Oh, yes, I vaguely remember something about that.'

'Well, I have need for just an enterprising man.'

'I'm afraid I don't understand. Your wife has been kidnapped and you come to me? Looking for – what? An enterprising man?'

'It's a little hard to explain, but yes, that's it exactly. What I need is someone who can be trusted to help me get my wife back.'

'Have you contacted the police? Kidnapping is something for the police, maybe even the FBI. Not anything for us here at the bank.'

'No, no, you don't understand. This kind of kidnapping is, well, it isn't really a kidnapping. It's a business transaction. What I'm looking for is the name of the man you were talking about that other time. I got the impression this fellow was, well, responsible. From what you said, he is someone who could be trusted and who was quick-thinking. I want to hire him for a few days. Just long enough to get my wife back safely.'

Gorman looked away from the other man, turning his gaze out of the window. He enjoyed the view out of that window. It was one of the benefits of being the head of the loan department. It had become his habit, when faced with a major problem, to look out over the bay towards Alcatraz Island. The sight somehow soothed him, thinking about the three prisoners who, history claimed, had escaped from there. None of the three men was ever seen again, of course. Their bodies, as had been expected, didn't turn up anywhere in the waters of San Francisco Bay. He liked to dwell on that while letting his mind solve whatever problem had been handed to him.

The question, he supposed, was whether or not to give this pompous businessman Steve's name. Steve Gunnison was the repo man he'd been talking about when sharing a humorous story. He'd told the little anecdote while waiting for the loan papers to be drawn up. Now he wished he'd kept his mouth shut.

Ah, well.

'I don't know if I should be handing out this man's name,' Gorman, being the officious banker that he was, said. 'You understand, I hope,' he added, quickly holding up a hand to stop the man in the client chair from cutting in. 'However, if you'd like, I could give him a call and let him decide whether or not to get involved. I have to be honest, though. I'll warn him about the dangers of getting implicated with something like a kidnapping. I feel it's my duty to an associate.'

'This is not a real kidnapping, I tell you,' Gussling said heatedly. 'It's . . . dammit, it's just a business deal.'

'I don't understand that. You claim your wife has been kidnapped but it's only a business deal?'

Gussling sat, clearly trying to get control of his emotions. 'Yes. It's hard to explain. But, OK. Please get in touch with your man and ask him to contact me. Tell him what you will, but assure him there is no danger, but a lot of money. All he has to do is be the go-between . . . just deliver the ransom and return my wife to me.'

CHAPTER ONE

Son was upset, more so than usual this time. I could tell something had happened out of the ordinary.

'They stopped me on the street,' he said, starting in without even a Hi there, Bernie, how are ya?

'Can you believe it? Right out there on the busy street.'

Son was scared. Not that it took a lot to frighten him. He was one of those people who were likely afraid from the first minute. I thought he was frightened of the light when he was born and it was made worse when the doctor slapped his bottom to start things working. Leaving the safe, warm, dark place scared the crap out of him.

Son Cardonsky and I go back a long way, clear back to Roosevelt Grade School. On that day we were both terrified. That's a tradition, isn't it, kids being afraid on the first day of school? My mom had been a little late in dropping me off, so when I crossed the playground things had already started. The class bully – and there is always one of those, too – was picking on a smaller, fatter blond-haired boy.

By the way, my name's Bernie Gould. If you saw me walking down the street you'd never think I was the kind of guy who'd stand up to a bully. And you'd be right. I'm just under six feet, well, maybe four inches under the six-foot mark. Skinny built, I tip the scales at about 175 when I'm eating regularly. My hair is the colour of faded sun-dried wheat, which I comb straight back. This hair is so thin that I can see my pink scalp through it whenever I look into a mirror. I try not to do that often. Oh, and it needs cutting. Normally I get cut every other week. That was my habit. Until Inez left. I needed a haircut then and haven't had the time or money to go to the barber's since.

I'm not a bad-looking man; just not one anybody would think was tough or dangerous. All I was was stubborn. That comes from being the youngest of three boys. To make matters worse, my brothers were twins. That meant, in that world, no matter what, it was always two against one. You think that didn't toughen me up? If I didn't stand up for myself I got what was left over. Every time. Maybe because of that I didn't like anyone pushing someone weaker around.

Well, as it turned out I only had to punch the bully once for three things to happen. First, Mr Bully went crying off like his world had ended. Second, Mrs Jordan, a stern no-nonsense old maid of a woman who turned out to be my homeroom teacher, only saw me hitting another boy, which wasn't a good start. And third, I became Bradford Cardonsky's hero and protector. I could easily have lived with the first two. The third became my lifelong cross to bear.

From the very beginning Bradford Cardonsky was called Son by friend and foe alike. Not that he had many friends. Son got his name when, as a child, his father, having the same name, took a dislike to the idea of having a Bradford Cardonsky Junior in the family. Until he could decide on whether or not to call him Brad, or maybe Ford, he simply called out 'Son!' whenever he wanted the child's attention. The name stuck.

By default on that day I became Son's best friend. Nothing I could do ever discouraged that and over the years I did everything I could think of, believe me. Even today when, we're both well into our thirties, both pursuing totally different professions, every time Son gets into a little trouble, here he comes, asking to get saved.

'Well,' Son was heard to explain when he got a lot older, 'I guess it's better than it could be. I mean with a last name like Cardonsky I could have ended up with a nickname like Cardy, couldn't I?'

Having Cardy for a nickname would have been ironic. That's because early in his first year in college he learned he had a certain knack for the game of poker. Being a professional gambler with a pet name like Cardy just wouldn't sound good.

'Yeah,' Son went on hurriedly telling me his latest woes, 'they stood right there and threatened me. Even with hundreds if not thousands of shop-a-holics streaming by. Nobody noticed a thing. Damn fools, everyone. I tell you, those two come up and stood right in front of me. They just stopped and stood right there, looking me in the face. Right in front of me. I mean it was just as if we were talking about the weather and how someone should be doing something about it. But it wasn't like that at all. They even smiled and went on telling me what would happen if I didn't make good on my IOUs.'

We were standing at the end of the dark wooden bar in Lou Lou's Bar and Grill, downtown Sausalito, my newest home town. Sausalito's a nice quiet little community just across the Golden Gate Bridge from San Francisco. Son lived over in the city. I couldn't live there, too many people doing too many things all at the same time. I mean, have you tried to get up on one of the many freeways that stream through that place at four in the afternoon? Everybody rushing like mad to get somewhere they think will disappear if they aren't there in two minutes? My policy is to relax. Enjoy life. That's why Lou Lou's is my favourite place.

The grill part of the business is focused on delicious special meat hot dogs, the best hamburgers this side of heaven and nothing else. That was the length of the menu. If you wanted anything else, you went somewhere else. Business at Lou Lou's was always brisk but it was the bar part that made Lou Lou's a profitable business. That was because of Fat Henry's practice always to make a big show of pouring extra booze in the customer's first drink and a lot less in all those following. Fat Henry is the owner and bartender. Nobody knew who Lou Lou is or was. That was the name of the place when Fat Henry bought it. Lou Lou's is my favorite saloon but all I ever drink is beer.

Listening to Son, all I could do was give him a shake of my head.

'Like what are we talking about here?' I said, not really wanting to know. 'What is going to happen if you don't pay up?'

'Man, there were two of them. One, the smaller guy, Murphy, he just smiled and mentioned what I could look forward to. The usual, he said. Break both my kneecaps. But then his buddy, Hugo, he's a lot bigger, he smiled like he was about to taste chocolate ice cream for the very first time, had his say. "We got to make it clear to any other gambling fool thinking about reneging on a debt. Do you know, some fools think being knee-capped is bad enough? Personally, I like the idea of cracking your elbows, too." Then he giggled. I swear, he actually giggled. "I like to think about making someone's life miserable. Not walking would be tough but think about not being able to feed yourself or wipe your ass." '

Son had brought his problems to me before; sometimes it was something to do with a woman who turned out to be married. Back when I was a reporter I'd get my buddy Steve to help. Steve was a deputy sheriff back then and he'd just show the husband his badge and the husband would back away. That didn't work any more.

I couldn't figure out what Son wanted this time. His troubles had to be money and he knew I couldn't help him with that. He knew I didn't have any extra cash, especially since getting fired from the newspaper.

'Christ on a crutch' I said, 'that certainly doesn't sound like fun. What the hell have you gotten yourself into, Son?'

'Ah, Bernie, it's just that my luck and the cards've been against me lately, I don't know.'

'So, what happened?'

'Nothing. I mean, nothing else. The shorter guy, he poked my chest with his finger and chuckled. That's all.'

'That's all?'

'Yeah. They just smiled and walked off down the street just like all the other shoppers. Like they were merely out for a stroll just like a couple tourists taking in the sights, you know?'

'Sounds like you stepped in it big time.'

'Uh huh. Now you see why you have to help me?'

'Help you? How do you figure I can help? I could raise a couple hundred bucks maybe, but this doesn't sound like a hundred-dollar problem. Kneecaps and elbows, you got to be talking lots of money.'

'Yeah. Lots and then some.'

'So, why are you knocking on my door?'

'Look, you deal with this kind of people all the time. You write about killing men, bad men, and these are like that. And the man who sent those two bums to scare me. He's a real bad man.'

All I could do was smile my little tired smile, which I could see in the mirror behind the bar looked more like a grimace, and slowly shake my head.

'Look, Son, get real. I'm a writer. A hack novelist, if you must, but you're dealing with people who hurt other people. That means to me you've got into a fix with real badasses while those baddies I write about in my stories are all make-believe badasses. Get real.'

'No, Bernie, you're way out in front when it comes to knowing how to handle something like this. Look, I know what you do, and you do it time after time. That's all I want you to do now: describe how to kill someone in such a way that even the police can't figure out who done it. You can write a story that leaves the law looking somewhere else for the killer. Well, that's what I want you to do now, simply write the story

11

about a man, me, caught in a trap, which I am, and how he gets out of it. God, Bernie, it should be a snap. I got it all figured out. You do this and there'll be a lot of money when it's done. Lots of money of which you will get half.'

Money. Or to be more precise the lack of it is the basis for things to go wrong. That deficiency was really the only part of my life, at that moment anyhow, that wasn't fun. Son's comment about lots of money caught my attention.

'And how is there a lot of money involved, pray tell?'

'It's like this. Right now I owe a certain shark a packet. OK, so if I don't pay I spend the rest of my life walking funny and with elbows that don't bend. You ever give any thought to how important your elbows are? Trust me, they are. Now I can't pay back the vig on what I owe, never mind the principle. The cards just haven't come through for me lately. I don't know what it is, but Lady Luck has changed her face; the title of the song is Let's Fuck Son. But that's the gamble, isn't it? If someone's gonna win then someone's gotta lose.'

'Hey, Son, get to it, will you. I do have other things to do today, you know.'

'All right, don't panic. It's like this, you do what you're good at, write me a story. I'll lay out the . . . what do ya call it . . . the plot and you make it come out in my favour. Now that isn't so hard is it?'

All I could do was sadly shake my head. Boy, if he only knew how hard it could be to drag every word out, kicking and screaming.

'Sure, as easy as pulling teeth. Get to the money angle, will you?'

'OK, OK. Here it is. The story would have me owing money to the leg-breakers. To get that much cash I get into a big – I mean really big poker game. Texas Hold 'em is the rave game right now. Lots of money on the table and I'm either winning or not. If I'm winning, then the story is that I pay off the debt, share the rest with my guardian angel, that's you, and that's that. End of story. If I'm losing then you write how someone, a couple men wearing masks or something, come in and rob the game. OK so far?'

I scowled to show my displeasure, causing Son to go on, now talking faster.

'Yeah, well, as these hold-up men leave they drop the sack of money or something. I pick it up and return it to the table. I'm the hero and walk away with a big reward. Pay off the sharks and split the rest with that angel I had before. Get it? You write how it'd work and I follow it like a script. It can't miss.'

'Son, that's the silliest thing I ever heard. What makes you think that by my simply writing something it'll happen?'

'No, think about it. You write the story and that becomes the blueprint. Easy as spitting watermelon seeds. You know,' he continues talking a mile a minute, 'the more I think on it the more I like the hold-up scene. Yeah. That way it's guaranteed there'll be enough money on the table. You write how the bad guys lose the dough and how I save the day and we're in. Now how hard can that be?'

I finished my beer, put the mug on the mahogany bar and climbed off the stool.

'Nope, Son, it can't be done. Sure, I could write a story like that about a big poker game, lots of cash on the table and a couple hold-up men. That story's been done a million times. But so you could use it to script what you do? It just wouldn't work. My advice is to come up with the money you owe the loan shark or start running. I understand San Diego is nice this time of year. Or maybe Denver. Winter's coming on and nobody in his right mind would head for Denver. They'll never look for you there.'

Quickly before Son could respond, I walked out of the place.

CHAPTER TWO

Walking up to the corner as fast as I could to get away from that fool, I slowed after turning on to Ontario Street. San Francisco is famous for a lot of things; the fog bank rolling over the hills in the evening is one of those. On this side of the bay the weather patterns are different. This time of year, here in Sausalito, the evenings are pretty darned nice, perfect for taking a walk. Anyway, I only had a couple blocks to go.

After the big break-up with Inez I'd moved into a small studio apartment on Ontario. I hadn't told anyone except my former partner, Steve, where I was going. I certainly hadn't told Son. Let him go out to the old house and bother Inez. She didn't know where I had gone and the way things had turned out, it was clear she didn't care either.

My apartment wasn't much. Actually it was less than that: a small kitchen with just enough room for a small under-the-counter refrigerator, a two-burner electric stove, a single sink with a draining-board that didn't drain back into the sink very well and just barely enough counter space for a cutting board. A shoebox-sized microwave did most of my cooking.

The bathroom was hardly that, being only big enough for the toilet, a tiny sink and a shower stall just wide enough to be able to turn around in without hitting the sides. The living-room was the joke. You know what a Murphy bed is? The inventor actually came from San Francisco. The way the story goes, a guy named Murphy started his bed company in the early 1900s and the one in my apartment is, I believe, one of the originals.

To pull down the bed, hidden during the day in the wall behind a pair of louvred doors, I have to move the metal-legged table I use as my desk and two chairs into the kitchen. Once the bed is down, to get to the minuscule bathroom I have to crawl off on the left side of the bed. It's off the right side if I wake up in the middle of the night and want to get a drink from the kitchen.

Right after moving in I began to have dreams of the bed folding up just as I and some young lovely were reaching the proverbial climax of a lifetime. Not that this is likely to happen. I haven't been close enough to a woman since Inez and I split up even to get an erection.

I have to admit my little home isn't much but it is quiet. That was one thing that couldn't be said about the house Inez and I had bought. The house that now was, thanks to the divorce settlement, all hers. The three-bedroom, bath and a half house over in San Rafael had been a place of fun and laughter. Inez, a tiny woman with a beautiful body, dazzling smile and long black hair, was full of fun and laughter. Only when things started on the downhill track did I discover the other side to the woman. That was when the three-bedroom house became filled with the sound of silence. Silence and frustration: Inez's frustration and my silence.

So now, as far as I knew she was in the three-bedroom and I was in the closet and a half.

On the way home from Lou Lou's I stopped by the little grocery on the corner to pick up a frozen dinner and a six-pack of beer. Safe from Son or anyone else wanting a piece of me, I snapped the cap off a bottle of Bud and lit up my computer. Walking home I'd been thinking about the idea of the robbery of a high-stakes poker game Son had talked about. It was an age-old story but maybe there was a new twist I could give it.

Sipping the beer I started writing. Much later, when things started to fall apart, I thought back to that night and wished I'd just gone to bed instead.

CHAPTER THREE

It was my only real friend, Steve Gunnison, who came to my financial rescue. What was left in the bank from the sale of the vineyard had disappeared with Inez and boy, did I need rescuing.

As mentioned before, it isn't all that easy to write 2,000 words a day. It's a lot harder to turn those words into cash money. That was the goal I had set for myself when I gave up my day job to become a novelist: 2,000 a day, five and sometimes when things were going good, six or even seven days a week. It's not that I had a lot of other things to do. Not that I had any choice in matters. I'd left my job on the editorial staff of the *Eureka Standard* under the same cloud as Steve. My best buddy turned to stealing cars and I started writing.

Yeah, it sounds easy, just fire up the old PC and start writing. The hard part is to pump out words that end up getting accepted by a publisher. Rejection is the name of the game. You got to know that going in. The stream of rejection slips can be a never-ending river. That's what got to Inez.

I had first met Steve Gunnison way back on the day we were registering for college. After graduating from high school, dear old dad had given me, his youngest son, a choice: either get a job or go to college. Both my brothers had gone to work in the same factory that employed Dad for way too long to think about. Without a doubt, Dad knew I'd never fit in there. He even offered to pay my first year's fees. I didn't hesitate and quickly accepted the offer. The nearest four-year school of higher learning was far enough from the hometown to get me out of dad's sight but was also a way to finally get away from Son Cardonsky. For twelve years he had been hanging around, sticking like cheap masking-tape. Back in high school, Son had failed a grade and was put back a year. It'd be a while before he could count on being accepted by any college admission office. There I was, signing up for classes knowing he was definitely part of my past and quite easily forgotten.

That left me all alone, standing in the gymnasium looking up at the board with all the courses listed when I heard someone grumble.

'How the hell am I supposed to know what to take?'

Glancing around, I saw it was a long-haired, straggly bearded guy about my age doing the complaining. I hadn't had time for the hippies in school and I certainly wasn't about to change that.

'That's what they've got councillors for.' I pointed. 'Over there at those tables.' Not looking to see if he took the hint, I went back to asking myself the same question. What classes to sign up for?

'Yeah, sure,' he hadn't moved, 'and what'll they tell me? Everything up on that list only leads to something else. All things I don't want to do.'

'So, don't,' I snapped and went back to studying the board. I didn't want to admit it, not out loud anyway, but going to college was just the better choice, better than taking some kind of job. I hadn't thought very far ahead and now the pressure was on.

'What're you signing up for?' The hippie wouldn't go away.

Looking at the list of classes still open, I thought I saw a way to get rid of the long hair. 'I'm thinking about taking that journalism class.' I lifted my chin with all the self-assurance I could come up with. 'Work towards a degree in journalism.' There, that should do it.

'Hmm. Ah, what the hell, I can't even spell my name half the time,' the kid said. 'Maybe I'll sign up for the police science course. Why not become a cop rather than go on being chased by them? My name's Steve, by the way.'

That was the beginning. After signing for the string of classes and getting our schedules, the two of us, one with a barbershop haircut and the other pushing his lanky hair to one side and out of his eyes, walked over to a nearby tavern for beer. It was while talking and getting to know each other that we met another new student, a pert little beauty named Inez.

Learning to become a journalist wasn't all that hard. In high school, English had been one of those subjects I didn't have to study for to get passing grades. It didn't take me long to understand that developing strong communication skills was the name of the game. Talk to people, write down what they tell you, use strong researching methods and write a news story that told the readers what they needed to know to make their world a better place. Or so the professor said. Basically I simply learned to rely on my skills and talents as a bullshit artist.

Steve on the other hand had found a home. The first thing he did was get a haircut. I almost didn't recognize him without his straggly beard.

'Hey,' I said, looking him over and seeing an example of Mr Straight and Narrow, 'what happened to the hippie fellow I used to know?'

'It's part of the dress-for-success deal. If you want to have people follow the law, you have to look like you're more on the ball than they are. Everybody left me alone when I looked like your average doper. Now they'll think I'm one of them.'

'Uh huh. And next you'll be telling me you're joining the Republican Party and voting for the next Richard Nixon.'

'Nope. Outside I'm wearing slacks and a tie but inside I'm still flinging my fringes and beads at everyone. I know it, they don't.'

I wasn't sure any of it made sense, but I had to admit he did smell better.

During the first semester the three of us met often to complain about the class work, the obvious mistakes we'd each made in choosing our individual career paths and the food offered at the student union. Over the weeks and months we became friends, and during the summer break between the first and second year of school Steve and I even went on to being business partners. The business was harvesting and selling the dope we'd planted up in the national forest. Except for what we kept for our own use, the crop we sold to other students was what paid for our tuition. And food. And booze. And, for me at least, dinners with Inez.

It was in the fall of that first year, after the harvest of the season's crop and the resumption of classes that Son showed up. I couldn't believe it but didn't really have any option. I had to introduce him to both Inez and Steve, both of whom took an instant dislike to the short, round, already starting to go bald first-year student.

As luck would have it, none of us ended up having much to do with Son Cardonsky. I had all but forgotten about him in my new life. Until, that is, he showed up one day telling me he'd registered for class. I don't recall what classes, he took no part of my journalism programme so I didn't stew about it for long. As it turned out Son was soon following his own path. He had discovered poker.

At first the penny ante games were played among a half-dozen other freshmen at a round table against the far wall of the student union. The game, usually five-card draw, was a means of spending time between classes. For the first few weeks it was hard to tell the winners from losers; it was a nickel-dime game, lose a dollar today, win a dollar tomorrow. That was the way of it until someone noticed that Son was winning a lot more than losing. An unspoken vote was taken and 'Slick-card Cardonsky' was asked to move on.

That didn't bother Son, he'd already found a higher stakes game in the back room down at the Elks Club. A fraternal organization, the Elks offered the members cheap drinks at the bar, inexpensive dinners in the restaurant and one-armed bandits in the back room. Behind the bank of slot machines were a couple of round felt-topped poker tables. Son had found his calling. For the first time since the first grade he had no time for me. To celebrate I took Inez out dancing.

Inez hadn't been part of the dope farm. She enjoyed a pipe now and again, sure, but she wasn't really into it. Even Steve and I lost our desire for it, especially after we graduated. Steve had heard about an opening in the Humboldt County Sheriff's department and drove down to take the Civil Service exam. Inez and I hung around our college apartment, searching job listings and eating lots of spaghetti and pizzas.

Neither of us really liked spaghetti and pizzas but it was cheap food. When Steve called to tell of an opening in the *Eureka Standard*, the regional newspaper for that part of northern California, we couldn't get out of town quick enough.

Hired and now with a good job, I proposed to Inez and with Steve as the best man, we were married.

It became a habit, Steve in his brown deputy sheriff's uniform and me in my Levis and worn tan corduroy sports coat complete with suede patches on the elbows. We even kind of worked together. That started when Steve invited me for a ride-along. I figured, why not learn what a deputy did and maybe I could get a feature story out of it? With notepad and pen in hand, that's what happened. Before long I was covering the cops-and-courts beat for the paper. When not working Steve and I spent a lot of Saturday mornings fishing out in the bay and Saturday afternoons at the apartment Inez and I had rented, cooking up whatever we'd caught that morning.

Before long we became known through out the county as partners. It was only natural, then, when Steve was caught growing pot, the plants intermixed with the grapevines on the ten-acre vineyard he and I had bought, that I was naturally painted with the same brush. Inez knew I had nothing to do with it and Steve knew it had all been his idea and that I hadn't even known about it, but to the outside world, we were partners.

The vineyard had been an investment. I had liked the idea of owning my own business, and having a vineyard was a good start. Steve, as it turned out, liked digging in the soil. Anyway, he said he didn't want to wear a badge for the rest of his life.

The previous owners, a couple of brothers, had been arrested for stealing cars. They had taken over the long shed on the property, which had once been used in the production of wine grapes, to repaint the hot vehicles before selling them to a guy who put them in shipping containers and trucked them across the border to Mexico.

The owner of a small local boutique winery, no longer able to get a portion of his grapes from the brothers, had gone by to find why not. Not getting any response at the front door, he had gone around back and had walked into the shed. Seeing the painting operation the two men were busy with, he simply turned around and called the police. As the property was outside the city limits, the call was transferred to the sheriff's department and two deputies were sent out to investigate. One of the deputies was Steve and, as usual, he called me to ask if I wanted to ride along. The deputies took one look and made the arrest. This time I had my little digital camera and got front page photos of the scoop. When the property went on the market to pay the brother's legal fees, Steve and I pooled our savings and made the down payment on the ten acres.

Inez was against the idea until I showed her how we could afford it and not have to refinance the little two-bedroom house we'd bought in town.

As it turned out, when someone let the sheriff know about the dope growing amongst the vines, he had Steve brought in. The sheriff, recognizing the years of service and the high arrest records his deputy had run up, decided not to take the matter to the district attorney. He did call my editor, though, and after talking it over with the sheriff, my boss went along. Partners to the end, we both had to give up our chosen careers. Steve handed in his badge and sidearm, I my camera and notepad.

CHAPTER FOUR

Losing my job at the newspaper wasn't the end of the world for me. Fact is I'd been thinking about making a change anyhow. Of course nothing had been said about it to Inez, she did like her security. When the managing editor explained how even the question of my being involved with a drug crime wasn't good for the paper, I wasn't worried. That was all it took to do what I wanted, to go on doing what I had been doing, writing. Only now it would be writing fiction.

When I explained it to her, Inez wasn't so sure she liked the idea. She didn't put up much of an argument, though, and even went along when I said I wanted to get away from the north coast, away from the rain. We didn't want to sell the house, so we rented it out, packed our stuff and moved. Our first place was a two-bedroom apartment in San Francisco. We both quickly agreed that big-city life wasn't for us and moved across the bay to San Rafael.

Money wasn't a big problem; we were living on the proceeds from the sale of the vineyard while I wrote. That's where we bought the nice three-bed, two-bath house. That's when I set the daily goal of writing 2,000 words a day. While that was happening, Inez got involved with three separate soap operas on our little television set. It didn't take long before we knew things weren't going to be easy for either of us. The rejections came in hot and heavy and Inez put on weight. There were days on end when I didn't even leave the house. While Inez lived life through the trials and tribulations of a series of beautifully dressed, clear-speaking actors, I was living the life of the characters I was busy writing about.

At about that same time Steve found his niche. He had grown to love wearing a badge; this was clear from the day he joined the county sheriff's department. I don't think it wasn't so much being a deputy sheriff he got off on, but the freedom that being an officer of the law gave him. Sure, he would freely admit he liked it when people waved as he drove by. And he knew it was not him personally they were friendly to but the badge. And the gun. And the patrol car. In his brown uniform he was somebody. Losing all that was, he told me later, the end of the world. Well, for a while anyway. As it turned out, it wasn't being a cop that turned him on; it was the thrill of the potential danger. That discovery, he said, came when he went to work stealing cars.

Inez and I had left northern California a little before Steve. He thought he'd stick it out until he found that living under a cloud wasn't fun. He packed up and followed us down to the big city. He slept on our living-room floor for a couple of days while trying to think of what to do next. It would be easy, he told me, to lose himself in San Francisco, maybe he could even find himself.

He did.

'When I was talking to the manager of a branch of my bank about moving my account,' he explained to us on his second day in town, 'all of a sudden I have a new career. And it pays a lot better than the sheriff's department paid.'

He moved into a small apartment on Gouch Street the next day.

To celebrate, he bought dinner for the three of us on the last night in our apartment: three large pizzas and a bottle of red wine.

With the empty pizza boxes in front of us Steve talked about his good luck.

'The guy I talked to in the bank, Frank Gorman, is the head loan officer for that branch. It's the largest branch and it turns out he's in charge of all the other loan departments. Anyway, when something was said about my having worn a badge he offered me a job. Man, I knew what money I had wasn't going to last for ever, not at big city prices for everything. So I listened and when that banker laid it out, I couldn't agree quick enough.'

The way it'd work was that Steve would be given only the repossession orders that others had not had success with. He would be working directly for the bank and that let him off the hook for having to get a state license. He wasn't sure the sheriff would keep quiet about growing the dope and that kind of black mark would not look good to the licensing board.

'I liked what the banker had to say,' he said with a smile, telling the tale after pulling the cork on another bottle of wine. 'No set hours to clock in for and nobody looking over my shoulder. I figure each morning I can take my time with a shower, have breakfast and then drop by the bank. There's an assistant branch manager I see who will have the updated list for me each day. I'm paid a commission for each vehicle I turn into the bank's lot.

'Now here's the good thing. I get the tough ones. That means my commission is higher, I get to work at my own pace and don't worry about how long it takes me to pick up a car or truck. Hell,' he chuckled, 'I haven't anything else to do.'

Well, that was fine and dandy. For him. In the Gould household things weren't going so nicely. I'll give Inez credit, only once did she say something about my finding a paying job. Why couldn't I do my writing at night, she wanted to know. I almost came back with the idea that she shut off that damn TV and go get a job if she was so worried about making the house payment. I didn't, though. Why stir the pot? I went on with my writing and she returned to *Days of Our Lives*, or something. And the tension started to grow. Right up to the day she drove off.

CHAPTER FIVE

Things were, as far as I could tell, going right along. Rejection slips were still the biggest showing for all my writing, but I felt I was learning how to write. Every rejection, one agent mentioned in turning me down, it was just another step toward being accepted. Uh huh. But I believed it and continued to write.

We didn't see much of Steve for a while. He was busy learning how the world of repossessing vehicles worked and for me, well, there were those 2,000 words a day to pump out.

My sales during those months were few and far between, a couple of short stories and even a feature article for a travel magazine. Not enough coming in to pay the bills for long.

One overcast fall morning, instead of turning to the TV set after washing up the breakfast dishes, Inez came into the bedroom I had turned into my office.

'Bern, I can't take it any more. Something's got to change.'

It isn't something I'm proud of, but I was right in the middle of trying to take control of the hero in my latest story and I kept punching the keys, not bothering to look up.

'I mean look at it from my point of view,' she went on. 'All day long, I've nothing to do but watch *As the World Turns*. Do you realize that damn world's been turning for years? Decades, even. I'm watching the third or fourth generation of actors doing exactly the same things others did before them. Something has to change.'

'Uh huh,' I vaguely recall agreeing, my fingers flying and fast. Hot on the trail of a sure-fire opus, my mind was somewhere else.

I can't be clear about this, but whenever I'm feeling down, I can picture Inez standing there for a long moment, watching me before sadly,

I hope, nodding and saying the fateful words. 'And the change is this: I'm leaving you.'

'Uh huh,' was more than likely my response. After all I was busy trying to keep up with my hero who was in deep doo-doo.

I do remember saying something like, 'That sounds like a good idea, your going to visit your mother.' Or maybe not. I don't know.

The rest of the conversation has also been lost but what was said became very clear a short time later.

'And,' Inez more than likely went on, not paying any more attention to me than I was to her, 'I'm going to clean out the bank account before I go. Plus,' her voice would have gained strength as she made her decisions, 'I'll be sure to get a lawyer that'll make you pay for all costs.'

My response? Well, I did want her to be happy on her trip to see her mother didn't I? I can hear it now, 'Uh huh, you go ahead. And take the car so you'll have a safe trip, hon.'

The day's 2,000 words were screaming to be written.

As I found out later, Inez did take the car.

That was the afternoon Steve called. I had finished my writing for the day and was feeling good about the latest effort to move my hero along in the story. I quickly accepted the invitation to meet at Alioto's for a drink. Later, thinking back on it, I recall being surprised not to find Inez sitting in front of the darkened TV. A quick look turned up an empty kitchen, too.

'Well, that's nice,' I eventually said aloud, a habit I'd lately picked up. 'I'll bet she's gone to get something special for dinner.'

That made me feel even better, a feeling that faded somewhat when I found the single-car garage empty. I left a note on the counter and walked down to catch the number 22 bus. It's only ten or twelve miles from San Rafael to the ferry terminal at Sausalito but it takes the bus, making six or seven stops along the way, damn near half an hour to make the trip. Still, it's worth it. Not the bus ride, that sucks. It's the ferry trip across the bay that is special.

Riding across the bay in a modern twin-hulled vessel that could probably make it all the way to Hawaii if the captain wanted to make a right-hand turn under the Golden Gate bridge, brought back my good humor. It was almost like taking a little ocean cruise and a hell of a lot easier than driving across the Golden Gate bridge.

Walking up from the San Francisco Ferry building, my good feeling grew. I mean, my story was going along pretty good and I was on the way to having a drink with my old friend. Plus my wife was out getting something special for dinner. It was a good day to be alive, was the song threading its way through my mind. The music died when using my bank debit card to get some cash from the ATM I discovered the account was dry.

At first it was concern that furrowed my usually smooth forehead. That changed with the furrows becoming plough-deep when I called the bank and learned that my wife had emptied out the joint account earlier in the day.

I found Steve sitting at the long mahogany bar in Alioto's.

'She's left me,' I said taking the empty stool next to Steve. The man and woman next to me didn't notice. They were just sitting there, looking deeply into each other's eyes.

Steve started to laugh, then noticed I wasn't talking to him. I was staring into the mirror behind the bar, really talking to myself. I could hear the surprise in my words. Poor Steve didn't know what to say, but I guess he really didn't have time to come up with something. Without missing a beat, I continued, going on, explaining to myself what had happened.

'That wasn't a visit to her mother she was talking about this morning,' I said, making the discovery as I said the words. That's when I noticed the couple sitting next to me. Giving me dirty looks, they got up and moved.

'Damn,' was my final word on the subject. Shaking my head, I turned to my former partner and only friend.

'Inez left me,' I said as a greeting. 'She took the car, cleaned out the bank account and left me.'

The news didn't surprise my friend, which was clear from his reaction. Steve actually smiled.

'I could see that coming. Couldn't you? I mean how long did you expect her to put up with your hanging around, beating that keyboard and getting back only slips of paper saying "sorry"?'

I looked away, blinking. He seemed actually to be pleased.

'Look, Bernie, it isn't the end of the world. I mean, it looks black right now, but give it some time. I'll bet if you were to get some work, start bringing in a pay cheque, she'd come back.'

'But that's not what we agreed on. When we moved down here, the plan was for me to write. There was enough money to live on until things started to click for me, but that's what we talked about. She was all for it. I don't understand.'

'No, Bern, *you* were all for it. Doesn't mean *she* was. Women like that feeling of security.'

'Ah, hell.'

For a while neither of us spoke, each thinking his own thoughts. I had just realized there wouldn't be anything special for dinner. Hell's bells, I said to myself, shocked at the thought, there wouldn't even be dinner. Thinking about Inez leaving, I was wondering what I was going to do about it when I caught myself thinking about how sitting at the bar drinking bottles of ice-cold beer with Steve and talking was almost like old times. Except that we weren't talking.

Motioning for two more bottles of beer, Steve turned to look at me. Probably gauging my feelings.

'Tell me the truth, Bern, how's the writing coming? You getting anything published?'

Everybody wants to know about getting published. Nobody understands the problems facing the writer, whether published or not.

People who paint seascapes are without a doubt artists. Whether the paintings are good, bad or hidden under the bed, just by slopping on the paint one is called an artist. Writing is different. Writers are either published or not. If you're published, then you are an author. If not, well, everyone writes, doesn't he? Letters, grocery lists and things like that? How hard can it be to write a story?

'Going pretty good,' was the answer I gave to Steve's question, thinking about my latest story and nodding, 'going pretty good. How're things with the car-stealing business?'

That was the opening Steve had been looking for.

'Damn good. I'm doing a lot more than just paying the bills. Yeah, fact is I've cut down a little and only take the ones that pay the most. Means I only have to work a couple nights a week, most times. Paying the bills and putting a little aside, you know.'

Paying the bills. I heard the words and felt my smooth forehead take on that puckered look again. Steve's claim reminded me that I barely had enough money in my pocket to get back across the bay. To make matters worse, the last addition to that now empty bank account was payment for the short story I'd written about the robbery of a high-stakes poker game. A hundred dollars, no more than short money for a short story. Well, at least Son hadn't come around asking for a commission for the story idea.

'So,' Steve said slowly after allowing for a suitable period of contemplative silence, 'you're making good money writing and that's why Inez left?'

I tried to see the bottom of my beer mug.

'No, I guess that's not the way it is. Let's talk about something else. I've got some thinking to do on that issue. It's too soon to be holding a conversation on it.'

'Hmm. OK, then, let's order a couple more bottles of beer and bowls of fish stew.'

The bar we were in, Alioto's, is a San Francisco tradition. Most of the long narrow building was taken up by the restaurant. The bar filled a section next to the big dining-room that looked out over the harbour, which was filled with fishing boats. As usual, the restaurant was bustling with more tourists lining up out on the street waiting for tables to empty. Those same tourists rarely came into the bar. The reason was that the bar part of Alioto's is small, dark and smelling of the waters of the bay, which surged with the tides under the pilings the place was built on. The bar is popular because it offers regulars a place to relax in quiet comfort.

Alioto's seafood restaurant is world-renowned for its cioppino. Most residents of the city turn their noses up at the idea of joining the tourists and eating at any of the restaurants in town that brag about being 'world famous'.

In actuality, Alioto's was one of the city's best eating establishments when it came to good food, and that's saying something. In a city famous for fancy restaurants, all too often the quality of the food served was of second or third importance.

According to the tourist bureau, the restaurant was started by a Sicilian immigrant named Nunzio Alioto back in the mid-1920s with a small fresh fish-stall. Over the years the fish stew he made, using whatever of the day's catch that didn't sell, filled the bellies of men working on the docks and fishing boats. In time his small fish market and ever bubbling stewpot became a tradition. Based loosely on his Genoese grandmother's recipe for fish stew, which she called cioppino, Alioto's restaurant gained in popularity. Add sourdough French bread and you have a meal fit for anyone, tourist or local.

When we first had come down to the Bay area it hadn't taken Inez and me long to find out this place offered a good meal. We even brought Steve here when he made the move. But still, for all of that, when Steve suggested getting a bowl of stew, I had to shake my head.

'Can't do it, Steve. To tell the truth, I don't know what I'm going to do. Have to give it a lot of thought, I guess.'

'What's the problem? You've got to eat, don't you? Look, all I'm saying is, let's have some dinner. We haven't been able to talk together for a long time. It's only a meal and a glass of beer. Or would you rather wine?' He was pretty good at keeping his smile to himself.

CHAPTER SIX

Steve was up to something. I could read the signs. During all those times we had sat in the little skiff, out on the bay dangling a fish hook, we had gotten to know pretty much everything about each other. My good friend wasn't all broken up over the fact that I was not only sleeping alone tonight, but that I was broke. Steve was poker player enough to keep a straight face.

'Look,' he said again after letting the silence grow a bit, 'there's a lot of things you're going to have to consider. That's a big change, having Inez take a runner. But there's no reason for you to take on the worry today. I told you, things have been going good for me. Let me buy dinner and a bottle of wine. You'll only make yourself sick worrying about things you can't change. Anyway, like I said, you got to eat, don't you? I do.'

Catching the eye of the bartender, he quickly ordered, fish stew, French bread and a bottle of Zinfandel. I sat staring out over the boat harbour, not talking.

It didn't take much, a good meal, a bottle of red wine and subtle reminders of my recently emptied bank account and I found myself agreeing to help Steve out. That's what he'd been after, getting me to help him steal cars.

I assured him I'd to be ready early the next evening and finding I had enough money to get back across the bay, made the walk back to the ferry building. The beer, wine, food and good conversation with my old buddy made it easier for me to overlook the emptiness of the house when I got home. After crawling into bed I was asleep in seconds.

The next morning, as I sat trying to write, the words just ignored me. All day I sat staring at the computer screen, my thoughts turning away from hero and his problems, focusing on Inez and my own. Supper that evening was whatever I found in the refrigerator. I didn't notice what the leftovers were, and it didn't matter much.

I wasn't happy about it, but after spending a quiet, solemn, sober day, thinking, my mind jumping from there to here and not finding answers or solutions, I was ready when Steve drove up.

Sensing my mood, Steve didn't talk much until we were nearly there. I hadn't been paying any attention and was surprised to find we were in a rundown section of a part of town. Looking around, I couldn't even tell you which town we were in.

'OK, Bern, here it is,' Steve said quietly after turning off the engine of his old Chevy and dousing the headlights. Sitting in the dark with the nearest streetlight half a block behind us, he glanced over to me.

'We're in South City, the international airport is over that way a mile or two so don't be surprised if a jet plane roars overhead. Up this street another block or so the pavement ends and a dirt road takes off. It's a six-month old Ford F-150 with a brand new yet-to-be-used cab-over camper on it that we're after.'

He sat waiting for me to say something or ask a question. I couldn't think of a thing to ask.

'It'll be a snap, Bern,' Steve said after a minute. 'All I need is for you to drive me on up there. The guy's a gyppo trucker, you know the kind, big, strong and not too bright but very cunning. Anyhow, all I'm asking is that you drive me up to a place I'll point out. Your part is to kinda keep an eye out for anyone while I hotwire the rig and drive it off. You follow along behind me and we then meet back at the bank parking lot and you've got an easy hundred bucks. What do you say?'

Since going to work for the banker, Steve had talked a couple times about these night raids. He loved it. He'd asked me a couple times if I could help him. There were cases, he said, where having someone along was a big help. I knew this was one of those times and he knew he had me by the short hairs. I needed the money and, I guess, somehow I needed Steve. Not saying anything, I simply nodded.

The night was a moonless one and standing in the shadow of a falling-down board fence all I could do was shake my head at the stupidity of it all as I watched my new partner walk up the road to a gravel driveway. You have to marvel at the man's nerve, I thought, and smiled. Doing it

31

just like he was at home. I watched as Steve quietly opened the driver's side door of the brand-new Ford pickup, quickly popped the cover off the interior light and removed the bulb. I could picture it in my mind, his making sure the gear shift lever was in park before pumping the gas pedal a couple times. In the weak glow from the light on the nearby porch I could only watch as my friend left the door open and quietly raised the hood.

Feeling like a bug about to get smashed, I caught myself paying more attention to the house; the flickering pale-blue light of the TV was noticeable behind a thin curtain. When the engine started, filling the night with a roar I nearly freaked.

Like a scared rabbit coming out of the woods knowing the pack of dogs was right behind him, Steve slammed the hood and was in the cab and behind the wheel in a flash. Hearing the front door of the house crash open and someone yell only made the repo man move faster. Putting the pedal to the metal and, hunched low over the steering wheel, the Ford was flat out as it made the turn out on to the dirt road.

I was quick to come out of my stunned trance, ducking back into the deeper shadows as a big hulk of a man came running out to the road. Standing still, the man pointed a long arm at the fleeing Ford.

'Christ on a crutch,' I muttered, realizing that it wasn't his arm. The bastard had a rifle.

Before the trucker could pull the trigger, I woke up and gave out what I hoped was a good imitation of a Rebel yell, or maybe the cry of a scared werewolf. The big fool must have thought he was under attack because he quickly scrambled back up the driveway.

Not waiting to see where the poor schmuck went from there, I took off, running down to where I'd parked Steve's Chevy.

'That tears it,' I muttered to myself as I sped away, catching up with the pickup which was swaying from side to side, top heavy from the brand new cab-over camper. 'You don't know it, Stevie boy, but this is going to cost you more than a hundred bucks and that I'll be damned if I ever do it again.'

CHAPTER SEVEN

'OK. Now are you finished?' The voice was calm and just barely loud enough to be heard over the rhythmic crashing of waves down on the beach. 'I didn't say anything and I let you have your disgusting fun, but it's late and I want to go home.'

Nothing else was said for a long moment. The girl was no longer pretty. In the tussle her hair had became tangled in the ground-hugging brush. Small twigs had become entwined in the blonde strands.

The man looking down at her body smiled and shook his head. An hour ago she would have been furious at the sand that stuck to her bare skin. That was then, this was now. Now and never again would her appearance matter to her.

Inhaling deeply, the man filled his lungs with air. He'd been finished for some time but when he spoke his words came out raspy, as if his throat was dry and as sand-covered as her legs.

'Yes. I'm finished.'

Silence made the faint roar of the surf sound louder.

'Well then, what's to be done with her? Can't very well just leave her here, not like that.'

The man frowned. 'Of course not, let me think.'

Looking around he saw the van was closer than he'd thought. In his excitement he'd only dragged her a few yards into the brush before stopping. Smiling at the memory he glanced down at the girl's body.

Her young, smooth, taut skin seemed to glow palely in the weak light. Pieces of her blouse, torn when she unexpectedly regained consciousness, hung from her arms, the bottom still tucked into the top of her dark-coloured skirt. A real beauty, he reflected, almost getting excited again. The fight she'd put up had been good, adding to the thrill. It was too bad when she sucked in air, ready to scream. He'd had to hit her. She was still good, *even then, but not as good as if she'd been awake. Or alive. He wasn't sure, but he thought he'd finished before his thumbs had choked off her breathing.*

Standing as tall as he could, all he could see was brush. Few people came along this stretch of the dunes. Searching for the right place, he'd found this section of Fort Funston. Too bad he wouldn't be able to use it again. It was a lot better than the last one. Situated high above the Pacific Ocean, the cliffs had once been part of an army base. He'd read that as part of his researching sites.

Even before the start of WWII, the US military had built a series of gun placements along the high headlands, the big 16-inch guns pointed out to sea, ready to protect San Francisco from invading enemy aircraft. Now it was popular for fools with their hang-gliders, dog-walkers and beach walkers. Hikers and dog people stayed down on the beach. He thought he could leave the girl up here. She wouldn't be found, not for a few days maybe. Better if she was over there in that thicket.

Back in the van he relaxed a moment, happy with the way things had gone. Everything happening just as he'd planned.

'Yes, be proud. However, don't forget. You promised. This is to be the last one.'

Smiling as he started the engine, he nodded. 'Yeah, yeah, yeah. The last one. I promise.' Laughing coarsely, he carefully turned the van around and headed back towards the city. 'You've been dinging me all night. Now, leave me alone.'

The complaining had started before the girl had even come down the street and he was tired of it.

Back on the street, while waiting for her to come along, it'd started.

'Are you sure you want to do this?' Sounding sarcastic but for all of that, demanding. 'Remember, you promised the last time it'd never happen again. Let's go home. I want to go home.'

'Shut up.' His whisper was rough and commanding.

Silence filled the darkened interior of the van. Faintly the click of heels came from down the night street, rhythmic, not hurrying but steady. The beat ran through his mind, left, right, left, right. Like a metronome as she came closer.

He'd chosen well, no more than two car-lengths round the corner of the well-lit street, close enough to streetlights and traffic to appear secure. A residential street, the nearest driveway was just beyond the dark blue van, black in the dark of the night. With the wide side door open, she shouldn't notice him crouched, ready.

The girl, about sixteen or so, was not your typical high school cheerleader type but was still attractive. He liked them a little overweight. Healthy. There had been enough of the too-little-to-eat skinny girls and he didn't have to settle for that any more. Not now. Not with all the healthy California girls to chose from.

Even before she came round the corner, he knew exactly what she'd be wearing, how she'd look. The fast-food restaurant gave its waitresses three sets of uniforms, short pleated skirts and white cotton long-sleeved shirts. A perky little cap the same dark-purple colour of the skirt was fixed to their hair by tiny black hairpins. This girl's hair was shoulder-length and sun-bleached blonde. Healthy and blonde. Hearing her getting closer, he smiled and tensed.

Timing was everything and his practised movements were perfectly timed. He let her get two steps past the open door, just barely ahead of him when he jumped out. Before she could react his right arm went around her waist, pulling her off balance as his left hand holding a cotton pad moist with ether smothered her face. Lifting her off her feet he swung her into the van. Holding the pad tight against her face he felt her body relax.

He closed the sliding door and flipped on the overhead light. Setting back on his heels he took a long minute to look down at her and smiled.

The anaesthesia was quick and when she came out of it wouldn't make her sick. When that happened it took all the fun out of things. The last time he'd had to use chloral hydrate and that often ended up being messy. Giving a girl a drink of booze with a quantity of drops in it often caused vomiting. The worst after-effect of ether was a little numbness and that didn't matter to him.

'Ah,' he sighed, looking down at her curled as if asleep on the thick padded floor. Her skirt had ridden up her thighs so he quickly looked away. It wouldn't do to get too excited now.

Closing his mind to anything else, he quickly secured her wrists and ankles with grey duct tape. Without wasting any more time he climbed behind the wheel and started the engine. After checking for traffic he simply drove away.

Yeah, it'd been a good night and now it was time to go home. Back on the well-lit streets of the Sunset District he hoped he wasn't stopped by a bored cop. There was no way he'd be able to hide his big happy smile.

CHAPTER EIGHT

I knew when Steve called and invited me over to Alioto's for a drink he would sooner or later bring up the subject of my going to work with him. He had been doing that, trying to get me to help him repo vehicles. Before, not wanting to stop the flow of words, I had always turned him down. Now things were different. When he asked, I said yes. I had to. Rejection slips weren't paying the bills. That became the pattern of my days, writing thousands of words in the morning and helping my once-again partner at night.

'Well, hell,' I told myself one morning while shaving, 'a man's gotta eat.'

I wasn't happy with the stark look I saw in the face staring back at me in the mirror.

Inez had said over and over that I was too wimpish ever to be successful as a writer.

'You write about people killing people,' she pointed out, 'men beating up on other men, but when it comes to standing up for yourself, can you? I don't think so. You're too nice a guy to argue when the girl at the check-out counter overcharges you. You gotta be tough to write tough.'

That didn't change anything. Here I was, spending most nights in the dark, stealing some deadbeat's car or truck and could I write about it? I tried. Oh, how I tried. But it just never came out right. Maybe my ex was right, I'm too passive. The face in the mirror wasn't smiling.

'But dammit, that's my nature.'

So, the little voice in the back of my head snickered, *helping Steve take someone's car is also in your nature?*

I didn't bother coming up with an answer. I did, however, continue to help Steve, and for the next few days I was able to put food on the table, beer in the refrigerator and still write my daily allotment of words.

It came as a surprise when I discovered one morning about a week or so after she left how I missed her. Not just the fact that half of the bed got a little chilly sometime in the very early hours but for a lot of other reasons. Sex wasn't the only thing, just one of the better things. Having someone to talk to, share things with, the other kind of things. And the apartment, small as it was, had an empty feeling. After more than fifteen years of marriage, I wondered how long it'd take to get used to being alone.

Life, I had read somewhere, was simply a series of adventures, one after another. Some might think going out at night, sneaking around in the dark, learning how to hotwire a car and then driving hell-bent for election to the bank's secure parking lot was an adventure. Even after four or five times, I didn't see it that way. Yes, the adrenaline surged each time but that just upset my stomach. I couldn't picture myself doing it much longer.

Worrying about my future came to an end when we pulled into the driveway of the address on the paperwork Steve got from the bank's loan officer.

'You know, people are fools,' Steve said slowly before opening the Chevy's door and climbing out. I hoped he wasn't talking about me.

'Look at it,' Steve went on, now looking at me over the top of the car, 'even after receiving the legal letters of warning, they always seem surprised when someone comes to reclaim whatever it was the outstanding debt was for. And they always take their anger out on me, like it's my fault.'

Shaking his head sadly, he slammed the car door and started walking towards the porch. I wondered about that. In some cases we'd had to sneak up and hotwire the vehicle being repo'ed and in others we just knocked on the door and asked for the keys. I didn't understand it.

This time it wasn't even a door-knocking situation. Sitting in a spindly looking rocking chair in the early evening dark was a big man.

'Hiyah,' he said softly, 'I kinda been expecting you.'

As he slowly pulled himself out of the chair, I tensed, ready to duck or run. The man standing on the porch was big. Looking up, I could make out a big, soft looking man. A teddy bear, I thought, and visualized that kind of beastie, one with drooping ears, huge eyes and sagging. I was afraid the guy was going to burst out crying.

'I knew you'd be coming,' the despondent man said miserably, 'I hoped she would come back and we could make up and everything would come out all right, but she didn't. Here, take the keys.'

Even his shoulders slumped. Neither Steve nor I had ever had anything like this happen and we weren't sure how to react. It would only add to the man's misery to simply get in the car and drive off.

'I don't understand,' Steve said at last.

'My wife left me. She knows how much I love that rig. It was our anniversary present to ourselves. Five years of marriage we celebrated by buying the car. That's where we made love the very first time, in the back seat of my old Ford Explorer. It was a big SUV, red, just like that one out there.' He lifted one hand just enough to wave out towards the driveway.

'We traded mine in for a sedan the first year we were married but always knew we'd made a mistake. So, on our fifth anniversary, that's what we did, bought another big red SUV. Even tried to make love in the back, but it wasn't much for comfort so we ended up in the house. Now she's gone and you're gonna take the car.'

Sadly he let his head hang down, remembering.

'Buddy, I'm damn sorry, but. . . .' Steve stopped when he couldn't find the words.

'Yeah, she left me,' the big man went on, not paying any attention to us. 'I haven't had the strength to do anything since. Just sitting here each day, waiting for her to come home.'

'How long has she been gone?' As soon as I asked, I knew the answer. Steve had said there hadn't been any payments made on the Ford in more than six months.

'I guess she isn't coming back.' If possible, the big man looked even more dejected.

I drove the red SUV back to the bank's lot, following Steve's old rust bucket. Thinking about the poor slob I almost laughed out loud until realizing there wasn't much difference between him and me. Maybe way down deep I expected Inez to come back and just didn't want to admit it. Maybe that was why I hadn't thought about replacing the car she took.

CHAPTER NINE

It was full dark when Steve dropped me off at my place. The first couple nights I had invited him in for a cup of coffee or a beer but I hadn't done that recently. All I could do this night was mumble something about seeing him later as I climbed out of his Chevy. Somehow the memory of the big bear of a man still bothered me. Maybe it bothered Steve too; he didn't waste any time driving off.

I was halfway up the walk when someone called from the blackness of the porch.

'You're coming with us, Gould.'

Surprised, I was once again poised to turn and run. I didn't have a chance to do either. There were two of them, one came up behind me and took my left arm just above the elbow.

'Let's go,' a hard, gravelly voice said softly in my ear. 'Mr Pistilli wants to talk to you and he doesn't like to be kept waiting.'

I had no choice, the pressure on a nerve in my upper arm was suddenly excruciating. Because of the pain streaking up my arm I wasn't really aware of being walked back down to the street. Only when the man squeezing my arm let go was I conscious of where I was. Rubbing my arm, I looked up in time to duck my head as I was pushed into the back seat of a dark car.

'What are you doing?' I asked, my chest tightening in panic. 'What the hell is going on?'

'Shut up,' the man seated next to me growled.

'Look, you can't just toss me into a car and drive off,' I said, which was exactly what they were doing.

The big man dropped his hand heavily on my shoulder and squeezed. Pain again filled my body.

'Shut up, I said. Just sit there and don't cause trouble.'

'But . . .' was as far as I got before the man gripped my shoulder again, pressing until I could feel the bones grate against each other. I shut up.

Sitting with my hands folded limply in my lap, I took a chance and looked sideways at my kidnapper. Not wanting to get caught, I tried to see as much as I could without moving my head too far. The man's leg resting inches away from mine was twice or three times the size of my own. Hands the size of tennis rackets with fat sausage fingers rested limply on his thighs. When streetlights flashed by illuminating the car's interior for the briefest of seconds, I could see that even the hair on the man's broad fingers was almost ropelike.

The back of the head of the man behind the wheel was all I could see of the other man. That didn't help explain anything. Looking ahead through the windshield I saw the lights of a freeway overpass coming up. The only sound other than the usual road noise was the rhythmic beat of the turn signal. My body was pressed back in the upholstery as the car went on to the on-ramp and smoothly sped up it. They were taking me south, across the Golden Gate toward San Francisco.

Sitting silently, I tried to figure out why I was being kidnapped. It couldn't be anything from my past, at least nothing I could think of. The only thing new was my helping Steve repo a couple cars and half a dozen trucks, mostly pickups. If it had to do with one of those it was more likely they'd be after Steve and not me. It couldn't be anything to do with Inez. I hadn't fought that, and anyway, her leaving wasn't worth sending a couple heavies after me. No. This was just some mistake.

What had the man said? Back there as he walked up to his porch, something about someone wanting to talk to me. A name. Mister someone. I couldn't remember.

The black sedan took an off-ramp after leaving the bridge and drove through a residential area. Since moving to the Bay area and before Inez drove off with the car, there had been a few times I'd driven over to the city but not enough times for me to become familiar with the streets. I had no idea where we were or where we were heading.

The driver knew. He didn't hesitate, driving confidently, stopping when a light or a sign told him to. Feeling drowsy, I lost track of things but woke up when the car headed up one of the steep streets that San Francisco is famous for. At the very top, the driver turned sharply, pulling into a narrow driveway. The car was stopped briefly to let a heavy-looking wrought-iron gate slowly slide into the high stone wall to one side. In the car's headlights I could see that the gate had been built more for security than artistry.

The driveway curved around in a big circle coming to a stop in front of a big, two-storey palace of a house. My first thought was the owner liked the old style Southern plantation mansions, all columns and wide verandas.

I didn't have to be told to get out, the driver had got out and opened the door for me.

'Up the steps.' He pointed. 'Mr Pistilli's waiting for you.'

Pistilli, that was the name I couldn't remember. Probably Italian, I thought. That didn't surprise me. Most gangsters, and that included kidnappers, were Italian. At least according to television and the movies.

Moving toward the steps, I glanced back to see that the big man had remained in the back seat. The driver, another muscle-beach type although not so big and muscular, was dressed in khaki pants, black thick-soled workman's shoes and a dark sports coat; he stood watching me.

Before I reached the eight-foot tall double doors, the right-hand door swung open and a man looking like a successful banker or lawyer stood looking at me.

'You Gould?' he asked.

I nodded and the man stepped aside, motioning me to come in.

'I'm Guido Pistilli. We got business to discuss. Come into the library so we can get to it.'

The man was shorter than me and I'm about five nine. So put him at five foot two or three. Studying him I put his age at about fifty. Looking him over as I took the chair the man motioned me to, I adjusted that thought. Maybe fifty, or maybe ten years to one side or the other of that guess. Somehow it was hard to get a clear picture of him. Pistilli, he'd said. Where had I heard that name before?

He wore his three-piece banker's suit comfortably. Upon closer inspection, I saw it was a pale-grey silk material, the kind of suit that costs more than I made in a month back when I was with the newspaper. The creases in his pants were ruler-straight and sharp enough to cut butter. The knot in the narrow crimson tie was perfectly tied. Black shoes, the tops polished to a brilliant shine, peeked from the bottom of his pants. Taking the chair I sat stiffly, taking up only about half the room on the seat. Too scared to sit back and relax.

I decided not to wait but to jump right in.

'What's this all about? Whatever you want, having your muscle-bound thugs kidnap me isn't the best way to get it.'

Pistilli's face was narrow, his cheekbones and thin nose all angles. Silvery grey hair covered his head, looking freshly barbered, pink skin showed through the thin hair. But even so, his smooth blemish-free skin looked soft, his lips lifted in a slight smile. I almost returned the smile, forgetting how I had been brought here and then I noticed his eyes. Hard, cold, unblinking eyes. Reptilian eyes, I thought. The older man may have been smiling, but all sign of that smile stayed with his thin, bloodless lips. I looked at the eyes again and thought about the look an iced-down fish in the market had.

'Let me tell you, right up front,' Pistilli said, his words coming somehow soft cotton wrapped around an iron bar. 'I always get what I want, so don't go telling me what is best and what ain't. You understand? I'm gonna tell you what's best and what ain't.'

Not waiting for an answer, he sat on the couch, facing me, his knees only inches away.

'I had Hugo bring you here because. . . . No, let's start this way. You know a punk named Son Cardonsky, right?'

That stopped me. I frowned but didn't say anything. Again the dapper-dressed man cut in before I could decide which direction to take.

'Look, Mr Gould, let me explain why you're here. A few months ago you wrote a script that was used to steal a lot of money. My money, and I want it all back.' Holding his hands out, palms upward, he smiled. Or he may have thought it was a smile. I thought he was grimacing. 'Mr Gould, I'm a simple business man and quite successful. The main reason for my success is that I take care not to get involved in ventures that lose money. When I do it is important to me to make good my losses. That's where you come in. Your little script cost me nearly eighty-five thousand dollars. That money appears to be unrecoverable. However, because you had a hand in its being taken from me, you will now have to make it up.'

'Wait a minute.' I quickly held up my hands to stop him. 'I don't have a clue what you're talking about.'

'Ah, Mr Gould. Let's start over. Do you not have a friend, a man named Son Cardonsky? I can tell from your expression you know who I'm talking about. Good, we got that outa the way. Now, did you or did you not create a kinda how-to script on how to hold up a poker game? See, once again your expression tells me you do know what I'm talking about.'

'No. I mean, yes, I know a guy named Son and I did write a short story about such a hold up. That's what I do, I'm a writer. But that wasn't a script or a how-to-do anything.'

'OK, that was one thing this creep said that was right. He named you as the writer. He said you had written the script for him. Mr Gould, the one thing I can not allow is someone to lie to me. Mr Cardonsky tried to, but Hugo showed him that it wouldn't work. Take that as a warning. Now let us discuss what I want from you.'

If I was tense before, my heart almost stopped now.

'Look,' I stammered, 'be serious. I don't know what Son told you, but you've got it all wrong. Go on ask him. All I wrote was a short story.'

'I'd like to ask him, Mr Gould. I really would. You see there was a lot of things I wanted your friend to tell me, but that friend has flown the coop. That leaves you holding the bag. You understand me now?'

CHAPTER TEN

'Hugo is a good boy,' Pistilli went on sounding more and more like an uncle explaining the facts of life to his young nephew, 'but he gets a little carried away, you know? So I told him not to hurt this creep, Cardonsky, too much. Just make him want to tell me where my money is. Hugo, bless his hard head, leaves him to get some water. The thief was all crumpled up and Hugo had thought he'd maybe hurt him. When he came back the crook had disappeared. To make matters worse, Hugo thought I'd be mad at him and didn't tell me right away. Well, when he did I was mad, madder than. . . . Well, I got over that. But one thing your friend did tell me was where he got the idea for knocking over the card game. From you. So there you are. Now Hugo is being very careful. He wants to get me off his back. And here you are, trying to tell me you don't know nothing. You understand the position this puts me in?'

I had been shaking my head.

'No. I don't know anything about what Son's been doing. I haven't seen him in quite a while.' I wasn't going to mention his recent visit if I didn't have to.

Without thinking, I got to my feet, and stood looking down at the scary little man. 'Anyway, all I did was write a short story. It was published and I forgot all about it. That's all.'

'Sit down.' Pistilli waved a hand, not raising his voice. I dropped back into the chair. 'Here it is. You been told. I want this Cardonsky. You're my link to him. It's as easy as that.'

'But I tell you, I haven't seen Son for some time and I sure as hell don't know where he is or what he's doing. Look, we were never friends. He'd talk to me once in a while, whenever he was in trouble. He always seemed to be getting into trouble. Anyhow, I don't know anything he's been up to. He goes his way, I go mine. Once in a while he'll drop around or we'll run into each other on the street. That's all. We're not friends, certainly not the kind that keep in touch, anyhow. I don't know where he is or how to get in touch with him.'

The last part came out fast, almost pleadingly as I felt a twinge of soreness in my shoulder which reminded me of Hugo.

For a long moment Pistilli sat in deep thought. The emptiness of the man's eyes as he stared at the far wall scared me even more.

'OK, I understand,' he said at last, looking back at me. 'A friend doesn't give up his buddies. I get that,' holding up a hand to keep me from interrupting, 'so we'll do it this way. Murphy'll take you back to your place. You think about things and we'll talk again in a few days. This Cardonsky gets in touch with you, you call me. I get him and you'll come out ahead. This writing you do, it can't pay all that good. Look at where you live, for Christ's sake. So you help me, I'll help you.'

Getting to his feet in one smooth motion, Pistilli stepped over and opened the library door, nodding to Hugo who had been standing almost at attention, waiting to be called.

'Get Murphy. Tell him to take this guy back to where you picked him up. That's all,' glancing back into the room at me, 'at least for now.'

I couldn't get out of that chair fast enough. He stopped me as I went out the door.

'Make sure when he contacts you,' he called loud enough for me to hear, 'you let me know.' I must have squirmed. 'Yeah, believe it, someone'll be around watching. Until I get my hands on your friend, you and me are connected.'

Driving back across the bridge, I sat up front with Murphy. Neither of us had anything to say until we were about halfway across.

'Who is this guy, your boss? I'm not familiar with any Pistilli. The name's somehow familiar but I can't place it.'

'It's a sure thing you read about Guido "The Pistol" Pistilli in the newspapers. His name's always making headlines?'

'Well, I can't place the name. So why is he in the news?'

'Don't you read the papers? The news is always writing about him. Mr Pistilli is a business man. He operates one of them Indian casinos, you know? Russian River Casino just off the Redwood Highway up in Healdsburg.'

'I don't pay much attention to the newspapers. What are the papers on to him for?'

'Ah, you know, those Indians up there, they think someone's skimming the profits. So who do they blame? The man they hired to make the place turn that profit. Shows you how those people think. It ain't so. Mr Pistilli doesn't need to skim anyone, he's got his own sources of income. Like that high-stakes poker game your friend stole from. He's got other things, too.'

'Cardonsky isn't my friend. I mean I know the man, have for a long time, but he certainly isn't my friend.' I sat silently for a few miles.

'When did Son Cardonsky hold up the game, anyhow.'

'Oh, a couple weeks ago. It took me'n Hugo that long to find him. I dunno if I'm supposed to talk to you about that. Don't talk any more.'

I nodded. I'd have to get a few back issues of the *San Francisco Chronicle* and bone up on who this man was. Christ, I thought to myself, what did I ever do to get involved with some high-end gambling outfit? Damn that Son.

CHAPTER ELEVEN

Steve knew a lot about Pistilli. When he came by later that night I asked him. He told me while we were on our way to repo a whole string of cars.

'Yeah, I know the name. You should too. Remember, oh, ten years or so ago there was a major investigation into the running of one of those Indian casinos somewhere up in Idaho? Back right after some federal judge said the Indians could do just about anything they wanted on their reservation? The gambling casinos in Nevada were fighting them, afraid they would end up with all those millions that had been pouring into the slots at Reno or Vegas. Remember any of that?'

'No, it doesn't ring any bells.'

'So what brought Pistilli up now?'

I told him.

'Oh, shit, man. Stay a long way away from that crowd. It's rumoured that "The Pistol" Pistilli either ordered a number of killings or did them himself. Man, he comes from a long line of badasses.'

We were heading south along the Bayshore freeway, riding in a big dual-wheel pick-up pulling an even bigger car trailer behind us. The trailer was long enough to take half a dozen normal-sized vehicles and had been waiting for us at the bank's parking lot.

The Bayshore, or as it was once known, the Bloody Bayshore, was at one time the major highway between San Jose and San Francisco. In the days when the population of the Bay area was about half what it is today, the Bloody Bayshore was a four-lane highway with just a double yellow line separating the north- and south-bound traffic. In those days, there were so many dangerous intersections and driving hazards that fatalities were constantly in the news.

Things changed in later years; today cars and trucks making the fifty- mile run up or down the peninsula have a variety of multi-lane freeways to choose from. Right off the top of my head I could count four or five; the 280, 680, 880, and the 380.

It was well past the evening's drive time and traffic wasn't that heavy. Thinking about the threats from Pistilli I turned my attention to the passing landscape. It wasn't much to look at. Anyone new to this part of the state would probably think this was just one city. They'd have a hard time telling where San Francisco ended and the next town began. On both sides of the highway was a continuous string of buildings and housing developments. Until we got on the other side of San Jose, that is. All of a sudden we were in farm land and the freeway dropped from eight lanes to four. The thin sliver of moon gave out just enough light so I could see a ways into the fields. I couldn't tell what was growing there though. Just long, almost straight lines of some kind of low, brushy plants disappearing into the distance.

'Now pay attention,' Steve said, breaking the silence. 'Forget that damn Cardonsky and think about what we got to do tonight. This one's going to bring in a lot more than usual. The cars are a special order, OK? That means a special payday.'

It didn't matter to me. I had other things to think about. A big-time gambling crook on my tail, my novel wasn't going the way I wanted and now we had a special event coming up. That's not my worry, I said silently, it's all yours and this one's going to be the last, I swear.

'OK,' I said at last, 'tell me what I need to know.'

'Oh, this one's a good one, all right.' I could tell Steve was looking forward to this job. 'There are three cars we've got to get. According to the story I was given, they all belong to one of the directors of the bank. It seems someone had cut the lock on the door to the warehouse his collection was stored in. The three classic cars had been loaded on to a trailer and driven off. Because of the way it was done, the banker thinks it was his ex-wife and her new boyfriend who had taken his vehicles.

'My banker friend, Gorman, says the cops can't be called in because the director doesn't want anything to happen to the ex. All he wants is to have the three vehicles found and returned. Gorman made it real clear, nothing is to happen to the boyfriend or his ex. Apparently the director has his own plans about them.'

'So where are these cars?'

Steve smiled, another sign of the pleasure he was getting out of this.

'I was given a photo of the former wife and the address where she used to work. The boyfriend's name is Leroy Anderson. He's the sales manager of a new car dealership down in South San Francisco. His photo's on the wall of the dealer's showroom. I stopped by to check it all out. Finding where he stashed the cars has been tricky. Ol' Leroy has stayed mighty close to the dealership.

'Now on the other hand, the ex-wife – her name's Sylvia Cummings by the way – she is a creature of habit. I've followed her three mornings and each day it's the same, from eleven until one o'clock, to the gym. I figured, sooner or later one of them would lead me to the cars. As it turned out, it was Leroy that gave it away.'

'Cut to the chase, Steve. Where in the hell are you taking us?'

'Hey, let me have my fun, will you?'

I didn't answer.

'OK. But I got to tell you, it was fun playing detective and all. OK, cut to the chase. Last Friday afternoon I was driving by the dealership when I saw a brand new Ford sedan pull out of the lot. Leroy was behind the wheel. I followed. We ended up down here, south of San Jose. Take a look out there,' he pointed with a thumb, 'we're damn near all the way to Morgan Hill. Well, anyway, I watched as he pulled off on to a long driveway and went back to a bunch of buildings. I drove past and found a place where I could watch him. He parked in front of the big double doors of a faded red barn, pushed open one of the doors and disappeared inside the barn. That's got to be where the cars are.'

'And that's where we're going?'

'Yep. We'll be able to get all three out of there tonight.'

I was sure there would be someone at the house. The white two-storey house stood out clearly in what moonlight there was like someone was blasting it with a high-powered searchlight, one with a fuzzy curtain over the lens. Having it so visible bothered me as we pulled off the pavement and drove up the drive. I could just envision a neighbour coming over with his trusty shotgun to check us out. No lights lit up any of the windows and as we went round to the barn no one came out to see what was happening.

'After Leroy drove back to town,' Steve explained with a big smile on his face, 'I drove up to the house like I had business there. Nobody's at home and there are half a dozen rolled newspapers lying on the porch. I figure these folks are somewhere, maybe on vacation.'

Steve was really enjoying himself. He was chuckling quietly as he climbed down from the cab and went to look at the lock hanging from the hasp on the barn doors.

'Whew,' he muttered, jerking on the handful of stainless steel lock, 'I hope the bolt cutters I brought are strong enough to cut through this.'

The bolt cutters were heavy duty but even with both of us straining, the lock was tougher. I have to hand it to Steve, he didn't give up. Instead he used the cutter to shear through the hasp, leaving the lock dangling.

Inside we stopped to stare. There was enough light from the moon to see the three cars all lined up as if they were on display. A regular showroom.

'I'll bet that's the plan,' said Steve, taking out the list given to him by his banker. 'It wouldn't surprise me if that super sales manager Leroy didn't have buyers all lined up for these little beauties.'

And beauties they were. Using a yard-long flashlight, Steve read them off as he went about checking the vehicle identification number.

'First off we've got a pristine 1945 MG TC, to be followed by this gorgeous red and white 1956 Chevy Nomad. Now that's a real classic. And last but by no means least we have a cherry 1955 Buick Roadmaster. Boy, drive anyone of these down the street and you'd have every eye on you. C'mon, let's load them up.'

I backed the trailer up to the door and let down the loading ramp. Steve was carefully pulling on a pair of thin leather driving-gloves.

'Cars like these should not ever feel the touch of a human's hands,' he said solemnly. 'We'll take the Chevy first. Gorman has penciled in in the margin of the sheet his estimate of the car's value. Want to take a guess?' I shook my head. 'He says it's got a forty thousand dollar price tag. Wow.'

'Are you going to have to hotwire these or did Gorman give you a set of keys?'

Steve laughed. 'Neither. According to the owner, the keys are always left in the ignition. I suppose it's that way with stored collections. I don't know.'

The '56 Chevy Nomad was painted a deep blue, so dark it looked almost black in the beam of his flashlight. The chromed bumpers and grill gleamed in the bulb's light. I remembered a guy back in high school having a Nomad station wagon. For some reason I could even recall being told it was loaded with a rebuilt custom 350 engine. You know, the funny thing is I can remember that but I can't for the life of me remember the kid's name. Cars then, as now, weren't a big deal with me as they were with most men. Still, looking at this car as Steve carefully drove it up on to the furthest spot, I had to admit, it was a real work of art.

The Buick came next.

'God, would you look at that?' Steve stopped and started lecturing me, sounding a lot like some museum guide. 'A perfect two-door hardtop with those distinctive four ports in the front fender. The Roadmaster had four ports and other Buick models of that year, lesser cars in the line, had three. Man, look at it, I'll bet it's been rebuilt and is in factory-fresh mint condition.'

I didn't give a damn, but I wasn't about to spoil Steve's fun. What I really wanted was for him to hurry the fuck up. I wanted to be a long way down the road before the sun came up.

The Buick's engine started right up once he turned the key. The sparkling blue paint job on the car had been given so many coats laid on that the colour looked inches deep. As Steve had said, a head-turner on any street, that was for sure. Or as old Uncle Andrew would say, a real pussy wagon.

'You know,' Steve just had to stop to talk once he'd got the Buick in place on the trailer, 'looking at these cars it's clear that the owner is a serious collector. Wonder what else he has stored away?'

Unlike the other two cars, the little MG was pure sports car, the kind you would look at and shake your head, saying boy, they sure don't make this kind any more.

All I could do was stand there and watch as Steve got behind the wheel and turned the key. When nothing happened Steve studied the dashboard until he found a button to push. Running, I didn't think it sounded right, it wasn't running very smoothly.

'Probably only a four-cylinder,' Steve called before slowly bringing the car around and up the ramp. 'And it sounds like only half of them are firing.'

Even if only two of the cylinders were working, it was enough. We quickly got the blocks in place and the small vehicle strapped down.

I wasn't wasting any time and was behind the pick-up's steering wheel before Steve had the barn door closed. The clock was ticking and I didn't want to push our luck too far. We still had to get these cars out of this part of the world and back to the big city.

51

CHAPTER TWELVE

The payday for that job was the best yet, enough for me to open a new bank account and dump most of the cash straight into it. Yeah, cash. I was paid in cash. I don't know how much Steve got but the next time I saw him he was driving a different car.

His old Chevy had been a real rust bucket; this one was in darn near new condition.

'You like it?' he said, standing by the front fender. You could tell he was proud of the car. I could remember my dad bringing home a new car once. I was just a kid but I can picture him, standing there, proud as Punch, talking to a neighbour, showing off his new car. Buying a new car didn't seem so important any more. Probably because most new cars looked like every other new car. Steve was proud of this one, though.

'Old man Gorman said Cummings, you know, the bank director fellow who owned those three cars we recovered? Well, he was happy with our work. Remembering the condition my car was in, and that when talking about the separation, Gorman said Cummings mentioned something about a year old Chevy Monte Carlo, apparently a car he didn't really need. Not a collectable one, but one he didn't want his ex to get her hands on. Well, Gorman said all he had to do was suggest to that the title be turned over to me as payment for getting his three fancy cars back. And here it is. All I have to do is transfer the title. Slam dunk. What do you think?'

Cars have never been a big thing for me but it was clear this one tickled the hell out of my buddy. What could I say?

'It looks new.'

'Yeah, and the best part of the deal,' he said laughing, 'is I earned it while stealing other cars. Well, we earned it, but you know what I mean.'

'Hey, it's not a problem. I've got money in the bank, so I'm happy.'

'You know the first thing I did? I bought a large bottle of Turtle Wax and buffed it down. Spent all morning on it. Sure looks good, sitting here in the sunshine.'

It was a sunny morning. Sausalito is just across the bay from San Francisco but they're worlds apart when it comes to weather. There have been times when I have watched the fog come in from the Pacific, rolling over the hills like a slow moving ocean wave. At the same time, the skies here would be clear and cloud free. This just happened to be one of those mornings and the sunshine did make the car's finish gleam.

No question, Steve was happy as hell.

He didn't stick around long. I invited him in for coffee but he was hot to go for a drive. 'I think I'll just get out on the highway and go, you know? Footloose and fancy free. Want to join me?'

'Just like a kid with a new toy.' I laughed. 'No, you go on and have your fun. My plan for the rest of the week is to hibernate and write.'

I was working on my second novel and was already thinking about it while watching him take off. The story I'd been working on was giving me fits. All I wanted was peace and quiet while I worked the plot line all out. Loading up the refrigerator with easy to fix meals and a couple bottles of wine, I unplugged my phone and started writing.

I got a day and a half in before Steve came knocking.

It was a little before noon and he didn't actually knock, he just swung open the door and barged right in.

'Hey, your phone isn't working,' he called out, inching round behind me and going into the kitchen. Opening the camp-trailer-sized refrigerator, he gave it one glance and swore. 'There's no room for any more beer. You've got too much food in here.' Kicking the door closed, he took two bottles from the sack he'd been carrying and twisted the caps off. 'Here, and tell me what happened. You stopped paying your bills? I've been trying to get you since late yesterday.'

I really didn't want the beer, I wanted to keep writing. 'No, the phone works, it's just unplugged. Anyway, I thought you were taking off. Don't I recall hearing something about hitting the open road, searching for adventure?'

'Yeah, well, I got as far as Clear Lake and turned back. Love that car, but driving loses it excitement after a few miles. Now, why in hell is your phone off the hook? Never mind, it doesn't matter. Look, something's come up, something that could easily make that last deal look like peanuts.'

'No way, Steve,' I said adamantly. 'I'm not going to go with you to pick up cars for a while. Not for another week, at least.'

'Hey, I'm not talking about repoing any car or anything. No, this one's something as far from that as it could be. Ready for it?' he asked and then didn't wait for my answer. 'A man's wife has been kidnapped and he's hired us to deliver the ransom. Man, we're going to make real money on this one.'

I took the bottle of beer he handed me, giving up on getting any more done today. Thinking about it, well, to be honest, that story still wasn't going the way it was supposed to anyway.

'OK, lay it out. How are you and I going to make money out of some kidnapping? Who is it we're going to put in the trunk of your new car?'

Steve didn't laugh.

'Nobody. The kidnapping's already been done. We are being hired to deliver the ransom, that's all.'

'That doesn't make sense. No cop, especially the nearest FBI agent is going to turn any part of any kidnapping over to people like us. What's a former reporter and an ex-sheriff's deputy got that any lawman would need help with? Who was kidnapped, anyhow?'

Steve didn't like the questions. He just frowned and shook his head. 'I'm not exactly clear on that. We're to meet Gorman over at his office at two. That gives us time for lunch. Where do you want to go? I'm treating.'

One thing about Steve, when he had money he was very willing to spend it.

We went down to Lou Lou's Bar and Grill for lunch. Steve had already told me everything he knew about the job Gorman was sending our way, which wasn't much, so we couldn't talk about that. Along with the hamburgers and beer, I was kept entertained by listening to my friend tell me about his love life. At least he had one.

Steve didn't believe in marriage or even engagements. His attention span under normal conditions worked fine. When it came to women things became hectic. We were sitting at a table over against one wall when he stopped talking about his date the night before. I looked up to find my friend staring off towards the front door. Glancing around, I saw why.

I'll be the first to admit, Steve has remarkable taste when it comes to women. This young lady was definitely worth his gaze. Until she turned to smile up at the big guy standing behind her, I enjoyed the vision of her smooth black slacks and white shirt, the shirt-tails tied in a knot under her breasts. She was too far off for me to tell much more than that about her but Steve never had a problem with that. A fairway beauty, he called them . . . most all women were, he would explain, beautiful when they were a fair way away.

Understand me, a guy couldn't ask for a better man to back him up than Steve. Big, strong, fairly good looking and usually filled to the brim with common sense. If there was a hiccup in the wood pile it was his inability to think with what was between his ears when what was hanging between his legs started up. And all it took for that to happen was for him to get close to a woman. I'll give him points, though. He rarely got chummy with a beast.

'C'mon, man,' I attempted to cut into his staring. 'She's got that big dude behind her to keep her company. Pay attention, now. You were telling me about a young widow you met?'

'Ah, yes. Husband killed in a car accident. Someone, she said, had been drinking. Funny, she never said who was at fault. Guess it doesn't matter. Any how, you'd love her. A tall willowy body, with small sharply pointed breasts and a firm looking butt under the white linen dress she was wearing. Man, I certainly wouldn't need booze if she were hanging on to my arm.'

'So, what happened? Was this a date, or what?'

'No. Turns out she's a full-time student over at UC-Berkeley. Man, she's young enough to be my daughter. Almost.'

'How old is she?'

'Well, a college student. That puts her at what, twenty? Maybe twenty-five?'

'What, ten years younger than you? And you let that turn you off? Steve, old man. You gotta see a doctor. That's the right age.'

'Yeah, and what're you doing about your sex life, old buddy. Huh? Still pining after Inez, the woman who not only dumped you but cleaned out your bank account and took your car? Don't go telling me to see any doctor.'

That stopped me. 'C'mon, let's get over to your banker friend and find out what all this bullshit about a kidnapping is all about.'

'It isn't bullshit. Don't take an attitude just because your sex life sucks. Or you wished it did.'

I didn't have a response for that.

Gorman is in my view typical of a man who has made a success from dealing with other people's money. Remember Ray Milland? How about William Holden? Both Hollywood stars of the mid-1940s and both cut from the same bolt of cloth; suave, debonair, perfect haircuts and able to smile or sneer equally well. That's Frank Gorman, loan director for one of San Francisco's oldest banking firms. Only this time he wasn't dealing for the bank.

'Look, let's be very clear on this matter,' he said, keeping his eyes on his fingers as he slowly uncoiled a paper clip into a straight piece of metal.

He had remained seated behind a long, wide desk when we were ushered into his office and simply waved us towards a pair of leather-covered client chairs. I wasn't able to tell how tall he was, all I could swear to was the colour of his lightweight wool suit coat and tie. His suit was black with a lighter very thin pin stripe; the knot in his dark-grey tie was perfectly centred. If asked I wouldn't be able to swear he was wearing the pants that went with the coat. His Ray Milland hair was dark with a faint hint of grey at the temples. Frank Gorman's smile, when he eventually looked up at us, studying first Steve and then me, was thin.

'I want to make it very clear, this . . . this affair,' he said, hesitating to find the right word, 'has nothing to do with the bank and nothing to do with me. Fact is, I really don't want anything to do with it. But . . .' and he let the comment die.

We sat and waited.

'All right,' he said after a long pause. 'A certain client, Theodore Gussling, by name, has a delicate problem. The company he works for is one of our bigger customers. In addition, many of the company's officers have their personal accounts with this bank. We, the bank that is, and this company have a long and very valuable relationship. A few weeks ago, Mr and Mrs Gussling came in and opened an account, moving a large sum of money from their previous bank. When he came in yesterday morning, asking to speak to me, I couldn't turn him away. He didn't specify the problem he was facing except to ask if I could recommend someone. He asked for someone who could be trusted to help him.'

Gorman had been twisting the paper clip metal wire, bending it and rebending it until it broke. I knew that if both Steve and I could keep quiet, sooner or later he'd have to tell us more. It was a favorite ploy for a newspaper reporter to use in an interview. Apparently it worked for cops, too.

'Well,' Gorman swept the bits of metal wire into the palm of one hand and reached around, dropping them into a waste basket, 'I told Mr Gussling that I'd have to understand a little more to know whom to recommend. The story he told was . . . well, I think it was quite odd. However, as I said, both he and the company he represents are important to the bank. I'd appreciate it if you'd find the time to let him tell you what is required.'

Steve broke the silence. 'When you called me, you mentioned something about his wife being kidnapped.'

'Yes. That's what Mr Gussling told me. As I indicated, this entire affair is odd and I don't fully understand it, so it is therefore my opinion that the less I say the better.' He slipped a sheet of paper across to Steve before finishing. 'I've written down the address and phone number. Mr Gussling can explain so much better.'

CHAPTER THIRTEEN

When we called the number Gorman had given us Gussling asked if we could meet at a coffee shop on Market Street. It took us no more than five minutes to walk there. The weather that morning was a little wet for walking but we weren't going far. A stiff breeze was blowing up from the bay and the air was filled with a typical San Francisco mist, not heavy enough to be called a rain shower but wet enough to bead up on every clean, waxy surface.

The man waiting just inside the door where Gussling had said he would meet us was a little older than he first appeared. This, I thought, was due to someone's having spent some serious money on upkeep. After the introduction, he waved his well-manicured hand towards the back of the room.

Since the very early days San Francisco had had a love affair with coffee. I could remember as a boy travelling with my parents to visit someone down along the southern part of the city and passing by warehouses that smelled of roasting coffee. Major brands of ground coffee were processed in factories in Hunters Point. I don't remember whom we went to visit, but I can picture the billboards advertising MJB and Folgers' coffee and the wonderful smell of roasting beans.

That was what this café smelled like; strong roast coffee.

Steve briefly caught my eye as we fell in behind the man. I had already decided there was something hinky about Gussling, something I didn't like. That glance told me Steve caught it too.

Well-dressed and clean-cut-looking as he was, I couldn't help seeing a sleazy used-car salesman with a nice pressed suit and a car lot full of worn-out 1970 Chevy Chevettes. That was the car, someone had labelled as the fifth Worst Car of the Millennium. "An engine surrounded by four pieces of drywall" was one description I remembered reading.

Gussling appeared slick in his banker's pinstripe three-piece suit and red power tie. No fleas would stick on this man, is what my dad would have said. When we had first shaken hands, I noticed that even the raindrops on his wingtip shoes had beaded and rolled off.

Settling around a small table against a back wall, we gave our order to the young waitress. For a moment no one spoke. I was hoping the silence would force the banker type to say something, would tell us why we were here. It didn't seem to bother Gussling. Even before our coffee arrived we were given a perfect "let's be friends" smile.

'When I talked to Mr Gorman he mentioned having one man in mind, I'm glad he found a second.'

Steve shook his head. 'Bernie and I work together at times to repossess vehicles for Gorman's bank. From what little we were told, it appears that it isn't a car or truck you want us to find for you.'

'No, it isn't a car I want to hire you to find. No, when I asked Mr Gorman to refer someone to me, he thought long and hard before giving me your name. He even warned me that you might not be interested in helping. However, it is possible that if that is the case, then you could suggest someone who could help me.'

'That's why I brought Bernie here,' said Steve, glancing in my direction. 'He and I have worked together a long time. Not understanding what the problem you want solved is, I thought it would be better if both of us were here to hear you explain.'

'Oh, if only it were that easy,' said the well-dressed businessman. 'Let me introduce myself.' He handed each of us a business card. Theodore Gussling, the card read, raised letters on a cream-coloured card. The very plush card said that Gussling was the vice-president for sales and training for a company called Havershack Industries, Inc. The company had offices in Berlin, San Francisco, Las Vegas, Macau and Buenos Aires.

'Havershack Industries,' Gussling said proudly, 'is the world's seventh largest supplier of gambling equipment. Our biggest selling items are slot machines manufactured in our German factories,' he added almost squaring his shoulders and sticking out his chest.

OK, so its slot machines you wanted us to repossess, I thought but didn't say the words. Gussling's next words dumped that idea.

'The problem I bring to you has little to do with my company, however. No, what I am looking for is someone to help me find my wife.'

'I'm sure your wife is dear to you, Mr . . . ah . . .' Steve hesitated, glanced at the business card, and went on, 'Mr Gussling. But finding people who have gone missing are a matter for the police.'

'I'm afraid I'm not making myself clear. She isn't missing in that sense. She's been kidnapped.'

I thought Steve was doing a good job and didn't interrupt with my questions.

'Well,' Steve said, smiling to soften the blow and then explaining as he would to a six-year-old, 'I'm sorry, but I still don't see how we can help. Kidnapping is certainly something for the authorities,' Steve held out his hands to show how hopeless it would be.

'I can't go to the police. Let me explain. My wife, Claire, and I just returned from Argentina. We had been down there for nearly two years. Opening up our house out in Saratoga has taken up most of our time the past three weeks and while I've been busy with meetings and the like at the office, Claire has been working at the house. Yesterday when I got home, the house was empty. A note had been left on the counter in the kitchen. Here,' he said, handing the single sheet of paper across the desk.

Steve took it and read the few lines before handing it to me.

Don't panic. Don't call the police. Your wife is safe with us and will remain so as long as you do as we say. Contact your company in the morning and inform them of this situation. We will contact you about how to make the necessary transfer arrangements. Remember, your wife is comfortable and safe as long as you follow the appropriate procedures.

'It's still as Steve says,' I said, handing the sheet back, 'the best chance you have of getting her back is to contact the police. We don't know anything about how to deal with kidnappers.' I stopped, thinking of something. 'Why would the kidnappers want you to contact your company?'

'That is the reason I can't call the authorities. Argentina is, sad to say, one of those countries where kidnapping is almost a way of life. American business people are among the targets most taken. Major companies doing business there typically take out insurance on their employees, to cover any ransom demands. In most cases it works, the ransom is paid and the kidnapped victim is returned unharmed. To the company, the insurance is part of the overhead. Down there the police are worse than useless in these matters. Too often, it is believed they could even be involved. Over the years the insurance companies have asked that they, the police, not be brought into it. They pay the ransom and everyone is happy.'

'But this is not South America, Mr Gussling. This is California.'

'Yes, but certain things remain the same. When I turn this over to the Havershack security people, they will put the wheels in motion. The insurance company will be brought into it and when the kidnappers contact me, they will make the ransom money available. Neither my company nor the insurance people will want any word of this to get out. They won't want to let anyone know how easy it is to get a payoff.'

CHAPTER FOURTEEN

Steve still wasn't sold on this and neither was I. Argentina is a long way away and here in the good old US of A when someone yells kidnapping the next words are always FBI. I wasn't sure of Steve's reasons but my explanation was simple; I just didn't like this man, didn't trust him.

I thought it was time to start turning the job down. 'That's reason enough to call the police in, don't you think?'

'Maybe. But if I'm to get my wife back safely, then I have to do as the kidnappers, my company and the insurance company wants. Can't you see that?'

I thought about what he had said for a moment. 'You may be right, as far as that goes. But that changes nothing. We can't help you and I don't know anyone who could.'

Gussling looked down at his hands folded on the table top.

'I had hoped you would at least try,' he said, quietly before going on with some enthusiasm. A master salesman closing the deal. 'My company and the insurance company will be focused on paying out the insurance money, I'm afraid my wife's welfare won't be the centre of their attention, early on at least. Not until the money is paid out. That part of it will take a few days to happen. What I'd like is to hire you to negotiate with the kidnappers for her return. I'm certain that once I've contacted the company with this . . . well, I had hoped you would have time to make a search for her. It's not the money I care about, that's just going to be part of a process. All I care about is my wife.' Slowing down now and going back to looking at his hands, he slowly shook his head.

'I don't know what I expected, but I can't just sit back and let the two companies do what they'll do. They are sure to be looking first at the bottom line, paying out the money and waiting for Claire to be freed.

Whatever you succeed with, finding Claire or simply delivering the ransom, you'll get ten per cent of the ransom amount once my wife is safe and sound. Plus your expenses, of course.'

Even not really liking the man, I felt compassion for him. 'You say the insurance company will simply dig up the cash and hand it over?'

'That's it. The insurance coverage on us overlaps our return to the States by six months. Both of us are covered with a policy specifically against being kidnapped. It is, I'm afraid, a little more for me than my wife.'

'I've never heard of anything like this,' Steve said, starting to stand up to bring this conversation to an end.

'And everybody wants to keep it like that. The insurance premiums are high, high enough to cover the ransom demands when they are made but that's all part of my salary package. Coverage for me is five million. For a spouse or child it is usually two.'

Steve sat back down. 'The insurance company will be willing to pay the kidnappers two million dollars for your wife's safe return.' It wasn't a question.

Gussling nodded. 'That's the sticking point for me,' he explained, his voice falling off, getting serious. 'When you're dealing with an Argentine kidnapper, you know it's strictly business. To stay in business the kidnappers rarely harm the victim. But here, well, who knows what these people will do? That's why I need your help.'

Steve was looking over the salesman's shoulder and out of the window at the rain. I knew what he was thinking about, ten per cent of two million, plus expenses.

'Maybe we should talk about this a bit more, Mr Gussling,' he said, bringing his gaze back to the man.

The three of us sat at that table for another half-hour or so before we finally shook hands on the deal. Steve and I would do what we could to bring the missus back. For all the talk, once that agreement was struck, there was little we could do except wait for the kidnappers to contact Gussling.

'I'll pass this note on to my superiors and that'll get that end of things started. A few of the upper-level managers have served in Argentina and have a good understanding about the situation. They will know how the process works. The insurance company will have to be notified and that'll get the ball rolling. I don't know whether their local people know how this kind of thing works or not, but they'll soon learn.'

'And it'd help us a lot, Mr Gussling,' Steve said slowly, 'if you could supply us with a recent photo of your wife.' He chuckled softly. 'It wouldn't do anyone any good to ransom the wrong woman.'

Gussling didn't respond with even a smile but said he'd get one to us.

I was thinking about the holes in his story. I thought that some at least of what he had told us didn't make total sense. Steve wasn't looking beyond the ten per cent payday. I gave up. Whatever it was about, it paid better than my novel or repo'ing any car or truck.

Thinking about what we were being told, I could see Steve and me approaching this from two directions. Not wanting to say anything, I waited until Gussling left us. Listening to the two go on talking, simply rehashing what had already been said, I sat sipping coffee, getting my arguments in order. Steve might have his own ideas on how to get this deal done. I could wait.

CHAPTER FIFTEEN

I didn't have to worry on that front. Steve beat me to it. Gussling stopped on the way out to pay the cashier, leaving the two of us just looking at each other. I hoped the man added a nice tip for the waitress, she hadn't bothered us once. Guess she was used to businessmen wheeling and dealing at the back tables.

'Can you believe it?' my partner said with a big smile, 'Ten per cent of two million. That's a helluva lot of cars we won't have to repo. Now look,' he went on hurriedly, 'it won't take both of us to carry the ransom money to the kidnappers. Once those bastards call to set up a drop off the rest is easy. But that could take a few days. I mean, Gussling there, didn't he say something about the insurance company not understanding how the Argentine kidnapping practice works?'

Actually I had missed that part and hadn't thought about how long it would take to get the money ready and available.

'OK,' when I didn't nod he just barrelled on, 'today is Friday. Most likely there won't be anything done before Monday. In so far as getting any hotshot bean-counter insurance claims manager to make a decision, I figure it'll take a few days and then it'll probably have to go up the chain of command to get the higher-up's approval. At least that's the way it is when dealing with the insurance companies over an auto claim.'

'So what are you saying?'

'So, let's figure out how we can find the missing Mrs Gussling. If the insurance company, or Gussling himself, is willing to pay ten per cent for simply delivering the ransom, think what they'll pay if we get her back and they can save that money. It shouldn't be that hard. I mean, the Gusslings have only been back in California for a couple weeks, right? Well, in that time the kidnappers had to set things up, didn't they? And that means at least one of them had to have a watch on her. And they would have to be familiar with the insurance angle. I'll bet that the list of people all that fits would be small.'

I liked the way his thinking went. I nodded and waited.

'Anyway, doesn't this sound kind of odd? I mean it sounds like someone is scamming the insurance company, doesn't it? Maybe it is a real kidnapping. Or maybe it's someone – hell, anyone who knows about that policy going after the pay-out.'

Again I didn't add anything to his thoughts. Let him ramble, I figured. Sooner or later he would arrive at the same conclusion I had already reached.

'It doesn't take a genius to figure out that the top two names on the list have to be either Mr or Mrs Gussling, does it?'

I had to smile. 'Or both? Or someone at Havershack Industries. Those folks would know when the Gusslings came back to the States and how much the insurance coverage was worth.'

'Boy, that does muddy up the waters, doesn't it.' He wasn't asking a question. 'OK, then,' he went on after a moment's silence, 'my suggestion is for you to deal with the money pay-off angle. Meanwhile I'll start searching for the kidnap victim. Even if old man Gussling and his wife are pulling a scam, or someone from his company is behind it, the bottom line is that dear, sweet Mrs Gussling is someplace. You deal with the mister, get yourself in position to do as he wants, deliver the ransom and at the same time keep an eye on him. That'll leave it up to me to see what I can turn up about any other person or persons who could get close enough to her to whisk her away. That OK with you?'

'Yeah, it makes sense,' I said at last.' You're a lot better than I am for investigating people. But there'll be information turning up that we'll have to share. That means you'll have to carry your cell phone and keep the battery up.'

Back when Steve was driving a department patrol car he had a bad reputation for turning the car radio down and switching off his cell. His favourite excuse was that he forgot to plug it in at night.

'Yeah, yeah, yeah, I'll keep in close touch. Now, what's your first move?'

'Well, I suppose the first thing is to let Gussling know what we're doing and then get him to introduce me to the insurance people. They certainly won't just hand a couple million in ransom money over to the first Joe Blow comes walking in off the street.'

'That's right. Man, wouldn't it be nice to get this little job done? Can you see it,' he moved his hands high overhead, spreading them out as if reading a bill board, 'Steve and Bernie, we repo cars, trucks and boats. Rescuing wives a specialty.'

CHAPTER SIXTEEN

Whatever training he'd had as a deputy sheriff – or maybe he'd been born with it, Steve was good at digging the dirt. Once upon a time I even thought it was something he'd been born with. You know, like Liberace had learned to play the piano while in the womb. Whatever it was, Steve was a damn good investigator. He did the hard work, searching, asking the right people the right questions and having a great memory.

'Naw,' he said more than once when recalling some obscure fact that nobody else could come up with, 'it's not a photographic memory I was blessed with; it's more like a pornographic memory.'

Then he'd laugh long and loud at the joke that really, when you thought about it, wasn't actually funny at all. But having said that, I'll be the first to admit: as an investigator he's a hell of a lot better than I could ever be. That's why I was overjoyed when he suggested he take that part of the deal. Delivering the money should be a slam dunk.

It didn't work that way, though. The first major hurdle, getting the insurance company that carried Havershack Industries policies to go along with Gussling's choice of associates, was more slam than dunk. Who in the hell is this guy? they wanted to know.

'Look,' Gussling said patiently. We were sitting in the offices of the American Underwriters Insurance Group. The office was on Maiden Lane, just around the corner and down the block from Gussling's office, home of Havershack Industries, Inc. I had called Gussling to explain the direction Steve and I were taking. At first the man wasn't too happy with our plan but when I explained about our approach being two-pronged, he gave it his blessing.

'Remember though, the first and most vital aspect of this is the safe return of my wife.'

I felt confident enough to smile when giving my assurances.

'To make this work,' I said, trying to overlook the feeling of sleaze he exuded, 'we'll have to have the insurance company's approval. That's the reason for my being here now.'

'I have notified my superiors here in the office and the insurance company has been notified. We can go over to the insurance carrier's offices right now and get that cleared up.'

Somehow I didn't expect it to be that easy.

The weather had eased as the afternoon progressed and while the streets and sidewalks were still wet, the mist had stopped falling. Gussling had picked up an umbrella but left it rolled up as we walked over to meet the insurance representative, using it like a cane.

According to the listing directory in the lobby of the Maiden Lane address, American Underwriters Insurance Group took up the entire third floor. Stepping off the elevator, we found ourselves standing in front of a long, chest-high counter. There were three women sat behind the counter, all three wearing tiny earphones and microphones so small as to be almost invisible.

'May I help you,' the prettiest of the three asked, looking up and smiling first at Gussling, then at me and then, deciding I wasn't the leader here, back to Gussling. I suppose it was his slick three-piece suit that did it. Dress for success had been the mantra, or so I'd heard. I didn't mind being sent to the back of the bus.

'Yes.' Gussling matched her smile with one he probably thought was as warm and friendly as hers. Personally I thought his smile was a lot like that of a not-too friendly crocodile. 'I'm Theodore Gussling and with me is Bernard Gould. We are here to see Geoff Frazier.'

'Do you have an appointment?' the woman asked, immediately looking down at the open pages of an appointment book. Why ask? I thought. She should easily be able to see if the big man had anyone booked in, shouldn't she?

'Yes.'

'I'm afraid I don't have any listing for Mr Frazier this afternoon. Would you like to schedule a meeting for tomorrow morning?' The smile behind her words was still warm and friendly. I decided that it was all part of the skills she brought to the job and had nothing to do with any real person.

'If you'd punch the correct buttons and mention the Havershack

Industries I would imagine he would take a few minutes to meet with us.' For a moment I liked the man a little more, he was able to show her he could maintain his own pretend version of an amiable smile.

Letting her smile fall a little, she did as he asked and punched three buttons. I couldn't hear what she said into the little microphone but when she looked up her smile had returned full force.

'If you'd care to take a seat, Mr Frazier will be out in a minute.'

Half a dozen soft-covered chairs over near the wall were clustered around a long, low table. Down the hall from the counter I could see a series of closed doors, each with a little label on it.

The magazines spread out in a decorative fan on the table before us included everything from *Environmental Weekly* to *Architectural Design*. Not one issue of *Readers Digest* or *Playboy*. Before I could make a choice, we were called and ushered down the hall and through one of the doors.

After being introduced to Frazier, another three-piece suit, power tie and smooth smile under a premature balding head, Gussling explained our reason for being there.

'Well,' Frazier said hesitantly, looking into his steepled fingers for the answer, 'it would be very irregular to have us turn over any ransom monies to someone we've no knowledge of.'

'Mr Frazier, I called for an appointment with you less than half an hour ago. When we arrived your young receptionist had no knowledge of that and suggested we make an appointment for tomorrow morning. Now I bring this to your attention because it makes me wonder about the workings of this office. We could be counting on a business where the right hand and left hand do not know what is going on. Understand me, this entire situation is very, as you say, irregular. My company has had to deal with it a number of times in the past. Your records should show this. You can believe we have the experience your people may not have. Let me ask you, what do any of your adjusters know about dealing with kidnappers? I'll tell you, nothing. Your people understand assessing a building damaged by flood, or the pay-out to a woman who slipped on a grape at the supermarket. But has anyone in this office ever had to conduct a negotiation with kidnappers before. Not likely. I want my wife back. You want to save your money. I think you'll find in the small print on that agreement that only a trained negotiator approved by Havershack Industries will be used.'

Frazier didn't like being talked to like this. Once more I had to keep from patting Theodore Gussling on the back.

'Now wait a minute; it is true our people in the field have little experience with kidnapping, which is something that the police and FBI handle. What you're expecting is that these agencies are cut out of the picture. That can't happen, I'm afraid. Kidnapping is a federal offence and must be treated as such. The fact is I have already set up an appointment with a member of a San Francisco Police Department task force trained in just this kind of thing.'

Gussling wasn't about to give it up. 'You had better read that policy again, Mr Frazier. This situation is well defined therein, not as a kidnapping but as simply a forced business transaction. Yes,' he held up a hand to stop Frazier from interrupting, 'we at Havershack Industries recognize that this type of business deal is more popular in certain South American countries. However the policy Havershack has with you covers my wife as well as myself, no matter where in the world we are. Now, let us get on with it.'

Frazier was weakening. 'I have never run into anything like this. We here at American Underwriters will have to research this policy. I assure you we will know what direction is to be taken, but you must give us time to get up to speed.'

Gussling stood and looked down at the insurance man. 'Just keep in mind, Mr Frazier; it is my wife's welfare we are discussing here. We will be waiting to hear from you.'

I followed the man to the elevator, shaking my head in wonder at the thought processes that men affect when putting on their fine suits in the morning.

CHAPTER SEVENTEEN

I didn't hear anything from Steve over the weekend and was glad. It gave me two more days to try to save the story I'd been working on. The weather stayed overcast and showery so I stayed inside, except for going down for the Sunday morning paper. Nobody bothered me all day Monday so all in all, it was a pretty quiet three-day weekend, I'd say.

Gussling called me about noon on Tuesday. American Underwriters had decreed that I would have to be bonded.

That, he explained, was more a formality than anything. The paperwork would be waiting for my signature and when signed I would officially be the representative for Havershack Industries, Inc. Now all I had to do was wait for the kidnappers to call.

A phone call to Steve went unanswered, so I texted a message to his cell telling him about getting bonded.

After a quick lunch I once again used the Golden Gate ferry to get me over to the other side of the bay. Signing the papers, and certain I was signing away not only my firstborn but probably my virginity as well, I decided to stop at a Starbucks for a coffee. That was where the police found me.

I was sitting at one of the small tables next to the window, watching people walk by when someone pulled the other chair at the table out and sat down.

'Don't mind if I join you, do you?'

'Depends on who's asking.'

'Very wise, don't talk to strangers is my motto. I'm Special Detective Jonathan Quincy, San Francisco Police,' he said, holding out a leather wallet to show me his badge. 'You are Bernard Gould and I hope you can help me out with something. Actually, with two things.'

'Well, make yourself comfortable and ask your questions. Any time I can help out the law, I consider my good deed for the day has been done.'

'Uh huh. Good. First let me explain that I'm a member of the city's Organized Crime Strike Force as well as the San Francisco Major Crimes Section. I always like to tell people that, makes me sound like I'm right in the middle of a lot of good juicy crimes.'

'And makes me wonder what any of that has to do with me?'

'Well, it seems as if you've become part of a couple things that are on my list. First there was a visit you had with a certain Guido Pistilli. We wondered about that but didn't give it much weight. Not, that is, until your name showed up on a suspected kidnapping. Or something that might be a kidnapping, it's not too clear. I decided maybe I should have a little talk with you.'

'How'd you know about my talk with this Pistilli?'

'Oh, the Organized Crime folk keep a close eye on a number of characters in the Northern District. Yeah, I know, it sounds like we don't have enough work to do and have to go out scaring up things. Trust me, it isn't like that at all. All of us have enough to do without bird-dogging a bunch of crooks. For instance, there have been at least two cases of young women being raped and murdered recently. You heard or read anything about that?'

I shook my head slightly.

'There've been two of them and I'll bet there'll be more. Young women, girls actually, both found in remote places. Both were taped up the same way and killed the same way. After they had been brutally raped, I might add. So we're starting to get pressure from the newspapers. That means the mayor's office will be calling. Any more and it takes on the label of being a serial killer we've got to deal with and then even the governor's office will get involved. At the same time there are the usual things, like what jerks like Pistilli are doing. Maybe you can help me out with that one?'

I didn't offer anything and after a moment the cop nodded, took a sip of his coffee, and continued. 'That's OK. It was having a call warning us of a possible kidnapping that I really would like to hear about. Your name came up on that and, well, hell, I gotta say, we just haven't got the time or manpower to be playing any games. What do you say?'

'OK, I guess it won't matter. First off, there has been no kidnapping. At least none that I know anything about. What I believe is that someone

73

is scamming an insurance company. A certain woman has gone missing. Her husband gets a note, not mentioning kidnapping, mind you, just advising him to start the process for an insurance pay-out. The man's company has a policy geared towards protecting employees and their families when working in certain foreign countries. The idea is to get a hold of one of these people and have the insurance pay for the rescue. The person is then released and everyone goes on their way. It's looked at like a simple business matter. I've been hired to make delivery of the insurance pay-out. That's all there is to it.'

Quincy shook his head. 'Boy, that's a new one. If the crims ever used their brains to go into legitimate business they could end up owning the bank. OK, I think. All I know is that a contact at a big insurance company made a phone call and then later called back to tell us it was all a mistake. So, no crime, no harm, no worry. Tell me about Pistilli.'

'Talk about being slippery, you got that in quite casually, didn't you?' I finished my cappuccino and put the mug down. 'A man identifying himself as Pistilli wanted to know the whereabouts of a guy I knew back in college, that's all. I haven't seen this guy in years and have no idea exactly what Pistilli wants to see him for. And after meeting Mr Pistilli I have to say I want nothing more to do with him either. A very evil man, I'd guess.'

'And you'd be right. Who is the man, your college chum whom Pistilli was asking about? Who's he?'

'Naw, there's no reason to bring him into it. He's long gone.'

The detective smiled, 'Let us hope he's simply gone some place Pistilli can't find him. As you say, he's one bad dude and if he wants your college friend bad enough, and finds him, you'll be right . . . he'll be long gone. Real long gone.'

CHAPTER EIGHTEEN

Steve ignored it when his cell phone vibrated. At the time he was talking to Theodore Gussling. Later he read Bernie's text and smiled.

Over the weekend he had thought about the kidnapping, mostly dreaming how he'd spend his share of the ten per cent. Beyond that, he did make the decision to see what he could find out about the kidnap victim, Claire Gussling. A good place to start, he thought, was to find out how she spent her time. It wasn't hard. He remembered something her husband had mentioned, something about their house in Saratoga. The Gusslings had been out of the country for quite a while, a couple years. No woman, after being away from her house that long is going to be satisfied with things the way she'd left them; she would want to redecorate at least part of it. Maybe there would be something at their house that would help. Steve decided to start there.

When he visited Gussling at the man's office there had been no problem in giving Steve the address of their house in Saratoga.

'Are you familiar with Saratoga?' he'd asked.

Steve shook his head. 'I know it's down the peninsula, one of those cute little commuter towns close to San Jose, isn't it?'

Steve was trying to get to the sales manager, hoping he'd say something useful. He succeeded. Saratoga, he learned, was an upper-class bedroom community some ninety miles south of the city, its residents too proud to accept being joined at the hip with a place like San Jose, though.

'I wouldn't describe it like that.' Gussling almost sneered. 'Our place is in Saratoga Woods, you know. Our little section is known as the Golden Triangle, with Cox Street on one side and Sunnyvale Road and Saratoga Avenue on the others. The Woods, as we call it, is protected by covenant to very stringent building regulations. You can be sure it isn't just anybody living there.'

Steve smiled, knowing that covenant building rules meant one thing: no blacks or Hispanics allowed unless they were there to mow the lawn or clean the pool. He'd have to wear a sports coat and tie when he knocked on the door.

When he pulled up in his Monte Carlo into the Gusslings' neighbourhood, it was certain he was being watched. Carrying a clipboard, he strode purposefully up the brick walk to the front door and pushed the discreet button.

Nonchalantly looking back over the street, he couldn't hear the chimes. He pushed the button again and waited patiently. Most of the houses on Cox Street, he figured, were in the million to a million-and-a-half dollar range. Nearly all were single-storey ranch style, with three or four bedrooms. From what he could see only a few were two-storey. Gussling's was one of these.

After waiting a suitable time Steve walked back towards the street before stopping to look back at the house, consulting the blank paper on his clipboard. Studying the house, he made a small mark on the paper before walking to peer down the side of the structure.

The steeply pitched roof peaked over the second storey which extended out over the double garage. Huge windows fronted that upper wall. Steve wondered what kind of view he'd get from that window.

Walking back along the side of the house, he stopped every so often to make another note on the blank paper. Any neighbours would know that the house had been empty for a long time, the owners having only returned a few weeks ago. Having someone come around to inspect the place, maybe getting an estimate for a paint job, would be natural. Taking his time, he moved close to the house, tapping on the siding before moving down between the wall and the fence.

Glancing quickly around when he reached a side door, he didn't think anyone could see him. Using a minimum of force, he slipped a thin metal blade between the door and the jamb right below the lock. The blade was part of a set of picks and toothed levers he had acquired while a deputy sheriff. It had all belonged to an elderly man of no visible means of support whom he had taken into custody. Feeling that the old man deserved better, and in return for a promise he'd pay the fine, get out of the county and not report the loss of his tools, Steve had given him a speeding ticket and let him go. The tools had come in handy a couple

times when getting into someone's car or truck, or when opening a side
door.

Putting pressure on the blade, he felt the door-lock tongue slide out of
the way. He knew there would be scratches on the striker plate but there
wasn't anything he could do about that. Chances were, unless he left a
mess behind, nobody would ever know he'd been inside.

Figuring he only had a few minutes, he knew he couldn't give the place
a thorough search. All he could hope for was to find some hint of what
kind of people this couple was.

Quickly bypassing the downstairs, Steve ran up the curved stairway,
heading for the room over the garage. That, he thought, would be the
master bedroom.

The king-sized bed was positioned so that anyone lying there with
their backs against the headboard could see out over the neighbour's
house across the street. Possibly the Gusslings got an added thrill making
love while looking out at their neighbours. Doors on each side of the
room were closed. Not hesitating, Steve opened one to find men's suits
and shirts on hangers. Shoes, the polish glistening in the morning
sunlight, were lined up in a row on the wardrobe floor.

A woman's clothes were jammed into the wardrobe on the other side;
Claire Gussling was obviously a woman who liked to shop. Her shoes,
unlike her husband's, looked as if she'd just tossed them after taking them
off. A tennis racket, the cover carrying the Wilson logo, stood in the
closet corner.

Matching dressers lined the wall next to the head of the bed, one on
either side. The dressers were bigger than any Steve had ever owned;
there were at least ten drawers in each one. Hurriedly he pulled out a
drawer to see what it contained before going on to the next one. He
found nothing until getting to the woman's side. He could tell it was hers
by all the little weirdly shaped bottles that covered the dresser top as well
as the piles of nicely folded panties in one of the drawers. What caught
his eye was the box of Trojan condoms half-hidden by the various
coloured, mostly transparent, thongs. Trojan Magnum Extra Large,
according to the label.

There had been that old joke about the kid going in to the corner
drugstore to buy rubbers and the guy behind the counter asking if he
wanted the small or large size. The kid naturally stuck out his chest and
said the largest you got. The joke was that rubbers only came in one size.

At least back then they did.

As he put the package back, he noticed that a Kodak photo envelope had been under it in the drawer. He picked up the envelope and looked inside, to find a dozen or so colour shots of young women. Actually from the angular shapes of their faces and their skin tone, Steve thought they were probably Mexicans and they were young, girls not women. All nudes, most with small pointed breasts and large bushes of coal black pubic hair and all with their eyes closed. Shaking his head, he replaced the pictures and closed the drawer.

He'd been in the house long enough and wasn't learning anything worth while. It was time to go. Hurrying down the stairs, he took time to give the living-room a quick look-over. Seeing a half dozen or so photos arrayed on the narrow ledge above a sparkling clean fireplace, he studied them briefly. Standing proudly in a double-hinged frame was a picture of a couple. The man was Theodore, so he figured the woman was the kidnapped wife. Another smaller picture of the woman was half hidden behind the grouping. That one he picked up, shoving the silver filigreed frame into his pants pocket.

Back outside the side door, he carefully checked to see that it locked before walking naturally back the way he'd come, holding the clipboard at his side.

'Hello,' someone called as he came round to the front. Turning towards the voice, Steve saw a grey-haired man standing next to a waist-high hedge, holding a pair of clippers. A nosy neighbour.

Steve smiled and returned the greeting. 'Good morning. Keeping things all nicely shaped, I see.'

'Well, you know if you turn your back very long it'll get away from you. The Gusslings got back from their trip, I see.'

'I wouldn't know about that. They've been gone?'

'Oh, yes. Mr Gussling works down in South America, some place. I can't remember where they said. My wife, Ethel, and Mrs Gussling are tennis partners over at the club, you know; they play a lot of doubles.'

'No, I don't know anything about who lives here.' Holding up the clipboard, Steve let his smile turn professional. 'I'm here to come up with an estimate for insurance purposes. Apparently the owners want more coverage.'

Remembering the tennis racket up in the closet, Steve smiled. 'Your wife plays tennis, huh? It's been years since I've played. Is the club private or do they have a pro who gives lessons?'

The old man smiled. 'Yeah, it's a private club and there is a pro. And Ethel says the kind of lessons he gives Mrs Gussling are private, all right, and frequent.' He chuckled, 'I guess I shouldn't be gossiping, but have you ever seen the woman?'

Steve shook his head.

'Well, if I was a dozen years younger, hell, maybe even a half-dozen, and it wasn't that Ethel keeps a close eye on me, then I'd offer to give a few lessons myself. She's a real looker. Big up front, you know, and all that tennis she plays keeps her rear end nice and tight-looking. Yes sir, a real neat package.'

Remembering the extra large condoms I wondered whether this old man had what it'd take, even a dozen years ago.

'I guess I won't worry about any of that,' Steve said, turning to walk away. 'It's probably too late for me to take up anything like tennis anyhow. Well, it's back to work for me. Nice talking to you.'

Maybe checking out the tennis pro might be the next stop, he thought as he started up the Monte Carlo. Somewhere there had to be someone who could tell him more about Claire Gussling other than that she liked getting a private lesson now and again.

CHAPTER NINETEEN

Tuesday evening

When we got together at Lou Lou's for drinks later that evening, neither of us was feeling good and both of us were sporting a black eye.

Fat Henry took his time inspecting the bruises, first on Steve's cheek before closely investigating my left eye which was swollen almost closed. It wasn't until then that he took our order for beer.

I knew what my face looked like; I'd studied it as much as I could with one eye before coming down to Lou Lou's. Steve's was more colourful. An area about fist size just to the side of his left eye was an interesting variety of shades ranging from bright pink to soft purple. Through out it all, the bartender didn't say a word, just smiled. I would have laughed except my ribs still hurt too much to even take a deep breath.

'What the hell did you run into, a quick tempered door?' was the best I could do, getting to him before he could question me.

'Ah, hell, Bern. It isn't funny,' Steve said, talking out one side of his mouth, 'My face feels like it's been flattened.'

'And you've got a beauty of a shiner. Do they still call a black eye a shiner?'

'You should talk. Anyhow, I said it isn't funny. Anyway, mine was just a mistake. Can you say the same?'

I ignored his question. 'A mistake when your face ran into someone's fist?'

'No. The guy thought he'd heard something and . . . the hell with it. Just believe me when I say it was a mistake.'

'So tell me how it happened, this mistake.' I said, forgetting myself and starting to swing around to pick up the beer glass the bartender had placed on the bar. The sharp pain from my upper chest made me flinch.

'Well, I found out where the Gussling's house is, down in Saratoga. I was looking for information about the missus. You remember what we were talking about? How there wasn't many people who would know about that insurance coverage that the Gusslings have? I think the Gusslings have to be in on it. So, I went looking. Well, as much as I could, but couldn't find a thing.'

I had to interrupt. 'Looked where?'

'At their house, where else?'

'You broke into their house?' I stopped to look at him before taking a long drink of beer. Some people don't like the tang of good beer. I guess it's an acquired taste. But after a day like I had had, that first sip was pure ambrosia.

'Well, yeah. I didn't stay long and they'll never know I was there. But it wasn't a total waste of time. I did find out that Claire Gussling plays a lot of tennis at a local club. That's where I ran into this,' he pointed at the side of his face.

'The Saratoga Golf and Tennis Club is a private club and I'd no more than parked the car and was getting out when this young tough-looking guy in a fancy green jacket came hurrying over to check me out. He wanted me to know this was a private club and that I couldn't park where I did. All I wanted to do was talk to the club's tennis pro. According to what I'd learned Claire may have been learning more from the pro than just tennis. The green jacket wouldn't tell me the time of day. He just wanted me and my car out of there. It was then that I got smacked.'

'The guy in the jacket smacked you?' I asked, moving slowly and carefully to pick up my beer.

'No. See, there was another guy, seemed to think I was the tennis pro. That's who he was looking for. He'd come around from behind the car I'd parked next to. When the green jacket turned away, this guy came around, yelling at me and before I could react, he dropped me.'

'Right out of the blue, he hit you,' I said in disbelief.

'Yeah. The green jacket came running over and for the first time I was glad he was there. He stopped the guy from doing any further damage. See, that's what the mistake was. The guy had heard only part of what I'd said, asking about the tennis pro. He heard the guard say something and somehow got the idea I was the pro. It turned out the guy's wife had been having it off with the pro and he was there to set things straight. See, what I mean? It was all a mistake.'

81

'The guy who hit you thought you were the tennis pro. How could he make a mistake like that?'

'Well, I had been told it was a private club. Saratoga's one of those kinds of places where things would be exclusive and selective. So I made sure I was dressed for success when I went out there to talk to the pro. I stopped and bought a pair of white tennis shorts and a matching shirt. A pair of shoes from a cheapo shoe store and I thought I'd pass. The poor guy thought I was the man he was after, so I guess I succeeded.'

'Yeah, except you didn't fool the guy in the green jacket.'

Steve's smile might have been lopsided but it was filled with pride. 'Nope, but I did find out what I wanted. I got the pro's name, Antonio Jardin, at least that's what he calls himself. Suppose to be some kind of Mexican hotshot tennis professional. Jardin doesn't sound very Mexican to me. Anyway, and here's the good part: according to what the fellow who beat me up told me, this Jardin hasn't been seen for the last six or seven days. Get it? That's about the same time since the wife of our Mr Gussling went missing.'

I had to admit: even getting punched Steve had done better than I had for the day's effort.

'OK,' he said, motioning for the bartender to bring us another beer, 'so that's my story, what's yours?'

'I didn't accomplish much. The insurance people got all huffy and it took a while to get that straightened out. I'm now bonded and waiting for the kidnappers to contact Gussling. I texted that news to you. Going to keep your cell on, weren't you?'

Steve ignored that. 'And what does that have to do with your black eye? And what's that stiffness in your side all about? Every time you move, you flinch.'

'That's something else. It doesn't have anything to do with Gussling and his wife.'

'But it has to do with . . . what?'

I took a second to consider how much to tell him about my run in with Murphy. After all, I didn't want to look like a complete idiot.

'It was the Pistilli hired hand, Murphy who stopped me to let me know I hadn't been forgotten. He came up to me when I got back to the house after talking to a member of the San Francisco Police Department. A Lieutenant Quincy. We had had a cup of coffee together. Too bad he didn't follow me home.'

'Wait a minute, you're going too fast,' Steve said frowning. 'Where did the police come into the picture? You said some lieutenant and you had coffee?'

'Yeah. Lieutenant Quincy was interested to know what Pistilli and I had in common. Apparently they're watching him, trying to catch him at something or another. I don't know, Quincy talked about Pistilli being a real bad man. Oh, and that fool at the insurance company had called the police to tell them about the kidnapping. That's what he wanted to talk to me about. Pistilli and the kidnapping.'

'What'd you tell him?'

'That there wasn't any kidnapping, as far as I knew. And that Pistilli had wanted me to tell him when a guy I knew made contact. He seemed happy that there wasn't any more to it than that. From what he said, the local cops are pretty busy. Seems there's been a couple young girls raped and murdered in the Bay area recently. He's afraid it's possibly a serial killer at work.'

'So he's not interested in the Gussling deal?'

'I don't think so.'

'OK, go back to what you were saying about Pistilli's man who caught up with you. He didn't think you'd run into your old friend Son, did he?'

'No. This guy, Murphy, just wanted to remind me. Mr Pistilli sent him around, he said, to remind me to make sure when Son Cardonsky showed up I'd be quick to give Pistilli a call. And he warned me to be sure to call him damn fast. Mr Pistilli isn't a man to fuck with.'

I stopped to take a long sip of beer before going on with my sad story. 'Steve, I didn't know what I could do so I did what I'd been doing and that was to deny talking with Son. "You and that boss of yours have got it all wrong," I told him, hoping I was talking to one of the more sane members of the Pistilli gang. I told him how Son and I know each other from way back but that doesn't mean we're friends. I tried to explain that Son is not my bosom buddy and I don't expect to hear from him. Ever.'

Steve smiled a lopsided smile. 'So what happened?'

'Murphy just smiled at me and went on as if I hadn't said a word. Mr Pistilli wants to make sure you got the message, he said. Then he said he'd been sent instead of Hugo because that big idiot likes to hurt people too much and Mr Pistilli doesn't want me hurt. At least not too much.'

I sat for a long minute, thinking. 'You know,' I said eventually, 'I can't remember the last fight I was in. The last fist fight, I mean. I guess that's why he caught me flatfooted. I didn't see it coming. He hit me in the face and all I could do was raise my arms. That's when he caught me in the ribs. Steve, it felt like he'd used a piece of concrete. It knocked me off my feet. I landed on my hands and knees, sure he'd broken a bunch of ribs. I didn't think I'd ever catch my breath. Every time I tried to inhale I could feel steel bands squeeze my lungs.'

I stopped, remembering how it felt. Steve frowned when I smiled.

'But that was when he made his mistake,' I said. 'I glanced up to see him smiling down at me. There he was, standing with his hands on his hips, looking all powerful. This, he told me, was only a taste of what would happen if I forgot to let Mr Pistilli know when Son contacted me. Oh, he was enjoying himself. At least until I brought my fist up as hard as I could between his legs.'

'You what?' Steve demanded incredulously when I told him.

'I hit him in the balls as hard as I could,' I said, chuckling at the memory. 'Doubled him right over. It took me a minute or two to get to my feet but he was still there, bent over, moaning, his hands holding his crotch.'

'Jesus, you like to live dangerously. He'll be after you now.'

'Maybe. But where I can hardly move now, it's likely he's having trouble hearing anything. While he was all bent over, I cupped my hands and brought them together hard against his ears. It must have hurt because he let go of his crotch and grabbed his head.'

'Bernie, you just don't treat those kinds of guys like that. They're the ones who have the guns and don't mind using 'em.'

'Steve, what was I supposed to do? Pistilli sent him around to give me a message. I returned the favour. Dammit, I haven't seen Son and don't want to. I've got enough on my plate right now, what with this Gussling thing and, to top it off, that story I'm writing isn't going that well.'

CHAPTER TWENTY

Gussling called me at home the next day, Wednesday. I still hurt but was at the keyboard trying to keep my mind on something other than my aches and pains. My mind was busy trying to build suspense in the story I was writing, it took me a moment to understand what he was saying.

'Frazier still isn't happy, you know. He's never had to deal with this kind of thing and doesn't understand our not calling in the FBI or the local police. I told him to go to BA and learn how this type of kidnapping is done.'

I interrupted. 'Uh, you told him to go to BA? What's that?'

'Buenos Aires. That's where my wife and I have been for the last two years or so, working in the company's Buenos Aires office. Anyway, as I was saying, he is in the process of putting together the two million. He told me the money will be in a good-sized briefcase. He's a real smart ass. Had to show off by telling me the money will be in hundred-dollar bills, packets of a thousand dollars each and the whole thing will weigh about fifty pounds. But I got the last laugh, I know that a million dollars weighs just ten kilograms or, as every good druggie knows, twenty-two and a quarter pounds. I was able to tell him his briefcase must weigh about five pounds. It shut him up.'

He couldn't see me shaking my head in disgust. 'So, what I hear you saying is that the money will be in a briefcase and when you hear where I'm to deliver it, I can pick it up at the insurance office.'

'That's right.'

'Today is Wednesday. What happens if the kidnapper doesn't call until the weekend? That office will be closed. Will the kidnapper sit on it until the next Monday? Wouldn't it be better if you picked up the briefcase and had it ready?'

'Hm, I hadn't thought of that. You're right. I'll take care of it.'

'And here's another thing you might do to help us out. When you get the call, you tell him that this isn't working like it would in Argentina. It's not as straightforward. Tell him that here you've got the local police to contend with. Let him know you've got the money, but to make the delivery it'll have to be a straight exchange, the cash for your wife.'

'What are you and your partner planning? This isn't going to put my wife in any danger, is it?'

'No. When your friend Frazier first heard the word kidnapping, he called the police. One of their detectives hunted me up and questioned me. I shared the bare bones of the deal, making sure he understood it was being treated as a simple business deal. Since then I've got the feeling I've had them all but following me. I just feel it'd be better if I have enough time to lose any tail I might have on me. That isn't hard, but it will take time.'

Gussling went silent. I wasn't sure he was still there and was about to check when he responded. 'OK, I can see how that'd be. I just don't want anything to go wrong, that's all.'

'Then that's it. You have my cell number so, if when you hear from the kidnappers you can call me, we'll get this show on the road.'

'Yeah. That's going to be the hard part now, waiting.'

I figured I could get in another couple hours writing but it didn't work out that way. After Gussling hung up I couldn't get back into it. There was no reason to call Steve, he had said he was going to follow up on the tennis pro lead and I didn't want to hang around the place for a couple reasons. First, this would be the first place Murphy or another of Pistilli's hoods would look for me. And second, this place was too confining. Don't ever rent a studio apartment, is my advice.

Lunch out would be a good way to spend the early afternoon. But, just as with my apartment, I'd had enough of Lou Lou's for a while. Anyway, I didn't want to be answering any questions or hearing any snide remarks about my black eye. Just as Steve had said, it was a doozy. Looking at it in the mirror, the colours were remarkable, ranging from a dull red where Murphy had hit me, changing to a greyish black closer to my eye, which was surrounded by purple with just a tinge of yellow. No, I didn't want to have to talk about it.

Maybe it was time for more fish stew. I caught the ferry across the bay.

That's where Son found me.

There was a light sprinkle of rain falling as I boarded the catamaran, so standing out on the deck was a bit uncomfortable. Only a few diehard tourists stayed out by the rails while I joined most of the other passengers, finding places to sit inside. This didn't upset me, although I liked standing at the rail watching the water of the bay slip by under the ship's hull.

I'd taken one of the window seats, so if the people watching weren't up to snuff I could look out at the world getting rained on. I'd been keeping an eye on a couple who I thought were interesting and were probably not tourists, when Son came strolling by like he didn't have a worry in the world.

San Francisco can, and does, have a lot of things that sets it apart from the rest of the world. The people-watching is, in my view, some of the best anyone could wish for. For instance, the couple who had caught my attention were both dressed in black: black boots, the kind we used to call motorcycle boots, black Levis, black T-shirts under black leather vests and black berets barely hanging on to dirty-looking long black hair, hair so flat black it had to be from a bottle. Somehow every bit of their black costumes they were so proud of had a dirty, greasy look.

What do the kids call it? Not grunge . . . umm . . . punk? No, Gothic. It was hard to tell how old the girl was but I got the feeling she was jailbait. Typical of that dress code, she was wearing black eyeliner and lipstick. Her partner looked old enough to have served a couple sentences as a guest of the state. He had on two more colourful items; one was a long silver chain, the links drooping down in a big loop from his belt to a long black-leather wallet stuck in a back pocket. The other was a startlingly white cigarette hanging from his lips. It was unlit, of course. The no-smoking laws were strict almost everywhere in the city, especially in any public place. But he wanted to make his statement. Actually, watching them I figured they were making a lot of statements, some impossible to decode.

Not wanting to be obvious, I let my eyes move on. That's when I spotted Son coming down the aisle between the seats, a big smile on his sorry-looking face.

'Hey there, Bernie. How's it hanging?' he called as he took the seat next to me. 'Man, what door did you run into?' I didn't offer an answer or move over to make room for him. He squeezed in next to me anyhow.

'Boy, you're one hard dude to hook up with, you know? Where you headed? Tell you what, we get off this wreck, let's stop by Alioto's for a beer. I'll buy. We got to talk, old buddy. By the way, what door did you run into?' I thought his laugh sounded like a wounded horse whinnying.

I ignored the comment about my black eye, trying to think of how he'd found me. How in the hell did he know where I was thinking about going?

'Son, do us both a favour and go away. A long way away.'

'Now that isn't being friendly,' he said. 'Here I went to all the trouble to follow you from that shitty little place you call home nowadays and look at the welcome I get.'

'You followed me?'

'Well, hell yes. You don't think I want any of you-know-who's people to see us together, do you?'

'You know who,' I said, frowning and taking a quick look at the people around us. If Murphy or Hugo were anywhere on the ferry I was dead meat.

'Don't worry yourself, pard,' he said. 'I checked it out pretty good before I came aboard. Unless you-know-who has a lot of new people, we're clear.'

I wasn't reassured but I must have relaxed a little because he chuckled. 'Of course, he could have put out the word that he's looking for you or me. I firmly believe he's got enough contacts in the Bay area for us not to last long if he did.'

That didn't make me feel good at all. Breathing deeply and feeling the bite of pain in my side I cursed.

'Damn you, Son. Why'd you go and tell him that I helped you with that little deal you pulled off? I had nothing to do with that and you know it.'

'Yep, I do. But you did help me, you know. Your plan was perfect. That little deal, as you call it, went off without a hitch. I've got your share and I'll be handing it to you in a little while. There's something else I want you to do. But,' he held up a hand, 'let's not talk about it now. Wait until we get to Alioto's and have a bottle of beer in front of us.'

That's what we did, riding the rest of the way not talking. At one point I did ask where he'd been keeping himself, but he just smiled and didn't answer. That didn't really matter, I really didn't want to know. What did concern me was thinking about the chances of someone from Pistilli's camp spotting us. Far as I was concerned he could have Son, but dammit, I didn't want any part of it.

CHAPTER TWENTY-ONE

We separated and left the ferry with Son going on ahead. The walk from the terminal to Alioto's is only a few short blocks but I was sure I spotted Hugo at least three times. Twice I was convinced it was him in cars that drove past, one time in an old rust bucket of a Toyota and the other I thought I saw him riding passenger in a pickup. The third time I saw him was in a crowd of people across the street waiting for the light to change. Nobody jumped me so I guess I was only being paranoid.

Son was sitting in one of the least popular corners of the bar, back where there was no view of the water or the boat harbour.

'Look Son,' I said, not giving him a chance to get in the first word, 'you're in big trouble with a guy who I'm told kills those people he doesn't like. I've been kidnapped, threatened and beaten up because you gave him my name. Now you're following me around. What does it take to persuade you to leave me the hell alone?'

'Ah, Bernie old friend, I want you to know I feel real bad about that. But with Hugo beating on me I had to tell them something. Something they'd believe or I was afraid they'd kill me. But look, it all came out all right, didn't it? I mean, we're both still OK and I've got the money I owe you. There wasn't as much on the table as I expected, though, but your cut is still a nice little packet.'

'I don't want any nice little packet. I don't want anything to do with you, don't you understand? If those friends of yours get any idea that we met and I don't tell them, I'm as good as dead. You don't get it, do you? They want their money back and a piece of you. A big piece. I don't want anything to do with them or with you.'

Son just sat back and smiled. 'Yeah, I know all that. Well, they're too late to get the money. I've had to spend most of it. Getting set up for the next little deal I'm working on. Anyway, they won't even know I was in town today. The only reason I'm here is that I wanted to let you know that you're not to worry. You and your little story helped me out before and you'll get yours from that deal. I don't want you to think I've forgotten you. You're my angel, remember? And here's the good news, the next one is bigger. Yeah, man, much bigger.'

'Son, leave me alone. You don't know these people. That damn Pistilli is a dangerous man. Hell, I even had the local police task force asking questions about him. As if I know anything. I don't and I don't want to.'

'Ah, Bernie, he's not as almighty dangerous as you think. And I do know about him, all about him.'

'C'mon, Son,' I interrupted his little tale. 'Just for once listen to me. I don't know about him and don't care to know about him. Go away and leave me alone.'

Son didn't pay any attention. He went on telling his story as if he was talking about his lifelong hero. Maybe, I realized, he was.

'Now there is something you will want to know about. For most of his adult life he's been working for his Uncle Bram. A big, and I mean almost the top guy in the city, he's Bram's right-hand man. A few years ago, when Bram decided to retire, he gave Pistilli the job of managing the Russian River Casino, you know, one of those Indian casinos. This one's up north in the wine country, up near Healdsburg. It's the one I'm going to knock over next.'

'Whoa, there. Don't tell me anything I don't want to know.'

Son laughed. 'No, you don't know anything, even though it's your plan I'll be using. That's why, when I've got everything taken care of, you'll be getting an even larger package from me. Yeah, talk about making my life easy, you're the man.'

CHAPTER TWENTY-TWO

Still Wednesday

Son didn't hang around long after dropping that bombshell. Whether he'd meant to or not, he'd scared the hell out of me. Oh, don't get me wrong. Anything that would enhance my bank account would be appreciated but not if it brought Hugo and company into my life.

No longer hungry, I decided to go see what progress Theodore Gussling was making. Normally walking the half-dozen blocks or so would give me time to think, time to clear the cobwebs from my mind. Not this time. Walking up from the harbour to the Havershack offices I was too busy looking over my shoulder to think about anything except the danger Son had put me in.

I could have saved myself the effort; the cute young receptionist minding the front desk at Havershack Industries informed me that Mr Gussling was out of the office and wasn't expected back until later in the day.

'Do you have the number of his cell phone?' I silently cussed myself for not having gotten it before.

'I'm not allowed to give that out. I'm sorry. If you'll leave your name, though, I'll let him know when he returns you were here to see him.'

'If that's the best we can do then ask him to call me, Bernie Gould, as soon as he can.'

'Oh, Mr Gould.' The young woman picked up an envelope from her desk, gave me her best smile and handed it to me. 'Mr Gussling said, if you came in to give you this.'

'Thank you. When did Mr Gussling leave the office, by the way?'

'I don't think he came in this morning. That envelope for you was on my desk when I came in this morning along with a note saying he would be in late this afternoon.'

The note from Gussling didn't help any. He hadn't yet been contacted, he wrote. There was, he went on to say, some out-of-the-office business to attend to, apologized for not being available but reminded me he had both cell phone numbers, mine and Steve's, and he'd call if he was contacted.

My day was turning out to be a big waste. Maybe Steve was doing better, but I'd have to wait to find out, he wasn't answering his cell phone.

Antonio Jardin, Steve discovered, was everybody's darling. At least the women members of the Saratoga Golf and Tennis Club could only say good things about him.

By taking a taxi to the club and mentioning to a different young man in the familiar green jacket that he was a guest of Theodore and Claire Gussling, Steve found himself waved through the double doors and into the plush lobby. If the thick carpeting on the floors and heavy dark-wood furniture lining the walls were meant to impress, it all succeeded. The silence of the place was deeper than one would find in any library or mortuary. Steve didn't have to ask directions, a set of discreet signs pointed the way, to the right for the golf pro shop, left to the tennis courts.

'May I help you, sir?' a white-jacketed young man asked as he pushed out on to a large covered patio. The young man was too professional to pay any attention to Steve's black eye.

Round tables, each with four chairs, were scattered all around the brick patio. Tennis players, all in white shorts and soft-collared shirts, were on most of the courts, the whacking sound of balls being struck filled the air. Steve almost smiled; green jackets for the outside staff members, white inside. If the obvious quality of the furniture in the lobby didn't make it clear this was a very upscale place, the abundance of helpful staff did.

'Well, not really,' he told the young man, gazing around at the line-up of courts just beyond the patio. 'I'm visiting the Gusslings and they suggested I stop in and look over the club. I believe Claire made dinner reservations for the four of us for later tonight.'

'Oh, yes, the Gusslings are new members. I think they'll get a lot of enjoyment out of their membership. Why, already Mrs Gussling has been out nearly every day, although I don't recall seeing her recently. But let me check and make sure of those reservations. For four people, you say?'

Steve nodded and the young man walked away.

About half of the tables were empty, the others had one or two people seated around them; most of them he saw, were women. Everybody's attention was out on the courts. A single woman was seated next to where Steve was standing.

'Excuse me, did I hear you say you're a friend of Claire Gussling?'

The gold emblem of the Saratoga Golf and Tennis Club rested on the upper left of the sparkling white tennis blouse worn by the woman. The emblem was, Steve noticed, almost horizontal as it rested on the top of her left breast. He visualized the bounce those breasts would have as she ran around the court.

'Well, don't tell anyone, but no, I'm not a friend. Teddy Gussling and I work in the same office up in the city. He and his wife just returned from South America and quickly joined the club. He mentioned it to me and suggested I stop in and look it over, thinking he might get me to join too.'

Boy, he thought, if you can't confuse them with footwork, befuddle with bullshit. The woman who sat looking up at him smiled.

'Are you married?'

'No.'

'Oh, goody. But how did you get that black eye? It looks painful.'

Steve ate up the sympathy in her voice. 'It was a simple misunderstanding I had with a door, can you believe.'

'Oh, poor baby. You're not one of those men who like to fight, are you?'

'No, and I don't play tennis either. That was one of the selling points Ted was using, that the club has a very good pro.'

She laughed. 'Well, I can attest to that. Antonio is good, but he's expensive. I think he used to play on the US Tennis Association circuit, although I've never seen any of his trophies.'

Steve hesitated. 'Is he teaching today?'

'No,' she said, looking out at the courts, giving Steve the opportunity to admire her long, sun browned legs. Like the furniture in the lobby, this woman was money. Good muscle tone, he saw, all tight and firm under healthy tanned skin, so smooth he wanted to run his hand lightly over it, or better yet, lick it. Tiny wrinkles around her eyes said she wasn't as young as he'd first thought and he updated her age to the other side of forty. Still she was years away from losing her nicely rounded and shapely body.

'Today is one of the club's competitions,' the woman went on, overlooking his lecherous examination. 'That's why there are so many of us just sitting around drinking. We've all been eliminated. Here,' she used a white tennis-shoe-covered foot to push an empty chair away from the table, 'you might as well join me.'

Steve had to wonder how long she'd been sitting there, sipping from her tall glass.

'What kind of guy is this tennis teacher?'

'Oh, the best kind. Tall, dark and very smooth.' She chuckled, the sound almost evil, before taking a drink from her near-empty glass. 'I would bet, though, if you wanted to learn the game he'd have one of his young assistants work with you. Our Antonio likes to instruct the women.'

'Ah, a ladies' man, I take it?'

'Yes indeed, he is that. And the latest is the wife of your friend.' Lowering her voice as if telling a secret, she ducked her head closer to his. 'And has she got the other women here pissed off. I don't mind telling you, our lady members are not ladies when it comes to our own Antonio. And until our newest member came along he was ours. None of us really cared because we knew that sooner or later we'd get our turn. Now we're not so sure.'

Sitting back she winked before going on. 'I'll admit it; I liked the attention I got from him. But your friend's wife gained the upper hand the minute she came through the door. She's a striking-looking broad and she knew how to get next to him. I think it was when he discovered they spoke the same language. Some kind of Spanish. You know, California is becoming more and more a part of Mexico every day. Christ, one can't even get a decent beauty treatment any more unless one speaks even a little Mexican. And I, unfortunately, don't.'

'I can't imagine your needing any such treatments,' he said, hoping he didn't sound like a third-rate movie script. If he did, she was too far gone to notice.

'Oh, you.' She smiled, looking sideways at him and letting her tongue play over her lower lip. 'Did you say you weren't married?'

95

'No, I've been able to outrun all likely candidates, so far. Just lucky, I guess.'

'Hmm, then you're probably gay. You know the old saying, if they're not married and look too good to be true, the chances are they're gay.'

'I like women too much to consider crossing that line. God, I can't get past the idea of playing kissy-face with a man needing a shave.'

'Well, it doesn't seem to bother me in the slightest. Tell you what, let's order another round of drinks and discuss the joys of playing kissy-face.'

Steve was afraid he'd let things go too far. Under normal conditions he'd go along and see how things turned out, but this kidnapping was worth too much to spend any time playing Romeo. Hoping he'd come up with a way to put this lady and her fine chest on standby, he wrote his cell number on a napkin. Before he could hand it to her, the white jacketed young man returned to save him.

'I'm sorry, sir, but I can't seem to find any reservation for the Gusslings.'

'Oh, well, I suppose I'd better take a look,' Steve said standing up. 'Excuse me,' he said to the woman, causing her to frown, 'I had better see to this.'

'You do that, but don't take too long. I don't like sitting here by myself.'

'Tell you what. Let me give you my cell phone number. That way if you think of anything that will help me – to get in touch with Mr Jardin, I mean – you can give me a call.'

Pretty ritzy and not likely to ever call, he thought as he followed the young man back toward the lobby. Boy, belonging to a club with women like that one hanging around the patio could be damn interesting.

'Look,' he said, reaching out to touch the young man's arm, 'I think I'll just wait until I get back to the office to ask Ted about the reservation. But while I think of it, can you tell me how I can leave a message for the pro, Antonio?'

'Well, he's not been around for a day or two. But if you'd like, you can talk with one of the other professionals we have here. I'm sure one of them can help you.'

The young man had been all smiles and perfectly formed white teeth, proud of his starched and pressed white tennis shirt. He had been almost eager to help until Steve asked for Antonio.

'He hasn't been on the court for a couple days. I'm sure, though, that anyone of us can help you with your game. We're all members of the US Professional Tennis Association, you know. The club is very proud of our teaching staff.'

'I'm sure, but it isn't exactly a tennis lesson I want to talk to him about.'

The young pro's eyes grew hard and cold and now he let Steve see him take in the wounded eye.

Seeing that reaction, Steve held up a hand. 'And I'm not an angry husband, either.' He chuckled to let the pro know he was friendly, 'No. This is something else. Look,' he said pulling a twenty from his wallet, 'I'm not after the man, just want to leave him a personal message. The front office won't let out his phone number so I can't call him.'

The pro studied Steve for a moment and the money before visibly relaxing. Glancing quickly around, he took the twenty from Steve's hand and nodded.

'That damn Antonio's a good teacher,' he said, keeping his voice low and confidential, 'and this is a great place to work, but sometimes the trouble he causes with all those women out there isn't worth it. OK, tell you what, I won't give you anything except to say he doesn't live in Saratoga. He's got an apartment down in Los Gatos. That's the best I can do for you.'

It was Steve's turn to nod and smile.

CHAPTER TWENTY-THREE

Los Gatos was once a nice, quiet village on the two-lane highway between San Jose and Santa Cruz. That highway, State Route 17, was a pleasant half-hour drive through the Santa Cruz Mountains to the coast. That was quite a few years ago, before the thing called Silicon Valley came into being. Los Gatos is part of that super conglomeration of high-tech industries that stretches from South San Francisco to, well, to Los Gatos. Today SR 17 is four lanes of heavy traffic and Los Gatos is no longer a village.

Steve made the short drive down to Los Gatos in less than ten minutes. Relying on the best friend an investigator has, the phone book, it took him half that long to find out where Antonio Jardin lived.

Lake Vasona Manor had a big sign out front telling the world there were apartments for rent. After spending ten minutes with the manager, a big, bluff Santa Claus kind of man, Steve said he'd like to walk around, maybe talk to one of the residents. Santa hesitated a moment, looking at Steve's eye, before smiling and nodding.

'Hey, that's OK by me. I'd rather you take your time and be sure than move in and then next week start thinking about moving out.' Santa laughed. 'Go ahead. I'll be over in the office when you decide.'

Jardin's was the last apartment facing the street. Steve strolled down the open corridor, taking his time and keeping his eyes open. He didn't see anyone or hear anything. It took him no more than a minute to slip the lock on the front door.

Inside the lay-out was typical of any town house, a short hallway with the living-room off to the left and a stairway to the bedrooms on the second floor straight ahead. The kitchen and a half-bath were just off the living-room. After a quick check to make sure he was all alone, Steve started looking for whatever he could find.

Giving himself no more than five minutes, he headed upstairs. Only one of the two bedrooms had furniture, furniture and lots of men's clothes lying about. This Jardin may be the great Latin lover but he was also a pig.

The only thing he found in his search was a brochure showing off the benefits of choosing to stay at the Best Western Inn in San Ysidro, down south of San Diego next to the Mexican border. The tennis pro had apparently looked into taking a vacation south. Or maybe that was where he'd been since disappearing from the club.

It was doubtful that anyone would know he'd gone through the place, so after making sure the front door had relocked itself he walked back to tell the manager he'd think about it.

It had been a good day. On the drive back to the Bay area, Steve decided he'd give Bernie a call. Maybe go have a pizza or something.

Not being able to contact Steve, and feeling deserted, I spent the rest of the day keeping out of sight in the city, dreading the idea of going home. After all, Hugo and Murphy had picked me up on my own doorstep, hadn't they?

After Son strolled out of Alioto's like someone without a worry in the world, I actually considered saving my bacon by calling Pistilli. That thought didn't last long. First because I couldn't do that even to someone like Son Cardonsky and secondly, there wasn't any guarantee that Pistilli wouldn't turn his two creeps loose on me. So I went for a walk.

Have you ever walked around San Francisco? It's a great place, full of art galleries, museums and parks, all spread out over a million square miles at least. I know because I walked over nearly all of them, not seeing a thing, worrying about Pistilli and his quick temper. It didn't even help when I thought about how things had turned out the last time I had anything to do with that crowd. My hurting Murphy as I had wasn't, as Steve so quickly pointed out, the best thing I'd done. I had enjoyed it, though.

Sooner of later I knew I'd have to go home, so just about dark I caught the last ferry of the day. Even after carefully checking out all the other passengers, I didn't relax.

My approach to my place was as filled with caution as I could make it, keeping to the far side of the street, hurrying past any lights and staying in the darker shadows. I stood across the street for long minutes, trying to make sure there were no surprises waiting for me. There didn't seem to be, but who could tell? At last, angry with myself for being so timid, I used the key to open my front door. There was nobody.

I was sitting at my little desk, trying to get creative but failing when my door slammed open and Steve barged in. I had been sure I'd locked it. So much for personal security.

'Hey, Bern, how's it hanging?'

How could he be smiling, I wondered? Didn't he know the trouble I was in?

I exhaled loudly, unaware I'd been holding my breath, 'Steve, how about knocking the next time? You scared the crap out of me, barging in like that.'

'Scared? Of what?'

Steve put the two flat pizza boxes down on the little table and opened the paper sack he'd been carrying. Until the smell of the pepperoni and cheese hit me I hadn't known just how hungry I was. Spending an afternoon being panicky takes a lot out of a guy.

I had to tell him.

'I ran into Son Cardonsky over in the city today. Actually, he followed me on to the ferry when I'd decided to go over for lunch.'

'And you didn't call Pistilli about it, either, did you. No, you wouldn't. So, what's the problem? If that thug or any of his men come sniffing around, deny you saw Son. It's as easy as that.'

'Oh, I'm sure they'd believe me. Sure. But that's not the real issue. Listen, Son is convinced a short story I wrote was actually a blueprint on how to hold up a high-stakes poker game. Pistilli thinks so, too. Now Son is planning on hitting one of the Indian casinos up north. I think he said it's called the Russian River Casino. And already he's thanking me for showing how it can be done.'

'Ouch. That'll make Pistilli happy. That's the casino he runs.'

'Yeah, Son thinks that'll make it a lot better. Getting back at the big bad casino manager for manhandling him. Dammit, Steve, how did I get involved with such losers, anyhow?'

Steve didn't answer, just started passing out the beer and pizza slices.

CHAPTER TWENTY-FOUR

We finished the pizzas and then sat around until the six-pack of beer was gone. With a full stomach, or maybe it was the beer, I relaxed and lost the feeling that I was on a short track towards a big drop.

'What did you write that would give that fool the idea he could get away with robbing a casino?'

'I don't know. All afternoon that's one of the things I was thinking about. Mostly though, I was thinking about ways to get out from under both Son and your mafia boss, Pistilli.'

'Hey, he isn't anything to me. It's your friend who gave out your name. Come on, think about what you've got published, what would fit?'

'Nothing I can think of. Let's talk about something else. What'd you find out today that helps us with this damn Gussling kidnapping?'

'Oh, yeah,' Steve sat up with a smile, 'got to thinking about your problems with Pistilli and almost forgot. Well, it's been a good day. Found out the tennis pro, Jardin, hasn't been seen in a week, is the main item of gossip and lust for many of the female members of the Saratoga Tennis Club, and that he's a slob.'

'Whew, this guy sounds like he lives an interesting life. What do you mean, he's a slob?'

'I happened to get into his apartment—'

I had to interrupt. 'You what? Man, you're playing it dangerous. What good would it do if you get arrested for a break and enter?'

'Naw, little chance of that. Anyway, I had to see what I could find out. So far I think he's our best bet for being the kidnapper,' he said, hesitating a second, 'that is, if there is a kidnapper in the middle of this thing. You know, I keep going back to the fact that the list of people familiar with the Argentine kidnapping insurance deal isn't very long and the tennis pro isn't anywhere on it.'

'Unless the kidnap victim herself is the genius behind it all. Anyway, what were you able to find out in your criminal activities?'

'Well, actually not much. Jardin is the play toy for quite a number of women with more time on their hands than what's good for them. Too much booze, too much spare time and there's this tall, dark-haired guy running around in white shorts. I got the idea even his assistants don't think much of him. Of course that could be that the one pro I talked to is jealous of the boss pro. Let's see, Jardin lives in a second-rate apartment in Los Gatos, doesn't pick up after himself and has a dirty kitchen. I guess the only two strikes against him are, one, Claire Gussling is his latest conquest and two, both have gone missing at about the same time.'

'So where does that leave us?'

'I suppose just about where we were, waiting for Gussling to get a phone call.'

Steve left just before midnight, not taking any of the empty pizza boxes with him. The smell of dead pizzas coming from the tiny excuse for a kitchen the next morning was almost overwhelming. That odour and the greenish bloodshot look of my black eye didn't make my morning a joyous one. When I sat down at the keyboard, after putting the bed back into the wall and dumping the garbage out in the bin, I found myself staring at the empty screen.

We've all heard about writer's block, but this was silly. It wasn't that the words wouldn't come, it was that the wrong words were floating around inside my head. Words like Hugo, and Murphy, and, oh, yes, Son. Damn the man.

At times like these one hopes for an interruption: any disturbance to take the mind off negative things will do. It was my cell phone buzzing that took me away from the PC.

'Keep ringing,' I called as I ran around looking under things for the phone. How in the hell could someone lose a cell phone in a place like this? The buzzing went on while I lifted pillows, a pair of shorts that had missed the dirty-clothes' bin, opened drawers in the kitchen and even pulled down the bed. The phone was in the center of the bed. How had I missed that?

'Hello,' I heard myself sounding pissed.

'Bernie? Is this Bernie Gould?'

It was Theodore Gussling. 'Yes, it is, Mr Gussling.'

'It sure didn't sound like you. I hope I didn't get you out of bed. I know it's fairly early, but I thought you'd like to know that I've heard from the kidnappers. It was a note in my mail box this morning. I was surprised to see there was no stamp or anything. It obviously was put there by the kidnappers themselves.'

I stopped him from rattling on. 'Don't bother telling me over the phone what it says. Steve and I will come across to your office as soon as we can get there.'

'No, it didn't come to my office. It came here, to my home. I had a busy night last night and, actually I'm not quite awake yet. I don't expect to go into the city today at all. Could you come down here?'

'Oh,' I had to think, was I supposed to know where their home was? It didn't matter. He'd told Steve and Steve had told me. 'Well, I guess that means we'll drive down the peninsula.'

'If you don't mind, I'd appreciate it. I'm afraid I'm not dealing very well with all this stress I'm under. Do you have the address?'

'I believe Steve has it.'

'Very well. Until later then.' He hung up and I called Steve.

I got into clean Levis and a collared T-shirt. Counting on the weather to be wet – this was that time of year after all – I pulled a lightweight waterproof windbreaker out of the tiny closet.

Waiting for Steve I played back the conversation with Gussling. The kidnappers had dropped the directions off at his house. OK, so they knew where he lived. That didn't tell us anything. We could only hope there was something in the note that would help us.

Steve was almost jolly, driving across the bridge and through the can of worms that best describes the series of freeways taking traffic south out of the city. By the time we pulled off State Highway 85, otherwise known as the Guadalupe Freeway, we had discussed everything we had learned so far. It certainly wasn't much.

'I wonder,' I said, thinking back to what the man had said. 'Gussling said he was busy last night and had no way of knowing when the note could have been put in his mail box. I wonder where he had been and what he had been doing?'

Steve thought about it but shook his head. 'Look at it like this: he

103

works in a big office, lots of business contacts, customers and the like. Of course he's out and about, it's part of his job, wouldn't you think? So he got a little tipsy and has a hangover this morning. And what does he find in his mail box? A kidnapper's note. What'll prove to be important will be the directions those assholes are giving out.'

'Yeah, maybe.'

'Remember, you're the one that'll be making the delivery. You know, Bern,' he said after a while, 'this might be a good opportunity to see if the overly worried Mister is part of the deal.'

'You think he's overdoing his concern?'

'Well, think about it. How many times has he mentioned wanting his wife to be returned safely? And how many of those times did he use her name? Not once. It's always been about making sure 'my wife' is safe. And does he say 'our house' or 'my house'? That certainly makes me wonder.'

I had nothing to say to that. It had gotten past me. But then, maybe Steve was just clutching at straws.

'Yeah,' I said as he pulled into the driveway of a two-storey house, 'let's both watch how he reacts to what the kidnappers have to say.'

The ransom letter didn't give out many clues. None, actually. Gussling was quick to put it in Steve's hands.

'They want me to call them,' he said, speaking hurriedly. 'At five o'clock sharp. Tonight. Why would they give out a phone number? Don't they know that number could be traced?'

'Yes,' Steve murmured as he read the brief note before handing it to me. 'But think about it. These people know about the kidnapping insurance, they know where you live; we have to assume they know quite a bit about you. It's clear they don't think you've brought the law into this or they wouldn't be handing out phone numbers. If it were me, this would be a phone booth somewhere. You'll call and they will give you the message, the directions for making the exchange. It'll be a phone they can see from some safe distance so they can watch if anyone is innocently hanging around at the time you're to call. They'll be long gone once the call is made, you can be sure of that.'

Gussling had motioned toward easy chairs but stayed on his feet, pacing back and forth as we talked.

'OK, is that what you think they'll do, give me directions for making the trade for my wife?'

'Well,' Steve went on, 'I imagine that's what their plan is. But that's not what we'll do.'

That brought the man's pacing to a halt. 'What? What do you mean?'

I wondered myself what Steve was thinking about.

'Well, first off, it'll be Bernie who makes the call. No, hear me out,' he said, stopping Gussling from interrupting. 'Bernie will tell the kidnapper that he has been hired to make the ransom drop. It'll only complicate matters to have you talk to them and then have to pass on the information. Better if Bernie, a non-interested go-between, handles this part of the deal. Bernie has the money and he'll be making the exchange.'

Gussling frowned, thinking, and then, dropping on to the couch facing our chairs, nodded. 'I guess that makes sense. I've got plenty time to drive into the office and pick up the briefcase. I suppose you'll be calling from here,' he asked, looking at me. I didn't know what to say.

'No,' Steve answered for me, getting Gussling excited once again. 'The first thing Bern will tell the kidnapper is that we have to be sure Mrs Gussling is safe and sound. That means having some type of assurance; say a photo of her holding up the day's newspaper. Something like that.'

'But that'll take days,' Gussling said, leaning forward. 'Why can't we just make the trade and be done with it?'

'We can and I suppose in Argentina that's the way it'd be done. But as you pointed out, this isn't Argentina and things have to be done differently. We'll tell them that the insurance company is demanding the photographic evidence before releasing the ransom. And it won't take days. The photo can be emailed. That way it'll only take an extra day, maybe two.'

Steve stood up and glanced at me, walked over to stand next to a brick fireplace. Glancing idly down at a pile of magazines, he frowned, getting his thoughts in order before going on.

'Look, today is Thursday. Your wife has been gone about a week, hasn't she? You've made it clear that the kidnappers only want the money. It's a business transaction to them and to the insurance company. OK, we all understand that. But this is the US, California even. Things have to be done a little differently. They'll buy it and it'll give us an extra day or so. Meanwhile, your wife, Claire – isn't that her name, Claire?' Gussling nodded. 'Well, there's really no worry about her. She'll be safe. The kidnappers will know we're all treating this as a business deal.'

*

Later, after assuring Gussling they would come back down to Saratoga in time to make the call, we left, stopping at the first Starbucks we saw for coffee and a talk. I could hardly wait to hear what my partner was planning.

'Today is Thursday,' he started in while we waited for our latte order to be served. 'When you make the call, you'll tell the kidnappers about the need for the photo. Give them Gussling's email address and have them email it. He's sure to have Internet service. OK, the quickest that can happen is tomorrow, or better yet if it takes even longer. It'll take a few more hours to get the photo back up to the city, to the insurance company to get their approval. Tell the kidnappers this. Lay it all out and sound like it was the most natural thing in the world.'

'OK, I can handle that. But what will it gain us?'

'Think about it. If this doesn't work we'll know Teddy Gussling has already let them know they're being set up. But, if it does work out this way, it could almost put Teddy in the clear. You see what I mean?'

That made sense. If the kidnappers went for the photo story, it could mean that Gussling had talked. Maybe. I sipped my heavy-tasting coffee before nodding.

'Yeah, but if it turns out Gussling is trying to pull a fast one, then what?'

'If it looks like he's behind this so-called business deal, well, we'll deal with him on that. But if he isn't, what'll happen is that we won't be able to get the ransom money until Monday. That gives us three or four more days to check out a few things.'

'Like what kind of things?'

'Something I just realized. You know, if it turns out old man Gussling isn't the mastermind of this plot to pocket two million dollars, we might come out of this smelling good. Either way, it's money in the bank for us.'

CHAPTER TWENTY-FIVE

Still Thursday

While on the drive back towards the city I thought about Steve's plan to delay things. By telling the kidnappers the insurance people would need the photo, we'd be buying time. Time for what?

'This extra day or two, what've you got in mind, Steve?'

'There're a couple things I'd like to check out. Back there in Gussling's living-room I saw a Triple-A street map for San Ysidro. I didn't think much about it at the time, but then as we were leaving I remembered seeing a brochure for a motel down in San Ysidro over at that tennis pro's apartment. Now, two of the names on our list of people with information about the kidnapping insurance coverage are Theodore and Claire Gussling. Dear innocent Claire Gussling is known by the women at the local tennis club to be playing games off the court with the pro and he's been missing as long as she has. Information about a place just a hop, skip and jump from an international border is seen in two places, Jardin's and the victim of the kidnapping. Wouldn't San Ysidro, right down there next to the Mexican border, be a good place for the kidnap victim to be held or possibly even to hide away for the few days it took to get the ransom money paid out? Get the money and head down to the land of sun and tequila. What could be better?'

'Yeah, maybe,' I said hesitantly, 'but that seems kind of slim to me. And even if it is where she is, whether hiding out or being kept there, how will having a couple extra days matter? What do you hope to prove?'

Steve sat relaxed behind the wheel of his Monte Carlo, driving with his attention focused on the traffic streaming around him, one elbow resting on the rolled-down car-door window.

'Why, by going down there and checking it out.'

'You're going down to San Ysidro?'

'Why not? If Claire Gussling is there, in that motel, I'll find her. If not, what have we lost? A little time and the air fare from San Francisco to . . . does San Ysidro have an airport or will I have to rent a car and drive from San Diego?'

'I don't know. OK, so we invest a little. And what happens then?'

'Well, I guess we play it by ear. It all depends on what I find. Look, Bernie, the bottom line doesn't change. If she's not there and Monday the kidnappers tell you where to deliver the ransom, you deliver it. The little wife is returned and we take our fee and go back to stealing cars. But, if we can mess up the deal, bring back the wife and return the money to the insurance company, the reward will have to be ten times as much and we won't go back to repoing. At least not right away. You can write to your heart's content and I . . . well, I can go visit a lady I met recently at a certain tennis club.'

'Somehow that all sounds too easy,' was all I could say, remembering what my mother used to say about counting chickens.

It worked out just about like Steve planned. I dropped him off at the San Francisco international airport leaving me to deal with Gussling and the kidnappers. There was no reason I could see to drive on home. Having his car I decided to spend the next few hours over a long lunch. Maybe enjoy the crossword puzzle in the *Chronicle*.

I'd barely got back on to the freeway when my cell buzzed.

'Hey, there partner.' It was Steve. 'Long time no see.'

'Yeah, all of . . . what, ten minutes?'

'Uh huh. Look, two things before my plane leaves. First off I got a flight on Virgin America and will land in San Diego in an hour and a half. I'll let you know later what I find. And the second thing is, remember that lady I mentioned? The one from the tennis club? Well, I'd given her my number and she just called me. Guess what? Never mind, I'll tell you. Jardin showed up right before lunch.'

'The tennis pro? Well, I guess that almost takes him off the suspect list, then.'

Over the background noise of the airport I heard Steve chuckle. 'Maybe and then maybe not. Think about how quick and easy it is to get to San Ysidro. He might want to show his face so nobody would tie him to his favorite student who's gone missing.'

'Or,' I cut in, 'he just might not have anything to do with this whole affair.'

'Yes, there is that. Maybe I'll find out when I get to the big city of San Ysidro. Talk to you later, *amigo*.' He hung up.

With a cell phone one doesn't actually hang up, you just push the little red button. I smiled, thinking of what people nowadays are missing, not being able to slam the phone down. This younger generation just won't know what fun that can be.

I was back at Gussling's two-storey palatial home by quarter to five. I didn't want to spend any more time with the man than I had to. Deep down, I really wanted to discover that he was the mastermind behind this whole deal.

As it turned out, he poured me a cup of half-way decent coffee and left the room, saying he had some paperwork to deal with.

'The office manager knows about my wife being taken but that doesn't stop business from going on. I've got a pile of orders left over from our stay in BA to process. I've got my office set up in one upstairs bedroom and will keep one eye on the clock and be back down in time.'

I got his email address from him, then sat back with the coffee and a magazine to wait out the next fifteen minutes.

Right on the money, as I was dialling the phone number listed in the kidnapper's note, Gussling came back down the stairs.

My conversation with the voice on the other end was brief. At first the person – I couldn't tell if it was a man or a woman, it was all muffled – didn't want any delay. Keeping my voice steady and hoping I sounded patient, I pointed out that the matter was out of my hands. I was simply the hired go-between, the one to deliver the ransom. When I got it, that is.

'Look,' I said, talking as if to a two-year-old, 'it doesn't do any good to fight me on this. From what I understand, in South America a thing like this is cut and dried. But, as it's been pointed out to me, this is California, not Argentina. Here the powers that be, and in this case, that's the insurance company, demand to have proof Mrs Gussling is safe and sound. Someone's been watching too much television, I'd say. So, you got a digital camera?'

'No.' Something told me I was talking to a man.

'Well, find one. A cheapie. Take a photo of Mrs Gussling holding today's paper so we can show the insurance people the front page. They'll see that and release the money. I'll call you and you tell me where we'll make the trade. That's not too hard, is it?'

'Damn it, that'll take a week to get a photo mailed to you.'

'No it won't. I'll give you the Gussling's email address. Take the photo to any Internet café and email it. That can all be done tonight. We'll have it up to the city in the morning, have the money ready for delivery, probably by noon tomorrow.'

The silence on the other end was thick. Then the voice came back.

'OK. But we'll have to find another number for you to call, that'll take some time.'

'Well, why not take my cell number and call me? Say around noon. I'll be the one bringing the money anyhow, so you can give me the directions then. It can't get any easier than that, can it?'

'Yes. It'd be a helluva lot easier if you had the ransom money already in your hands. All right. Give me your number.'

I did and the phone went dead. I wondered if he tried to slam it down.

CHAPTER TWENTY-SIX

Gussling was getting a bit antsy, I could tell. He'd only heard my side of the conversation with the kidnapper and it probably didn't make him feel good.

'I don't know what the hell you think you're doing but I don't like it. That's my wife we're talking about, and all I can see is that you're putting her life in danger with all this playing around. What the hell is going on?'

'Mr Gussling, you called us to do a job for you. That's what you're paying for. Now to you, and apparently to the kidnappers, this is a straight trading deal, the insurance company pays up and your wife comes home. That is what this is all about. OK, and as I've heard over and over, that works fine in Argentina. This isn't Argentina and I can't believe we're dealing with kidnappers from that country. The guy I just talked to didn't sound Mexican. Whoever he is, he's as Californian as you or me.'

'So, he's a local, what does that mean? How does that get my wife back? You and that friend of yours are up to something and I want to know what it is. No, I demand to know what it is.'

'Demand all you want but let me lay it out for you. There's a question that has to be answered before any money changes hands—' Once again he started to butt in. 'No, you want to know what's happening, let me tell you. There's a fly in the ointment. You and your wife return from Argentina. A couple weeks later your wife goes missing and you get a note telling you to get the kidnapping ransom process started. This type of thing doesn't happen in California. It might be business as usual in other parts of the world, but not in Southern California. That means someone familiar with that kind of kidnapping insurance is at the centre of it. How many people do you think are on that list? Uh huh, I can see what your first thought is. The list begins with Mr and Mrs Gussling. Well, add a few people from your company and a few more from the insurance company and that's about it. So, if that's the case, and it is, guess what that means.'

I stopped to watch him work through the options.

'Hey,' he said, near panic in his voice, 'don't for a moment think I've set this up. No way, dammit, I'm the one who hired you, remember?'

'Yep, you did. Could that have been because you wanted someone in between you and the kidnapper? Might be. Or it could be by hiring me, if anything goes wrong there is someone to put the blame on? Another way might be that your wife is truly a victim and neither of you has anything to do with the entire affair. Now, we could simply get the money, set up the drop and trust your wife will be released, unharmed. End of the deal. You go back to work Monday morning and your wife goes back to playing tennis at the club.'

'But you don't think that's how it'll happen?' He was thinking about it. The man had stopped wearing out the carpet and was leaning where Steve had leaned earlier, against the unused fireplace.

'Well, maybe, maybe not. One thing is clear. The kidnapper is going to be emailing you a photo in a few hours. Then he is going to call me to set up a procedure for making the trade, ransom for wife. Nothing has changed. It's just been put off for another day. Kidnapping, California style, would call for something like this, don't you think? Remember, kidnapping for ransom is a one-time deal. It isn't likely that the kidnappers will know exactly what they're doing. Everyone knows how it's done on TV and that's the common instruction manual. OK, so we're all following the script. It's logical that the insurance company wants proof. That's what we're getting. That is what we're up to. Now, are you satisfied?'

I left Saratoga with Gussling set to meet me at his office the next morning, email and photo in hand. He had to accept the plan I had shared with him. He'd heard me contact the kidnappers and make arrangements to make the swap. He wasn't a hundred per cent convinced but my explanation had a strong enough thread of logic running through it for him to go along with it.

Driving back to the city in the late-evening going-home traffic, my feeling was that Steve had better come through or we'd be sharing the promised ten per cent. Which wasn't all that bad, was it?

It took almost an extra hour of driving to get over to Sausalilto. Fighting traffic on the freeways through San Francisco at any time of the day is not fun but during the evening drive time it was almost the worst thing a person could do. My day had been a long one and I was so tired that I'd parked the Monte Carlo and had the key in my front door before the thought of Pistilli crossed my mind. My sigh of relief when the minuscule place I called home proved empty and non-threatening could probably be heard all over town.

Dinner was quickly out of the way, a frozen hamburger helper kind of thing in the microwave washed down with a glass of some inexpensive red wine. I'd eaten the meal, every tasteless bite of it, out of the package it came in so there were no dishes to wash up. With that out of the way, and starting on the second or third glass of wine, I was sitting there, staring at my laptop screen when my cell phone rang.

'Hey there, buddy. How'd your day go?' It was Steve, sounding upbeat and happy. That, I'd learned a long time ago, didn't mean much. His habit when it came to talking on the phone was to plaster a big smile on his face and start talking. The smile, he said, carried over and made whoever was on the other end feel good. I could just see him making a call to let someone know their mother had just died, big smile coming down the line, making the newly orphan happy.

'Well, things went about like we expected. Gussling fought it a little until I gave him some gobbledy-gook about keeping ahead of the kidnappers by requesting a photo of the Missus. He didn't like it but had to take it. How about you? Find the aforementioned kidnappee?'

'Not yet. I'm in a room of the motel that was advertised on the brochure I saw in that tennis pro's place.'

'There're a couple things you should remember,' I said. 'First, you don't know what he looks like and second, didn't your tennis-club girlfriend say he was back at the club?'

'Ah, yeah. I called her when I got off the plane. Among the other things I found out was that Jardin came striding through the place like he owned it, talked to a couple of his former lady friends, had a bit of jabber with a staff trainer and then walked back out. She said she hasn't seen him since.'

'This girlfriend of yours sounds like she's a real lounge bunny. You sure she knows anything about tennis?'

'Hey, you ought to see her chest. She doesn't have to know the game to play the game. Trust me. Anyway, what I'm saying is that he could have flown in, let himself be seen, then caught another flight back down here. I don't think he's out of the frame. Not by a long shot. Oh, and I do know what he looks like, there was a series of photos in the lobby identifying the various club pros, both tennis and golf. Each with the name listed underneath.'

'So all you think you've got to do is watch the women by the pool? You know what he looks like from a photo so any female sitting by him will be Mrs Gussling? I don't know. What happens if she is being held captive?'

'No, I don't expect to find her sitting down by the pool but you never know. Remember, I've got that photo that Gussling gave me. Oh, and another one I picked up when I visited her house.'

'You never mentioned that. What happens if Gussling sees it's missing?'

'I doubt that would happen. How often do you ever really see things? Photos on the shelf just become part of the shelf after a little while. Anyway, I'll get started in the morning and find out if she's checked in here. Which I don't expect, but you never know.'

'I still think you're on a wild-goose chase.'

'Yeah, maybe. But have you got a better idea?'

'Nope. Anyway, we'll go on, playing it the way we planned.'

'OK. Now, I'm off to find some dinner. I'll talk with you tomorrow about this time.'

'Let's hope we've both got good things to report. Talk to you then,' I said, pushing the little red icon on the cell, hanging up. Once again I had a brief internal discussion on whether one actually can say that 'hanging up' applies to cell phones.

CHAPTER TWENTY-SEVEN

Friday

The next day was almost a total waste of time. I met Gussling at his office just before noon as we'd agreed the day before. He had the photo that the kidnapper had taken and the briefcase filled with money. The photo didn't tell us much except that she had been alive and well the day before. I recognized the newspaper's front page she was holding up, a three-column-wide shot of a train derailment somewhere up in the northern part of the state. Looking at that took me back to when I was a journalist. A train derailment would be a good story to work, lots of good photos. Any disaster makes a good story, especially one that can be milked for a couple days.

I studied the photo of the woman holding the paper but the background didn't give anything away. Mrs Gussling had been posed sitting against what appeared to be a blank concrete block wall. She wasn't smiling but didn't look bleary-eyed or tired either.

'Damn, I still don't like this,' Gussling said, staring at the photo. He'd printed it out in black and white; I couldn't tell whether the original had been colour.

'No,' he said when I asked, 'that's the way it came, just a lot of black and white and grey. It could be anywhere in the state.'

I nodded, thinking or anywhere 500 miles south, down near the motel where Steve was staying. I'd have to remember to ask him whether there was such a block wall anywhere around.

'OK, so now we know she's safe,' I said, folding the photo carefully. 'I'll wait for the kidnappers to call and find out where they want to make the exchange.'

He watched as I undid the snaps and opened the worn leather briefcase. The packets of money had been placed in perfect order, each wrapped with a paper band that had the amount, date and someone's signature written on it. I didn't take the time to count the packets, but just closed the brass snaps and stood up.

'I want to go with you.'

I hadn't counted on that. 'Then why do you think you need me? No, I can't see how that would work. My suggestion is that you take the rest of the day and stay at home. Keep close to your phone. As soon as she's safe, I'll call and let you know how long it'll take to get her to you. There's no way of telling exactly where this swap will take place. It could be anywhere in the state and they might even hold off until dark to make it impossible to set them up.'

'I hadn't thought about that. But anywhere in the state? Why not just someplace here in the city? I can think of a lot of places, the San Francisco Zoo, for instance. Is there something you're not telling me that makes you think she's being held somewhere outside the Bay area?'

'Nope and if it were me the zoo would be the perfect place. Or even over at the Museum of Modern Art when one of the tour buses drops a load of tourists. I just want to impress on you that we don't know and can't plan until I make contact with them. Let me do the job you hired me to do. Go home and wait by the phone. It'll be hard, but that's the best thing to do. Best for both you and your wife.'

'All right, but I'm still not all that comfortable with this.'

'We've been through this, haven't we? None of us, you, me or the kidnappers has ever done any thing like this before. Let's play it out just as planned. This is Friday. It's almost all over.'

It might be getting to the end of the week but I was sure it wasn't almost over. I was right.

Having a couple million dollars in one-hundred-dollar bills locked in the trunk of the Monte Carlo bothered me a little. I had visions of being stopped by the highway patrol and them finding the briefcase.

'Now looky here,' I could imagine one of them saying. There always seemed to be two whenever I had one of my little mental movies. 'How do you explain this?'

What could I say? Obvious they would think it was drug money, wouldn't they?

That was the scenario that was going through my mind as I wedged the briefcase upright between the spare tyre and the back of the trunk.

Ever notice the spare tyres the car manufacturers are putting into their new cars now? Little almost flat tyres marked clearly with the warning that in any emergency you're not to drive more than sixty miles before replacing. The Monte Carlo's spare wasn't like that. This one was as big and robust as the four already hitting the pavement.

And the jack wasn't one of those weak-looking ratchet things that came in three parts: a flat slotted base, the tall pole that fitted into the slot with the ratchet mechanism on it and the jack handle. Again, when Chevrolet produced this car they did it in style: they included a hefty scissors jack, one that looked as if it could lift three cars. And the jack handle was good steel too. A couple feet long, flattened on one end so you could prise off the hub cap and a socket on the other that would fit the lug nuts. Now, this was a real man's tool. Good for the Chevrolet designers. I used the tyre jack to hold the briefcase firmly in place.

By the time I drove across the Golden Gate Bridge I'd nearly forgotten the briefcase and was worrying about other things. Namely, Hugo and Murphy.

There was no sign of them when I got home. After carefully locking the car I checked the street before heading up to my apartment.

The phone call I was expecting came exactly as the noon whistle blew. I let it buzz for a bit before picking it up.

'OK, you got the ransom money?' The same voice as before, muffled. I figured it was a man talking through a handkerchief. We had both probably seen the same thing done on one of those television crime shows.

'Ah, no.' I tried to speak hesitatingly but at the same time convincingly. Remembering Steve's theory about smiling while talking on the phone and having the smile come out on the other end, I was attempting to look believable.

'What? What do you mean, no. You're not trying to pull something, are you?'

'No. Most definitely not.' I was talking fast now, trying to sound frustrated and helpless. 'Believe me, I've been talking until I'm blue in the face but these bean-counters just won't let go. All morning they've been passing the buck, saying someone higher up the food chain would have to be consulted. Look, I just got through with some vice-president or another. He assured me that the money would be released in an hour. These guys have been going over the insurance forms with a fine-toothed comb. I've accused them of reneging on their obligation but they swear they aren't. They say they just want to make sure this is all in order. Remember, this is coverage like none of the bozos have ever seen before. Another hour, that's the best I can do.'

Silence on the line.

'OK, one hour. I'll call.' He hung up.

I sat at the laptop, reading the part of the story I'd been working on, trying to recapture the train of thought I'd been following before. The basic story, really no more than an outline, had been rattling around in my mind, only needing for me to punch the keyboard, filling in the blanks. Somewhere that train had become derailed.

Keeping one eye on the little clock down in the corner of the screen didn't help me concentrate. In less than an hour I was going to have to take up the act again. Think about sounding frustrated, helpless with a touch of anger, I instructed my inner being. This time will be a little harder so the tone will have to be just right. I wasn't quite finished with my self-lecture when the cell started buzzing again. The caller ID didn't indicate who was calling. That made sense.

After some moments, breathing heavily like I'd just run a four minute mile, I punched the correct button.

'Yeah, just a sec, let me catch my breath.' I counted to five or six. 'All right, sorry about that but . . . anyway, hello.'

'You got the money yet?'

'Oh, it's you. I wasn't expecting you to call for another fifteen minutes. That's what I was doing, over in another office. No. They're still dicking around. Someone, nobody seems to know exactly who, is dragging his feet. Look, give me a number I can reach you at. That would save a lot of stress on both of us.'

'No. That wouldn't work. This way I can use different phones. What the hell's the hold up, anyway? This is a straightforward deal. This insurance company has dealt with dozens of these kinds of things over the years. Who's jacking us around?'

'I don't know. Really, all I want is to get the money to you, get the woman back and go home. I didn't sign on for this kind of BS. By the way, is she still all right? This delay must be damn hard on her, as well.'

'You tell those fools that the woman is starting to panic. That's because we're starting to panic and she knows that won't be good for her.'

'I've been using that as leverage, trying to get someone to sign off on that policy. Look, they're saying it'll be a while. Now it's a bunch of attorneys. Dammit, you got to believe, I'm doing the best I can.'

'Get that idiot Gussling. I want to talk to him.'

'Hang on. He's in the next office.'

I let the cell knock the table top as I put it down, leaned back and counted to twenty-five. Silently I got up and went over to the furthest wall and, keeping my back to the cell, presented my argument.

'What can I tell them? They want to talk to Mr Gussling.' I waited and then slammed the flat of my hand against the wall. 'OK. I'll tell them, but they aren't going to like it. Don't forget, this is Mrs Gussling's who's in danger here.'

Coming back to the phone, I picked it up and started apologizing.

'Gussling's not in the office.' I now sounded as harried as I could. 'Hello, you still there?'

'Yeah. I'm here, and I'm not very happy.'

'I know, I know. But there's nothing I can do. They said Gussling threw up his hands and after yelling at them, stormed out of the office. They want me to tell you that it'll take a couple more hours. They're saying four o'clock.'

'This is shit.' His frustration didn't sound as fake as mine. 'OK. Four. But that had better be the end of it. I'm warning you, that had better be all.' Again I had the feeling he was slamming the phone down.

Now all I had to do was wait a couple more hours and go into my final act. This was turning out to be hard work. I decided the best thing to do was relax over a cold beer.

Lou Lou's was mostly empty. Four men were sitting at the bar, each a couple stools from his nearest neighbour. Back at one of the pool tables, two men were watching a third lean over the table lining up a shot. I didn't see anyone that looked familiar. I pulled the stool the furthest away from the others and climbed on, ordering a draught.

Draught beer always seemed to taste fresher than anything from a bottle. Beer in a can, in my view, should be outlawed. Steve didn't believe me when I said I could taste the aluminium from the can. It was the solder they used to put the thing together with. When I said that, he'd only laugh at me.

119

Thinking about Steve, I wondered how he was getting on. With all this telephoning going on, if the tennis pro was part of it and if Steve had the right motel, he should be easy to spot. I wasn't as sure about the tennis pro as he was. From what I could see, it could as easily be a scam being run by the Gusslings. Maybe he'd have some news when he called later.

Sipping the beer, I gave some thought to what we could do if none of this worked out. Nothing. We'd simply turn the ransom over to the kidnapper and, as Steve said, go back to stealing cars for the bank.

The first time I'd asked for salt the bartender had frowned, not knowing what I was up to. It was something I'd learned years back, while I was working up in the northern part of the state. Up there people often dropped a few grains of rock salt in their glass of beer. The salt caused the beer to foam a little, but as it dissolved the taste of the beer changed. Not much, but enough.

Red beer was another favourite of beer drinkers up there. I hadn't seen anyone in this part of the country ask for a red beer. It hadn't been one of my favourite ways of drinking beer, filling half the glass with tomato juice before pouring in the beer. Salt was a good addition but I could pass on the tomato juice.

I had two glasses, taking my time with both, before deciding it was time to get back to the phone. This time it was going to be really tough. If the kidnapping was anything like they showed in the movies or on television all these delays could be dangerous for the kidnap victim. Neither Steve nor I thought there was any danger for the victim in this case. Mrs Gussling was money in the bank for someone. She wouldn't be harmed and the kidnappers were going to put up with our postponements, at least for a little while longer.

CHAPTER TWENTY-EIGHT

'C'mon, you're not taking me seriously. What are you trying to pull?'

'Nothing. I'm not trying to pull anything,' putting a lot of emphasis on the 'I'm' part of it. 'I'm just the go-between. It's these fools holding the ransom money who are holding things up. I've made it very clear to them the danger they're putting Mrs Gussling in and I think they really care. But they seem to care more about the money.'

'Something has to be done. I'm not going to be put off any longer.'

'No, don't do anything foolish. Look, I don't know what to tell you. Apparently there is some big shot who has to sign off on a pay-out this size and he's off on some holiday or a conference or something. All I know is they have been on the phones all afternoon, trying to trace this guy down. I honestly don't know what else to say, other than we got to wait.'

'How long. I want a time. A definite time.'

I waited for another ten count. 'I don't know. I really don't. Look, there isn't anything we could set up this late anyhow. How about nine in the morning?' I hurried the next part, 'that way you'll have all day to make the exchange work. I'll tell them this is your final cut-off time. They'll have to release the funds by nine or. . .' I let the sentence die.

'Yeah, or they won't be seeing the lady again. You tell them that. Nine o'clock in the morning. No more bullshit.' Once again he slammed the phone down. Or I believed he did.

So far so good. It was all up to Steve now. I went back to staring at the screen on my laptop. Maybe there was a jinx in all this that was causing my mind to be a complete blank, the story not going anywhere. I didn't have much time to concentrate though, when someone started knocking on my door. It was quite possible, I thought getting up and taking the two or three steps to answer it, that I wasn't suppose to get any writing done.

Opening the door, ready to tear into whoever it was, I stopped, recognizing the San Francisco detective I'd last seen in a Starbucks over in the city.

'Hey, there, Mr Gould, thought I'd stop by to see how you were.'

'You're that detective who was asking me questions a few days ago. Quincy, if I remember right. How'd you find me over here?'

'Yeah, Detective Jonathan Quincy, San Francisco Police. And you could ask me in, offer me a cup of coffee or something, and I'd tell you.'

I hadn't opened the door but now did. 'Sorry, Detective Quincy, I guess my mind was on something else. Sure, come on in.' Pointing towards my only chair, the one facing the laptop, I retreated into the kitchen area. 'Sit yourself and I'll see about coffee.'

'Naw, don't bother. I won't be staying long. Say,' he said. 'What's the story on the black eye?'

'Oh, you know how it is, I ran into a door.'

'Yeah. For someone who claims to be innocent, you sure have a lot of secrets going on.'

Glancing around the apartment he smiled. 'It's a good thing you're not a big bruiser of a guy or suffer from claustrophobia. This place could get a little crowded if three people tried to get in.'

I didn't appreciate the comment but couldn't argue about it. He was right.

'It is a little cramped but it'll do. Now, what can I do for you, and how in hell did you find me?'

'Oh, that. Well, I've sorta been keeping an eye on you. You and your friend Steve Gunnison. Look, don't get in a huff. I'm cool with your repoing work. That's none of my business. It's that kidnapping that's bothering me.' He quickly stopped me from interrupting. 'No, don't bother denying there isn't something going on. There is and I know it.'

Not sure of my footing, I turned my back on the man to give myself time to think and filled the pot that I used to boil water in. Flicking the switch on one of the burners of the stove, I set out a jar of instant coffee and a couple cups before looking back at the cop.

'As I understand it, our business with repossessing cars and trucks is all legal. We're under contract with a bank. As far as any kidnapping, well, I thought we'd already discussed that.'

'Uh huh. You're right, we did talk about it. But now I understand you've picked up the ransom money. Why not tell me about it? You could end up being charged with obstruction of justice, you know. Or the district attorney's office might want to think that by not calling us you're part of it. Kidnapping is very serious stuff, and you're right in the middle of it. Now would be a good time to come clean.'

The water was boiling so I poured a couple spoonfuls of coffee into the cups and set out the sugar bowl and spoons. I got the bottle of milk from the little refrigerator and handed it to the detective.

'Thanks,' he said, adding two heaped spoons of sugar to the coffee and splashing in a dollop of milk. 'I don't see how anybody can drink this stuff. But on the other hand, it's a lot better than that stuff we get out of the machine back in the office.'

I fixed my cup and nodded. 'Yeah, but it's easier than perking up a pot that won't get drunk. And as far as any kidnapping goes, all I can say is what we talked about before. The wife of a man who is high up in a prestigious local company is part of a business deal. That deal calls for a certain insurance policy to pay out a premium. My part is to make the delivery of that premium, and that's all. Nobody's crying kidnap, nobody is making any threats. It's a simple business transaction.' I sipped the coffee and burned my lip. 'The last time we talked you were interested in that big name hood, as I recall. Anything new on that?'

Boy, I thought, wouldn't it be nice to hear Pistilli had been found guilty of something terrible?

'Nope.' He said, sipping from his cup. The hot coffee didn't seem to bother him. 'I don't suppose he's been in touch with you since then, has he? Or any of his thugs?'

I shook my head and tried the coffee again. Still too hot.

'Look, if you don't want to talk to me about whatever you guys are in, that's cool. Either it'll work out and I won't be involved or it won't and I'll be all over you like shit on a shingle. And that'll be OK, too. I got too many other things to deal with. Remember I told you about young girls being raped and killed? Well, there was another one. Her body was found early this morning. Sixteen years old. She was last seen coming home from doing homework at a girl friend's house. Found by an early morning dog-walker in a corner of a city park. The experts say she was killed sometime late last night. After midnight is his best guess at this stage. That means she suffered for at least two, maybe three hours. It was the same as the others. The crime scene boys spent all day at the place, trying to find something, anything. They came up empty. That makes three and the DA's office is thinking serial killer.'

He drank more coffee and then looking tired, shook his head.

'I hope to hell it isn't another serial killer at work but all the signs are there.'

'What are the chances? And what signs are you talking about?'

'Officially a serial killer is a person who murders three or more people over a given period, usually a month. The timing is one sign, the sexual element is another. If the killings are done in a similar fashion, stabbing or strangling, the pattern is a sure indication there's a serial at work. What clinches this up for us is that the vic's are all the same, young girls and all with long hair. Boy, when the newspapers get a hold of this, we'll really get the pressure.'

'So keeping a watch on Steve and me isn't top of your list, then?'

'Hell no. You guys are just one of a dozen things I got on my plate right now. Like I said, you'll either rise to the top, or not.' He got up and put his empty cup on the table next to the laptop. 'But don't let things get too out of hand, whether it's about Pistilli or this so-called business deal. Here's my card. You want to share anything, give me a call. My personal cell number is on the back.'

I quickly cleaned up the two cups after Quincy left and was thinking about giving it up and going out for some dinner when again someone knocked at the door.

'What the hell,' I muttered, going to open it. 'How in hell did I get so popular?'

I opened the door and stood there with my mouth open in total shock. The cop, Quincy, was probably right, there were too many things going on that I had little or no control over. Whatever made me think I could simply walk out and go have a nice quiet dinner? I mean, who did I think I was that the gods of fate would leave me alone? I should have known better. There I was now, feeling suddenly like the deer caught in the headlights. Standing in the open doorway was my ex-wife, Inez.

'Hello, Bernie,' she said, smiling faintly.

I was speechless. Oh, I wanted to say something, but all I could do was stare. Inez. How many times had I dreamt of seeing her again, of hearing her soft voice, seeing the sparkle that made her eyes seem to shine.

'Aren't you going to ask me in?'

I stepped aside, holding the door open for her. There she was, after all this time, walking softly past me, her flowing skirt brushing against my leg.

Thinking back on it, what was said the next few minutes isn't clear to me. Inez had come back, had taken the trouble to find me and had come back. Why? I don't remember her ever saying. Later thinking about it, the only comment I could recall was that she missed her Bernie.

From where? That didn't matter either. She mentioned something about her parents' place up in Seattle but couldn't stay there.

'You know how mother can be. She always liked you and thought my marrying you was what saved me from myself. Well, you can guess how she reacted to find me coming back home without you. From there I went down to Reno and got a job. That was OK for a while. Did some traveling and, ah, hell, Bern, I still thought about you, you and me, you know? So I came back out to the coast and asked around. You're a hard man to find. But I did. And how did you get that black eye?'

I didn't answer. For the longest time I just stood there like a dolt, not saying anything. How many times I had thought about her I couldn't say. When she had walked out, a big part of me had gone too. I didn't realize how big a hole she'd left until she came through the door just now. And here she was, looking just like she did the day we met. What the hell could I say?

My silence didn't go unnoticed.

'Maybe I shouldn't have come back,' she said after a long moment. 'I turned back a few times, thinking of how you must feel about me, but, you know, I have to make sure. So here I am.'

'I don't know what to say, Inez. I really don't.'

'That's OK. To be expected, I guess. After all. . . look, I took a place over in the city, a little apartment on the third floor of what was once a hotel. It's been broken up into apartments and caters to single women. This has come on too fast. I know you remember, and know you'll have to think long and hard about my popping up like I did. I apologize for that but I didn't know what else to do. I'll leave my phone number. You think about it, about us, about me. When you have it figured out, what you want, call me?'

She had a business card ready, a phone number pencilled in on the back. Everybody wanted to give me cards today.

'I don't know what I'm doing,' she went on handing me the card, 'but

125

damn it, things aren't worthwhile out there by myself. I keep remembering the good times we had and want more of them.' Pointing to the card I held, she went on. 'Think about me, us, and when you've got it all straight, call me. Please.' The last word was almost a question. I just nodded.

I stood on the porch and watched her walk away. I followed as she went out to get into her car, a little white Honda. She smiled and waved before driving away. All I could do was stand there and watch, all thoughts of dinner forgotten.

CHAPTER TWENTY-NINE

I have to admit it. I'd been thrown for a loop. One I never expected. When Inez had walked out I had actually felt relieved. Before she left she hadn't actually said anything but I knew she wasn't happy. Back when we were up in Eureka and I was still with the newspaper there had been times she let me know she'd feel better if I had a normal job. It was the hours I had to keep that upset her. But what could I do?

If there was a major five-car pile up out on the Redwood Highway, it was my job to grab my notepad and camera and go cover it. Even if the damn fool tourists chose Sunday afternoon when the entire family was just sitting down to dinner, I'd have to go. Of course in those days the entire family would be the two of us and Steve and his latest girlfriend.

Steve understood. Hell, he'd be right there with me, both of us doing what we were paid to do. Most times weren't like that but it happened often enough. More than once Inez had suggested that I do the course work and get a teaching credential.

'You could teach journalism out at the junior college,' she pointed out after reading something in the paper about a shortage of qualified instructors in the state system.

I didn't say much about that idea, but when I did my usual response was 'Those that can't do, teach.'

To be totally honest, I liked being the hot-shot reporter that I thought I was. Having my byline on the front page nearly every edition was a major point of pride for me. She never understood that. Probably because I didn't think it sounded good for me to declare it, so I didn't.

Anyway, I had to give her a lot of credit, she had put up with me and the job. Even when I had left the paper and turned to writing fiction, she stood by me. At least she had for a while. Thinking back I could see that neither of us had any idea how difficult it'd be, getting into print, getting published and getting a pay cheque. But when she left I wasn't exactly devastated. No, I was more relieved than anything. Now I could focus on my writing and not have that guilty feeling buzzing around in the back of my head.

So she'd gone, taking everything in the bank, and I'd had to go to working with Steve. Burying myself in story after story that didn't go far and then out most nights repoing some poor dead-beat's vehicle didn't leave me much time or energy. The instant I saw her standing there, I knew one of the reasons I'd kept full of activity was so I wouldn't have to think about her.

Maybe it was subconscious but I didn't want to admit to myself how much I had screwed up my life.

That all changed before she even had time to say hello. Now I could see it clearly. The question was, though, should I do something about it?

So now what was I supposed to do? Before my inner know-it-all could reply, my cell buzzed.

'Hey, good buddy.' Steve sounded far too happy. 'I was hoping I'd catch you before you went out dining and dancing.'

'Not likely, Steve. Not likely at all. Give me the good news, you've found the missing Mrs Gussling.'

'Well, no, not yet. But let's give it another day. There're a couple people I want to talk to. You know, the day clerk might remember seeing her.'

'Steve, old man Gussling is giving me the shits. He wanted to hand the ransom money over the minute he got the briefcase. Talking him into letting us hold off for a day took all my arguments. Now you want to let him sit and stew about his wife for another day? It's not going to happen, old son. Just not going to happen.'

'Ah, yeah. I guess you're right,' he said slowly. 'OK, You call the kidnappers and set it up. But don't go meeting up with them until I'm back to cover your butt, you hear me?'

'I hear, I hear. I'll call them first thing in the morning. Work it around so any exchange will take place, say, early afternoon? Can you catch a flight and be back by noon?'

'Yeah, I suppose. Dammit, I was so sure they were down here.'

'They? You're still going on the assumption that the tennis pro is part of it?'

'No reason not to, is there?'

'Maybe. But no reason, no real proof that he is.'

'Yeah, maybe. OK, anything else you heard today?'

'Well, yes. Guess who knocked on my door a little bit ago?' I didn't give him time to guess. 'Inez came by.'

I had said it quietly. I wasn't sure at first he'd heard, he didn't say anything for a long minute. Then, as if it suddenly hit, he responded.

'Inez. You don't mean the former Mrs Bernie Gould? That Inez?'

'Yeah, that one. The only one, you idiot.'

'What did she want?' I didn't have a chance to answer. 'After all this time, after the way she just up and walked out, you're telling me she had the balls to come waltzing in and. . . . What did she want, anyway?'

'I don't know. She's living over in the city. Gave me her number and left.'

'Gawd, I can't believe it. I really can't.'

I didn't want to, but I had to ask. Something had been bothering me.

'Steve, you didn't happen to tell her where I was living, did you? I mean, how in the hell did she find me? You're about the only one who knows.'

The stillness on the line grew. I swear, when he answered I could see the worrying frown clouding his face.

'Yeah. It was almost like an accident, Bern. She apparently got my number from someone up in Eureka, one of my old girlfriends from up there. Hell, I wasn't keeping my whereabouts a secret, you know? Anyway, she called and said she was living nearby and could we have coffee. At first, I think she just wanted to know how you were, kinda like, is he OK? You know, wanting to make sure you're taking care of yourself. Stuff like that.'

'And you blurted out my address?'

'No, not right off. I mean, you told me how she'd left you, how she emptied the bank and took the car. That pissed me off, that she'd do that. But when we got to talking, I could see she really felt bad about all that. Anyway, I wasn't going to tell her anything and all I told her was that you were doing pretty good, working with me. Had a nice little apartment, but I didn't say where, honest I didn't.'

'Uh huh.'

'Well, all I said was you were getting on. I didn't tell her about that hovel you're living in. I just said you had a "small" apartment.'

129

'But she came knocking on my door.'

'Well, I wanted her to think you weren't hurting. You know, about her leaving and all. So I said that you'd got one of your novels picked up by a publisher and, well, I might have made it sound bigger than what it was. You know. I wanted her to know what she threw away.'

'And told her where I lived.'

Silence.

'Yeah, I guess I did. But Bern, all I wanted was for her to know how good you were doing without her.'

'So you told her where my little – what'd you call it? – my little hovel was. So she could come knocking on my door. So she could screw up my head again. Thanks a lot, buddy.' The sarcasm was dripping from the last part.

'Look—'

I cut him off. 'No. Never mind. Let's not talk about it any more. We've got this damn kidnapping deal to take care of. I'll call the kidnapper in the morning and get that going. Have to call Gussling too, I suppose. You just get your ass back here as early as possible.'

'OK, Bern, I'll call as soon as I get a flight to let you know when I'll be landing. I'm sorry about, well, I'm sorry I messed things up.'

I didn't say a thing.

'Bern, what are you going to do?'

'By the time I pick you up at the airport I should have the directions from the kidnapper. We can discuss it all then.'

'No, I mean about Inez.'

'I don't know. Haven't thought it all out, yet. Probably nothing. Anyway, I want to get this damn mess straightened out first.'

CHAPTER THIRTY

Thursday evening

Dinner that night was a couple scrambled eggs, a piece of toast and the rest of a bottle of red wine. When I got up Friday morning ants had found a bit of pale yellow egg and a tad of crust on a plate in the little kitchen sink. The size of the kitchen didn't slow the little bastards down any. The wine bottle was lying on its side on the minuscule counter, empty, and my head hurt, the throbbing centred back about where my skull joined my neck. I must have slept crooked and on my right side because my shoulder and upper arm had its own aches. Those were on top of the aching of my sore ribcage. Looking in the mirror I was pleased to see my black eye was now various shades of pale yellow, light blue with highlights of wishy-washy green and pink. I must be healing.

I was drinking my second or third glass of water when the buzzing that filled my head changed tone. It was my cell phone.

'Hey, buddy, guess what?' Steve, this time yelling happily in my ear. 'They're here. Both of them. Right here. I'm standing at the railing outside my room, looking down through the palms and watching them as we speak. Down by the pool. Man, I can see why Gussling's so hot to get her back. She's something, Bern, I mean, mighty nice even from here. The swimming suit she's got on is a little bit of nothing, hiding very little of that smooth-looking brown body. I'll bet she's got the most even all-over sun-tan I've ever seen.'

'And the tennis pro, what's his name? I can't remember, he's there too?'

'Antonio Jardin. Yep, he's lying back in one of those banana chairs face up to the sun with his eyes closed. He's browner than her. A different kind of brown, if you know what I mean. Got to be some Mexican blood there, I'd say. Yeah,' he chuckled, 'I spotted them when I came out of my room. They don't have a clue. Probably figured nobody'd ever think they'd be this far south. I figure they're here so all they have to do is hang around until the ransom is paid at which time she and her lover will disappear across the border. If he's originally from Mexico it'd be damn hard ever to find them and they'd have that two million to live on. Two people could live pretty damn good down there on that much Yankee *dinero*.'

'OK, so you're sure it's them?'

'No guessing. I called down to the office and asked if Mr and Mrs Jardin had checked out yet. The clerk said they hadn't, that they were out by the pool. Did I want to talk to them? He said he would take the phone out to them if I wanted. I thanked him and said not to bother. I'd come down and talk to them in person. Bern, what'll I do now?'

'Let me think.'

What to do? OK, so the kidnap victim is sunning herself by the pool. She's in no danger, except possibly from attracting melanoma. Was that right? Could someone get a melanoma by becoming a centre of attention for the thing or did that kind of cancer come on merely from getting too much sun. All I knew about it was reading that this cancer was one of the worst kinds to get. You're blabbering, I said to myself. Think. What would happen if I got the money and drove down? I'd like to see his face if I didn't say anything to the kidnapper when I called him to set up the exchange. Just dropped in and said, 'surprise ... here's the money' but then don't give it to him. Take the missus and come back to the City. Hand her over to her husband, the ransom briefcase back to the insurance people and we accept their reward. That'd work.

'Steve.'

'Yeah?'

'How's this?' I laid it out. 'What'd you think?'

It was his turn to be quiet. 'OK, that'd do it. But you sure you want to drive? It's only a couple hours by air.'

'Uh huh. And how do we bring the kidnapped victim back, will she come willingly on the plane? With the scare this country's in about terrorists, I can just see us bringing her on the plane, you holding her arm on one side and me on the other. No, I can drive down. Say five hours to LA, then another two or three to San Diego. Eight hours. Leave just after midnight, no traffic, get in by daylight. I can sleep on the way back.'

'Hmm,' I could almost hear the little wheels turning. 'Well, I can't think of anything better. OK. Give me a call when you get close, though, all right?'

'Yeah. See you tomorrow morning. Keep an eye on them.' I said and pressed the hang-up button.

I sat and thought about it all. Somewhere along the way my head stopped hurting, maybe it was all the water I'd been sucking down. So what now? Wait for the kidnapper to call to set things up and then drive down. Have to make sure Steve's Monte Carlo was all gassed up.

About then was when someone knocked on my door. 'Damn it,' I jumped then headed for the door. 'why *am* I so popular, all of a sudden?'

Wait a minute, I said silently, the last couple times it hasn't been good news coming in. Looking around, I tried to think of something that would make a good weapon. Nothing.

'Hey, Gould,' the caller yelled, beating on the door again. 'Open up, it's your favourite police detective.'

Detective Quincy.

'Now what?' I asked, stepping back when he pushed his way in. 'Twice in as many days, people will start to talk.'

He ignored me. 'I've got news for you. You'll definitely owe me one for this. I'm on my way up north, to Healdsburg. Ever been in Healdsburg?' I shook my head as he went on, not paying any attention to my denial. 'It's a small town, a nice town, someone said. It's also the location of the Russian River Casino. You know the Russian River Casino?' I shook my head again. All of a sudden my headache was back.

'You should. It's run by your old friend, Guido Pistilli.'

'All I know about Healdsburg,' I managed to cut in, 'is that it's one of those little towns alongside the Redwood Highway.'

Quincy stood there, his feet spread apart, his hands shoved into the pockets of his jacket. 'OK, if you say so. Now here's the good part,' he went on, 'the place was robbed last night. From the report there were two, maybe three men, all wearing Hallowe'en masks. Hit the armoured van just as they were picking up the day's take. The robbers got clean away.'

He stopped, not taking his eyes off me.

I shook my head again. 'If you're waiting for me to break down and confess, you're wasting both our time. I told you last night, I haven't had anything to do with *your*,' I stressed the word, 'friend or any of his friends. Why in hell do you keep coming back? Just because I had one run in with him doesn't mean a thing. Damn, I wish people would leave me alone.'

His smile was cold and humourless. 'OK, OK. But think about the good deed I'm doing you by stopping here before I head on up to the crime scene. If Pistilli came after you when someone hit one of his illegal poker games, think what he'll do now that his casino has been knocked over. By the way, that black eye of yours is starting to look good. Be careful that you don't get another one. Or something worse.'

CHAPTER THIRTY-ONE

Sunday morning

It was the 'something worse' that bounced around in the back of my mind as I packed an overnight bag with a change of underwear. I'd Googled a road map of California and found that it was 470 miles from San Francisco to San Ysidro. The expected drive-time was slightly more than seven hours. If I left at midnight traffic down the interstate would be light and I should be pulling in by breakfast time.

If everything went as planned, and when did that ever happen, we should be back on the road heading for home by noon at the latest. I only put one pair of socks and an extra T-shirt in the overnight bag before heading out for a late Sunday brunch. I'd miss the nine o'clock call with the kidnappers but that didn't seem to matter much any more.

I made a complete circuit around the Monte Carlo before unlocking it to make sure it hadn't been broken into overnight. Feeling good about the way things were going, I was clicking the seat belt when the passenger's door opened and Murphy slipped into the seat. He was holding a revolver.

It is very strange how things like that happen. Hearing the door open, I looked up and saw the gun. Just that. Somewhere in the recesses of my brain I was aware of what was happening, but it hadn't registered up front yet. Somehow time seemed to have stopped for me. Before glancing up at the man or having time even to react, I had the weapon he was pointing at me all figured out.

The revolver he was holding had an unusual barrel; it was smaller in diameter which made me think it was probably a .22 calibre weapon. The barrel was a lot longer than would be normal, and a lot bigger towards the end. That had to be a suppressor. Not taking the time to consider why anyone would need a suppressor, my inner voice handed out a brief, silent lecture on the topic.

Most people think silencer when they see an extension on the barrel of a weapon but in reality that would be incorrect. When a bullet is fired, the gunpowder turns to gas, creating huge amounts of pressure forcing the bullet down the barrel at enormous speeds. As the bullet leaves the barrel, depending on the amount of powder in the shell, it can travel at supersonic speed. This produces the loud ballistic crack. The more powerful the gun and ammo, the more chance the bullet will travel at supersonic speed and the crack will be louder. A .22 calibre bullet is much slower and the sound of the bullet leaving the barrel is much quieter.

In any case, even with a high-powered weapon, there is no such thing as a silencer. One can suppress the sound with the use of baffles in the extension to the barrel, which will absorb some of the gases from the powder. Typically the device has a lot more room than the tight barrel of the gun so the suppressor has about thirty times more space for the pressurized gas to expand into. A high-quality suppressor may remove all the muzzle blast and nearly all the ballistic crack. Without thinking about it, I could see this was not a high quality piece of equipment. Which, if he pulled the trigger, wouldn't matter to me very much.

'Good morning, Mr Gould,' Murphy cut into my daydreaming. 'If you'd be so kind as not to do anything stupid, I won't have to use this piece.'

I sat there, open-mouthed, staring at him.

'That's right, keep both hands on the steering wheel and we'll be fine.'

He was speaking in a normal, conversational manner. That helped. Even with a gun pointed at my chest I wasn't really frightened. After all this time of worrying about meeting up with these two, I had to marvel at how relaxed I was. Thinking about Hugo, I glanced over my shoulder. The big man was standing in the street outside my car door, bending over to watch me. His smile was the kind that would cause nightmares in children.

'Go on, Hugo,' Murphy called, not taking his eye off me and continuing to smile. Even while pointing a gun at me, I felt his smile was friendlier. Hell, even a tiger's smile would be friendlier than the one plastered on Hugo's face.

'What's this all about?' I was surprised at how calm I was taking it all.

'Oh, Mr Pistilli wants to talk to you again. We're going to go for a little drive so he can enjoy your company. Actually,' he chuckled and that definitely wasn't friendly, 'I suppose it'll be me and Hugo that'll be getting the most enjoyment out of it. Hugo really enjoys himself.'

Again without looking away, he raised his voice. 'OK, Hugo. Get the car and follow us.'

Still with the smile, he tipped the gun up a little. 'Start it up and drive. Don't do anything stupid. Stay within the speed limit and go where I tell you. Fuck up and I'll pot you and be out of the car and gone before you discover you're dead.'

Unlike the last time, Murphy had me take the north on-ramp up to the Redwood Highway when we left Sausalito. Any discussion with Pistilli would take place at the casino. I didn't need any more information to understand that Son and the robbery would be on the vile little man's mind. Glancing in the mirror I saw a late model black SUV crowding my rear bumper. It was close enough for me to be able to make out the Chevrolet emblem on the hood. The windshield had been darkened, though, and I couldn't make out the driver's face. But I didn't have to. It had to be Hugo.

'Where are we going?' I asked, keeping both hands on the wheel in the prescribed ten and two positions. With the gun barrel just inches from my chest I didn't want any doubt in Murphy's mind. I didn't even look to see if he was watching me or the road.

'Don't be stupid. And don't go thinking we're dumb, either. You got away with it last time, you and your gambling friend, Cardonsky, but not this time. This time Mr Pistilli isn't going to take any shit. This time he really got hurt where it counts, in the pocketbook, and he'll want to know where his money is.'

I shook my head. 'Just like last time, I don't know and don't care. Son Cardonsky isn't now and never has been my friend.'

'Yeah, and that'll not get you anywhere. You'll tell us, no question about that. Now shut up and drive.'

The Redwood Highway stretches from the Bay Area up into Oregon. Mostly two lanes, it hugs the rugged California coast and is popular with vacationers in their RVs. I was keeping my eye out for a cop car but nearly all the traffic seemed to be either heavily loaded logging trucks or tourists in their home on wheels.

I'd driven the highway a time or two but was most familiar with it further north. Sitting behind the wheel with a gun pointed unwaveringly at me was unsettling enough to ensure that my thinking wasn't clear. I was trying to remember the map and was drawing a blank.

That detective, Quincy, he'd said the casino's armoured van got held up last week. Thursday night or maybe Friday morning, early, I couldn't remember exactly. The casino would be where we were heading and that would be Healdsburg. I recalled seeing the name of the casino on a road sign but had never been there.

'Look,' I tried again, 'I had nothing to do with who ever held up the Pistilli's casino. Just like before when he thought I had something to do with someone sticking up a poker game, I don't know anything about it. When the casino was hit I was busy down in the San Jose area and I can prove it.'

Murphy actually laughed. 'See? Already you're not being truthful. How'd you know it was the casino that was hit? I mean, how in hell did you know anything about the casino ever?'

'Because I was told about it. There's a San Francisco cop, a Detective Quincy who came around yesterday to ask me what I knew. He's part of a task force that's been keeping an eye on your boss. Quincy heard about the last time, when you took me to see him, and came calling. Yesterday morning he wanted to warn me to watch out for you and your friend. He told me about the casino hold-up.'

'Boy, you've got some interesting friends, a big city cop and a cardsharp. Anyway, your cop friend told you wrong, it wasn't the casino that got hit, it was an armoured car that was picking up the night's take from the place. Pistilli don't care about that, it's the armoured car company's problem. He'd like to get his hands on the missing cash, all right, but what he's mostly worried about is that everyone'll think his outfit is an easy target.' He chuckled but glancing down I saw the revolver hadn't moved. 'And then there's the problem of having the cops swarming around the place. I guess you know that we can't have that. Too many snooping cops could spoil the soup. I guess it don't matter if I tell you that Mr Pistilli's interests go far beyond that dinky little gambling club. That's nickel-and-dime stuff. The place is just a front for his real business and having the place filled with cops investigating something like a robbery slows things down. That's what worries my boss.'

'Well, what the hell do I have to do with any of that?'

'He thinks that if he can turn up some information about the guys who knocked over that armoured car the cops'll leave him alone. That's where you come in. You tell him where he can get his hands on Cardonsky and the badges'll go away.'

I wanted to laugh at the stupidity of it all but couldn't. My throat had dried up.

'Man, I don't know where Son is. I don't know how to get in touch with him and I certainly don't know anything about any robbery, whether it's the casino's money or not.'

'Sorry, that's not what we've heard. Somebody heard something, something about how you had designed the plan. Mr P didn't take much notice until the armoured car was hit. Then he did, and sent us to get you. Now, like I said, shut it up.'

'But I never designed any plan, not for anything.' I couldn't help it if it sounded like I was whining. I was scared.

The gun barrel poked me hard in the side. 'I said, shut up.'

CHAPTER THIRTY-TWO

I hadn't been paying much attention to the time or, to be honest, even to the road or traffic. Having someone hold a gun on you will do that. I wasn't expecting it when Murphy told me to slow down and take the next off-ramp. The big sign advertising the Russian River Casino was all lit up, the bright-red neon letters looking ten feet tall. Spotlights were angled up at it from the ground, making it even more visible in the late-morning sunshine. The feathers on the Indian headdress that topped the sign had to be at least twenty feet long.

Murphy directed me to pass up the four-lane entrance to the huge parking lot in front of the long, single-storey building and follow the pavement round to the side. The parking lot in back was about a quarter filled, mostly with parked RVs, some as big as Greyhound buses, others simply campers on the back of pickups.

'Go down there,' he said, pointing with the gun barrel. It was the first time it had been pointed at me since leaving Sausalito. 'Stop at that big door and wait.'

There were two huge doors built into the concrete side of the building each with a short loading dock. He directed me towards the single-vehicle door, no wider than a regular garage door, and told me to stop in front of it. The black Chevy Tahoe pulled up behind me and I watched in the side mirror as Hugo climbed out and came round. Not bothering to look in our direction, he used a key from his key ring to unlock the door. He pushed it up into the overhead, then stepped back and waved me on.

Slowly, not knowing what to expect, I drove out of the bright sunlight and into the darkness. Flipping on the headlights I went on down a concrete ramp and into a long, narrow, parking garage.

'Put it over there against that wall and shut the engine off but leave the headlights on.'

I did as he said, then sat and waited. Maybe, I thought, when he got out I would have my chance. Looking around, I changed my mind. From where I sat I could see the ramp at the other end. There had to be a garage door at the top of it, but it'd be closed. The underground space was too narrow to turn round.

Murphy chuckled. 'Yeah, this is the last stop. Now, slow and easy, open your door and step away. Keep your back to me and stop. I'll be right behind you.'

Knowing the revolver was aimed at my back I did as he said. The lights from the SUV swung down and round as Hugo parked on the other side the Monte Carlo.

'Get the damn lights, Hugo.' Murphy yelled out the order. I wasn't able to see how close he was behind me.

I heard the door to the SUV slam closed and in a few minutes overhead lights filled the long room with cold, hard light.

'OK, over there,' Murphy said, pointing with his free hand toward a series of open doorways set in the wall. 'Take the first one.'

I stepped through the door and into an unlit room. I stopped when a single-bulb light hanging from the ceiling came on. The room, I saw, was a simple concrete box, about a dozen feet in each direction. A pile of wooden chairs, all low-backed and some with broken legs or backrests were piled against the wall.

'Take one of those,' Murphy ordered, 'and set it down in the middle of the floor. Get one of the good ones.'

I didn't like the sound of that but couldn't think of a way around doing what he said.

'Now sit down and put your hands behind the back of the chair.'

'Now, damn it. . . .' I started to turn only to have Hugo slam me in the chest with the heel of his hand, forcing me into the chair. It rocked but didn't go over.

Before I could catch my breath my hands were pulled round and held tight. I was sure he'd crushed my chest and I was fighting to get air into my lungs. Looking through my watering eyes I could only watch as the big man wrapped grey duct tape around my legs, fastening them to the front chair-legs.

I looked up to see Murphy standing in the open doorway. He smiled as Hugo finished the job; then, checking his wristwatch, he nodded.

'We've got some business to take care of so I'm going to close the door for a while. You can yell all you want, won't nobody pay any attention. Hell, we're in the underground parking garage. Those fools up there,' he flipped the gun barrel at the ceiling, 'couldn't hear you and if they did, they're too busy losing their pay cheques to care. We get things taken care of out here and then we'll invite Mr Pistilli down. I know he's sure looking forward to hearing what you got to tell him, isn't he, Hugo?'

The big man didn't answer, just laughed.

Maybe it was part of the softening-up process, but when they closed the door one of them flipped the switch, leaving me in total darkness.

For a long time all I could hear was the sound of cars coming into the garage. Sitting there with nothing to do I listened and realized that the cars, and a few motorcycles, didn't park. I could hear them come down the ramp, stop for a couple minutes, then drive on by the cubicle where I was and accelerate up the other ramp.

I had no way of telling how long it'd been since they had put me in the chair and no way of knowing when they'd come back. All I could do was work at the tape.

Don't get the idea I was sitting there doing nothing except waiting to see what Murphy and Hugo would do to me next. No sir. At first I spent all my strength trying to get some slack in the tape holding my wrists together. That didn't work but even while listening I was trying to get even a little movement in the tape. Damn the man who'd invented the sticky stuff.

One thing I did notice, and silently cussed myself for not paying attention to it earlier, was movement in the chair. Listening to the cars going by and focusing on the tape holding me in the chair, I didn't realize at first that I was instinctively holding my body to keep from falling over. The damn chair wasn't as solid as I'd thought. Maybe the amount of movement I was making in trying to tear the tape had loosened something. I caught myself involuntarily tensing, trying to keep my balance. Damn fool me, what was the worst thing that could happen if I did fall?

Well, I could break a bone. But it was quite possible that if given the chance Hugo would do that for me. Or, I smirked in the darkness, I could break the chair. Wiggling my butt a little, I thought I felt the back of the chair move a bit while the seat was solid. OK, what did I have to lose?

I leaned as far as I could to the left and crashed to the floor.

Pain shot through my shoulder but it was my head slamming against the floor that caused a bright flash behind my eyes. Closing them tightly I lay there on my side for a long moment, feeling the world spin first one way and then the other. From somewhere I heard myself groan.

It was the sound of a motorcycle, a Harley for sure, roaring up the ramp that brought me back to my senses. I couldn't afford to just lie there. Once more I tested the tape binding my wrists. The tape held but when I tried to sit up, the back of the chair fell away. The fall had broken the damn thing.

Inching around until I was sitting upright I discovered that with nothing holding my arms from my body, my arms felt looser. The tape holding my arms together wasn't as tight any more.

I almost had to laugh as I twisted my wrists first this way and that, to realize that I was squeezing my eyes shut. As if it'd help me better feel what was happening in the dark. Things were happening. The tape had loosened enough so that the only thing holding my arms behind my back was the stickiness of the tape. Gritting my teeth, and squeezing my eyes shut, I jerked at it and came free.

Now, dammit, let's see what was what.

Tearing my legs free, I stood and stretched. They had left me tied up for so long that my legs felt like cramping at first. Stretching helped.

Again, it was the sound coming from outside that brought my attention back to reality.

Feeling around the floor, I picked up pieces of the chair. I tried to remember what I'd seen before Hugo had pushed me back into it. A wooden kitchen chair, I thought. I picked up the back and ran my hand over the four spindles attached to the upper part. None of them was heavy enough to do much damage.

Kicking out with my foot, I bumped against the bottom of the chair. By feel I determined that the four chair legs were thicker. Twisting, I was able to free one about two feet long. I swung it through the air. It didn't feel as good as a baseball bat would but all of a sudden I felt good. I wasn't going to go quietly into the night after all.

It took me a while to feel my way around the room. After sticking my makeshift club though my belt so I wouldn't lose it, I put out my hands and took baby steps until running into a wall. Keeping my fingers lightly against the rough concrete I moved until coming to the doorframe. The doorknob was solid. Locked from outside.

I was feeling for a light switch and finding only blank wall when someone outside grabbed the door knob. Moving quickly back, I heard the lock click as the lights came on.

'Hey, Hugo. That's all for now,' I heard Murphy call as he opened the door a little. Blinking my eyes to adjust them at the suddenly bright light, I saw I was standing behind the opening door. Murphy was standing there, looking back over his shoulder.

'Close down the door and I'll check on our friend here,' he ordered. As usual, his voice sounded light and friendly. He came on in, taking a couple steps into the room before stopping to look at the wreckage of the chair on the floor where he expected to see me.

I swung at the back of his head as hard as I could. Without a sound, he crumpled to the floor. Not wasting any time, I swung again, catching him squarely on the side of his head just above his ear. Murphy didn't make a sound.

He'd been holding the silenced revolver but had dropped it when I hit him. It felt good in my hand.

'Hey, Murphy. C'mon, let's go. I don't like it down here.'

Crouching down, I stuck my head out to look round. Hugo was coming down the ramp, brushing his hands like he'd just been handling something dirty.

'Hey, dammit, c'mon. Let's get this over with. I got things to do this afternoon,' he yelled, not looking up, still wiping at his hands.

Keeping my eyes on him, I slowly stood up, staying behind the doorframe as much as I could. Hugo must have seen something, or maybe he was expecting to hear from his partner. I don't know, but he stopped and for an instant stared at the open door. I ducked back out of his sight and crouched in the far corner of the room.

'Hey, Murph, everything OK in there?'

Murph wasn't answering.

I kept my eyes on the door and the revolver up and ready. Without thinking I'd eared back the hammer with my thumb. Maybe that click was what he'd heard. I don't know, but when Murphy didn't answer he knew something was wrong. When he came through the door he was holding a short square-barrelled-looking gun out in front with both hands.

I shot him in the chest. The little .22 calibre slug didn't stop him. I don't think he even felt it. He must have felt something, though, because he halted and looked down at the front of his shirt. I pulled the trigger again, and again. When the third one hit him I actually saw a little movement of the material covering his chest.

He must have felt that one; he looked up, a questioning frown building on his forehead. Suddenly his eyes widened and, as he took another step into the room, his leg gave way and he fell. To be safe, I kicked the weapon away from his outstretched hand. I didn't have to look any closer to know he was dead.

I did touch a finger to Murphy's throat but there was no pulse there. The chair leg had done its job all too well.

I picked up the black automatic. I'd never seen one before but I knew what it was. In the research I'd done for one of my stories, I'd Googled automatic weapons and found the world-famous Mac-10. Big Hugo had armed himself with the rapid-firing automatic and Murphy, being a smaller man, had chosen the little nine-shot .22 revolver. I had to smile. From what I'd read, the Mac-10 was a piece of crap but still a better weapon for killing people than a .22 calibre. Although the little bullets had done their job, hadn't they?

I stood there for a bit, looking down at the two dead men. One thing was certain, I couldn't spend much time just standing around. Sooner or later Pistilli or another of his men would come looking for these two.

I stepped outside the little room and looked around. Steve's Monte Carlo was just where Hugo had left it, parked against the wall next to the black SUV. Next to where I was standing a rickety-looking folding card-table had been pushed against the wall. A flat electronic scale was on it, along with an open box of quart-sized plastic bags, a box of thin disposable gloves and a pile of rubber bands. Sitting next to one of the table's legs was a squat leather briefcase, its sides worn and scratched from long usage and its top open. Glancing down, I saw it was filled with bundles of money, each bundle bound with a rubber band.

A big cardboard box was on the floor up against the wall. Looking inside I saw sacks of white pills. Piled next to the box were stacks of rectangular wax coated bricks. Those, I figured, would be high grade dope. It'd been years since I'd smoked any. While I remembered enjoying the buzz, in recent years I found I liked the taste of good single malt Scotch or a fine wine better. Thinking of that brought me back to what I was doing.

This section of the underground garage was a drug dealer's stockroom. I didn't know enough of how the market worked but it was obvious that Pistilli was deep in the business. Thinking back I remembered Murphy saying something about the casino not being his boss's main source of income. That was down here, supplying the street dealers.

Now what? Standing in the open doorway, I took time to think about it. There were two bodies here. So far I don't think I'd touched anything except the two weapons. And that chair leg. With that thought, I reached over and took two of the disposable gloves out of the box and pulled them on.

OK, so an anonymous call to 911 and the cops come and find the boys. It then becomes a murder scene. Forensic experts would be called in to try to discover who killed Hugo and Murphy. Was I sure all I'd be leaving behind were my prints on a few things? Television shows about the art and skill of those experts scared me. No, I couldn't be sure. OK, so, what do I do?

If Quincy's task force came rolling in, they'd be looking for answers to the drug angle. Do they have forensic experts? More than likely, but wouldn't they be focusing on the drugs and not the bodies? I nodded, especially if the bodies weren't here. Without the bodies this wouldn't be a murder crime scene, would it?

One would think that living near the bay would make disposing of a body or two an easy job. But first you'd have to have a boat, then something to anchor the bodies down with. In a couple of my many unpublished stories I'd used the bay and the ocean beyond to dump bodies but that wouldn't work here. We were too far from the ocean and I didn't have access to a boat. Where else could one leave a couple bodies so they weren't likely to be found? And if found, not be traced back to me?

Thinking about it I smiled. I knew of somewhere.

I took a long careful look around the place. Nodding to myself, I reached over, closed the briefcase and took it over to throw it into the front seat of the SUV. After rolling Hugo's body out of the way, I dragged Murphy's body over to the back of the Chevy van and, grabbing the shoulders of his jacket, stood him up, letting the weight of his body tip him into the space behind the rear seat. Hugo was another matter all together. Not only was he bigger and heavier, there was some blood so I had to be extra careful in moving him. I had to strain to pick up the dead weight and roll it in. I closed the doors and rested my body against the SUV for a long moment, letting the perspiration dry on my body.

Back in the little room I'd been locked in I spotted a little drop of blood. Using the edge of my shoe I scraped enough dirt across it. It wouldn't fool anyone looking for it, but it might make it less noticeable that someone had been shot there.

Hugo had closed the ramp we'd driven down but the other ramp was still open. I ran up to the top and looked around. Even though it couldn't be much more than late afternoon, the parking lot was about half-filled, still mostly with campers but now with a good scattering of cars and pickups. Nobody would notice the Monte Carlo among them.

The black SUV's keys were still in the ignition and the engine started right up. I stopped before driving out and thought over what I might have missed. I wondered if there was a lock on the down ramp, the one Hugo had just closed. Quickly I jogged up and saw it'd been secured by a big chrome padlock. That meant the outer door on the up ramp would likely have one, too. Driving the SUV up the ramp I stopped and smiled. It was equally certain that somewhere in the pockets of those two lying quietly in the back there would be a key.

CHAPTER THIRTY-THREE

Traffic coming off the Redwood Highway and into the entrance to the casino was heavier than that which was leaving. So many people I thought, as I turned north on to the on ramp, rushing to spend Sunday afternoon and leave their money at the tables. I wondered whether they had gone home to change out of their best church clothes before heading for the slot machines. I didn't think anyone would notice one more SUV joining those already heading for home.

The highway was four-lane along this stretch, the California Highway Department had apparently wanted to make access to the little town of Healdsburg easy. I set the cruise control for seventy and relaxed. Having two dead bodies in the back didn't bother me and the luxurious seat of the Chevy Tahoe was too comfortable to not take advantage of as I drove.

There was little traffic on the highway north from the casino and my passengers had little to say. It was a quiet peaceful moment, time to relax a little after all the excitement. Sitting behind the wheel of the big SUV was, I had to admit, quite comfortable. You'd think that with nothing to do but keep the SUV in the right lane I'd start to feel panicky about what I had just done. Or nervous about what I was planning on doing. All I was feeling was relaxed. And safe.

The way I saw it was that right now Pistilli would be thinking his two tough guys would be softening me up. No reason to worry. After all, even with the hold-up and all, he still had a casino to run, didn't he? It'd probably take him a couple hours, well, an hour or so anyway, before he started wondering. So, what would he do? Send someone down to the little section off the big underground garage to see what was what. The black Chevy Tahoe would be gone, so would Hugo, Murphy and yours truly.

For a while he might wonder what had happened, but what could he do? There was no way he could know I and his two men were heading north.

The sunlight was coming in and even with the darkened windows I could feel its heat. That made me drowsy and remembering I'd missed breakfast I started looking for a place to pull off. The exit to Geyserville was my first opportunity. I wasn't more than a half-hour away from the casino but thought I'd be safe.

Geyserville, as it turned out, didn't have much to offer travellers. Signs pointing the way to a number of wineries and a small grocery store on the opposite side of the main road from a pair of rusty railroad tracks were about the only things. It was enough. With a large container of rank-smelling coffee and three candy bars I thought I would be able to stay awake and still not lose too much weight.

I wasn't sure how far it was to Ukiah, the town I was headed for. East of there, up Little Horse Mountain was my destination and the only times I'd been there I'd driven down from Eureka. One of the California Highway Department's green-and-white signs answered the question: the Ukiah exit was another thirty-eight miles ahead. Thirty-eight miles and I'd be turning off, heading for tall timber.

The national forest country that covered almost all of Little Horse Mountain would, I figured, be a good place to dump the bodies. It was remote in the wilderness of Mendocino National Forest, and the few narrow dirt roads cutting through the woodland were rarely used. About the only time anyone was liable to go driving in that nearly inaccessible country was during deer season. That was later in the fall. By that time little would be left to be discovered by any sharp-eyed hunter.

At Ukiah I ran into trouble. I couldn't remember exactly where to turn off to get to Little Horse Mountain and the only gas station I saw was yet to open. I certainly didn't want to be remembered asking for directions in case the world had more eagle-eyed Daniel Boone types walking the back trails.

I didn't panic, and I'd never admit it to anyone if I did, but I was relieved to find a Triple-A packet of maps in the glove compartment. You have to hand it to the American Automobile Association: they do provide quality road maps. My search also turned up a Nokia cell phone that had been left under the AAA packet.

State Highway 20 took me from the Redwood Highway east across to

Upper Lake. Not much had changed in the years since I'd been there and the further I went the more I remembered. I thought I knew where to go from there.

The Mendocino National Forest was only a few hours' drive from Sausalito but it was a totally different world. Living in Sausalito, or even back when I was working further up north in Eureka, I was in town. Up here I was soon all alone. This was rugged mountains terrain. From Upper Lake the highway got narrower and the pavement more needul of attention from the California Highway Department. At the even smaller community of Vann I found Forest Service Road 17N11, marked on the map as the Elk Mountain Road.

Seventy-five years ago or so, the mountains I was driving into had been criss-crossed by a maze of logging roads. That was back when the forests were all being logged off. Sometime in the middle 1950s, when all the best of the trees had been taken out, the US Forest Service decided on the Roadless Conservation Area programme. Huge tracks of USFS-controlled forests were let go wild, nearly all the logging roads and trails were closed off and any other indication of human habitation was erased. The few unimproved logging roads the Forest Service didn't block carried enough traffic each year so that a four-wheel drive vehicle could get up into the back country. About the only reason for that traffic was to get into the prime deer hunting areas.

The first time I found myself in this remote part of the state was back when I had been invited to go deer hunting with a couple guys. As I recalled the hunting trip had consisted mainly of us sitting around camp all day drinking beer and telling lies about past hunting trips. The four of us, three young men each equipped with high priced, big calibre hunting rifles and me, were serious about what we were doing. I was the odd ball: I didn't have a deer rifle. I don't remember what reason I gave, but the truth was I wasn't into hunting – or shooting, for that matter. After the first morning I didn't remember any of the rifles being taken out of their lined cases.

But things had changed and having reneged on my vow not to cause trouble and not to go shooting up things, I was back. Now, driving up a narrow rural stretch of highway with thick growth of tall trees lining both sides of the pavement I was glad to have been included on that earlier trip. I had to laugh as I glanced at the dark forest surrounding the road; just as then, any time now I expected to see Daniel Boone step out from behind a tree. He didn't. Except for the quiet passengers in the back I was alone.

As the sun was dropping, at times going out of sight behind the higher forested ridges, I had the Chevy Tahoe in four-wheel drive and was snaking around axle-deep chuck holes, carefully making my way past places where the spring run-off had cut through the bare dirt roadway. Where once huge diesel logging trucks would be noisily straining up and down this rutted washboarded roadway, the Chevy's V-8 was quietly and smoothly floating along.

Choosing a good site was easy; after more than two hours of driving on the old logging road I simply pulled off into a little wide place at the top of the tree-shrouded ridge I'd been climbing. The road continued on, dropping down into more thick forests on the other side. This was far enough. Looking out, as far as I could see there was nothing but trees and brush. Down in the valley below it was all tall pine trees, the ground hidden under the spiky greenery.

Backing the SUV round, I reversed as far into the trees as I could, stopping when the rear door came up against some low-lying bushes. Both men's bodies had stiffened and were still going stiff. I quickly gave up trying to lift Hugo's body and simply let it fall to the ground after opening the rear doors and pulling. There were a few dark spots in the carpeting under where he had lain but I wasn't going to worry about that. Murphy was easier to get rid of.

The forest floor was heavily covered with pine needles which made dragging the two of them further back into the trees easy. I decided not to make it simple for whoever found them, I removed their wallets. It was doubtful that they would be found soon, probably not until nature and whatever wild animals were around had had their way.

'Sorry fellows,' I couldn't help saying out loud, 'but for once I do hope there is the kind of heaven you both believed in. And I hope I've got you far enough away from it for you not to be able to find its front door. Enjoy the scenery.'

I used the pocket handkerchief from Murphy's jacket to wipe the surfaces of both the Mac-10 Hugo had been carrying and Murphy's little revolver. Walking back out into the road, I slung the Mac-10 as far down hill into the tree- and brush-covered hillside as I could. I wound up and threw the .22 in another direction. My throw would have made Willie Mays proud.

The drive back down FS Road 17N11 seemed quicker than the ride up and I wondered if I shouldn't have hidden the bodies further back into the woods. Too late for that, I decided and didn't stop.

Getting rid of the Chevy was part of the plan I'd come up with. On returning to the casino's parking lot I pulled up next to the locked Monte Carlo. The lot was more than half-full now, but as I looked around I didn't see anybody. Even if there were anybody about it wasn't likely they'd pay me any attention as I used the handkerchief again to wipe down every surface on the SUV I thought I might have touched. Even wearing the gloves, I wasn't taking any chances.

After making sure I had the Nokia cell phone, I locked up the black SUV. On the way back to Healdsburg I'd given the question of whether to keep the briefcase bulging with drug money a lot of thought. In the end I decided the best thing to do would be to leave it and the two wallets on the floor of the van, lock it up and drive away. Which is what I did.

CHAPTER THIRTY-FOUR

According to the dashboard clock, it was only a little after seven. Once again the pangs of hunger made me aware that I hadn't really eaten all day. My first stop was about twenty miles south of the casino, in Santa Rosa.

California is a big, long state stretching from the dry, barren landscape around the Mexican border up to the thick, lush forests in the northern part of the state. A couple hours ago I had been up in the wilds of those forests; now, in Santa Rosa, I was in a different world. Santa Rosa looks like Hollywood's version of life when Father Junipero Serra was on his mission-building rampage a couple hundred years ago. I almost felt culture shock the minute I left the freeway. But maybe it was only hunger. Getting out of Steve's Chevy, I looked around the parking lot of Angelino's restaurant, I stood for a moment, flexing my back and looking over the building, a typical flat-roofed Mexican hacienda. I almost expected to hear a *mariachi* band start up.

Angelino's restaurant, as I recalled from times past, offered a mid-priced menu full of outstanding food. Having opted for one of the booths along the back wall, I picked up the menu. Nothing had changed. The meal was delicious and mother would have been proud of me: I cleaned up everything on the plate. Feeling full and happy, I even ordered a cup of fresh-brewed coffee and a nice slice of apple pie afterwards. Taking my time to enjoy it, and, as my mother would say, to give the meal time to settle, I called Detective Quincy.

Everyone who has watched even a single police show on television knows how easy it is for someone to trace a phone call and find out not only where the call came in from but later to identify the particular cell phone the caller used. I used the Nokia I'd found in the Chevy Tahoe to make the call.

'San Francisco Police.' The dull voice of a computer-generated answering machine sounded loud and clear. 'Please choose from the following menu so that your call can be directed to the appropriate office.'

I listened through the half-dozen choices before given the direction to hold the line for a live operator.

'Sergeant Lewison,' a woman answered at last. While waiting I had finished both the coffee and the pie. I was glad I was using someone else's cell. 'How may I help you?'

'I'd like to speak to Detective Quincy, if I may.'

'Do you know which department the detective is in? We have a number of officers with that surname.' She sounded either very tired or very bored.

I quickly read the card he had left with me. 'Yes, its Detective Jonathan Quincy with the city's Organized Crime Strike Force.'

'Thank you, and may I tell him who is calling and what the call is about?'

'Just mention the name Pistilli. He'll know.'

'One moment please.'

Again I was put on hold and again I was glad it wasn't my cell that was being charged for it.

'Yeah, this is Detective Quincy. What can I do for you?'

'I want to make a bargain with you. I'll tell you how you can nail Guido "The Pistol" Pistilli and you won't look too closely into how you came by this information.'

'Uh uh. It doesn't work that way. You tell me who you are and then we work our deal.'

'Uh uh,' I echoed him. 'If you want Pistilli, you will simply say, thank you, John Doe, for the information. Then I'd say if you and your drug investigators move fast enough you'll get everything you'll need.'

'Like what, exactly?'

I'd watched enough TV to visualize him motioning with one hand, writing a note to direct someone to put a trace on my call, all the while trying to keep me on the phone long enough. Did that work with cell phones? I didn't know and really didn't care.

'Here it is. If you look closely in the back parking lot of the casino run by Pistilli you will find a black Chevy Tahoe SUV. It's locked. Inside there are a couple wallets taken from the pockets of two of Pistilli's boys. The men themselves are not there. You'll also find a briefcase filled with money. That'll be drug money. Now, in the casino's underground garage, not the main one but in a secure section off to the left side of the loading docks, you will discover a drug supermarket. I would hurry, if I were you. Once Pistilli discovers his two main men are missing, he's liable to start moving things. That's the lot. Now it's all up to you.'

I touched the red icon before wedging the cell out of sight between the seat and the back of the booth. Feeling fat and well-fed I left a nice tip when paying the tab.

CHAPTER THIRTY-FIVE

Before getting back on the highway, I sat in the car and thought about things. If I was going to meet up with Steve in San Ysidro for breakfast I'd have to get on the road by midnight at least. Taking on that big meal might not have been a good idea, I felt like it was time for a nap. God, was this what getting old was like?

No matter. There was time to stop and get a couple hours' sleep. Nodding in agreement with myself, I headed for home.

Home, the little hovel, never looked so good. After making sure the car was locked as tight as I could make it, and knowing I wouldn't have to worry any more about Hugo and his friend, I hurried up to the apartment.

I pulled down the bed, set the radio clock to come on at midnight, kicked off my shoes and flopped. I was asleep before my head hit the pillow.

There has to be at least a million better ways to be woken up than to hearing Willie Nelson warning the nation's mothers not to let their kids grow up to be cowboys. I'd left the volume on the radio too high and Willie's nasal voice cut through my dream like a buzz saw ripping up hardwood.

After a quick wake-me-up shower, and knowing I had a 500-mile drive to make, my first stop was at the Starbucks down next to the ferry terminal for a large Americano, no sugar, please. Midnight is a good time to travel on Interstate five, the north-south freeway that cuts right through the middle of the state. I mean if one must drive it the late night traffic is the least worrisome, being mostly semi-trucks and buses. To get on that freeway from Sausalito was the tricky part.

From the Oregon border, some 500 miles or so north, to the outskirts of Los Angeles, I-5 bisects the state north to south almost perfectly. To reach the closest it comes to where I started out meant taking the Richmond-San Rafael Bridge across the bay to get on 580. This stretch of highway, all eight lanes of it, goes inland, passing through a continuous stream of east bay cities, the biggest being Oakland. Except for the signs you'd never know when you left one suburb and entered another.

The first break in scenery, not that you can see much while on any of the freeways, came when 580 angled away from the Bay area and headed inland. The highway cut through or, I guess to be correct, over, a small mountain range. Actually, the only way I became aware of it was that for once there wasn't a continuous spread of lights stretching out on both sides. Obviously no one had yet been able to figure out how to build the kind of housing development that California is famous for in that rough countryside.

I had turned the radio on to a quiet music station. Whatever the format was didn't matter, all I wanted was background music.

Fields looking empty and dark took over for the next forty miles or so. With nothing to look at I concentrated on the traffic, of which there wasn't much, and my thoughts. Of which there were far too many. It had been a very busy day with a lot of travel involved. It wouldn't do, I felt, to spend too much time thinking about what I'd done to Pistilli's hired hands. By now, well maybe not until early in the morning, even Pistilli and his threats would be only a memory. That led me to thinking about Son Cardonsky.

I still didn't understand how he figured I'd drawn up the plan for sticking up a poker game. Smiling in the weak light of the Monte Carlo's dashboard I had to chuckle about the casino robbery. Detective Quincy had said it was the armoured car picking up casino money. Now how in the hell could Son find a blueprint for that in one of the stories I wrote?

My first string of short novels that were published was straight out of the old Saturday afternoon movie matinée, back in the days of Roy Rogers and Gene Autry. You know, cowboys and Indians. Shoot-'em-up-bang-bangs, we called them when I was a kid.

When Highway 580 melded almost seamlessly into I-5, instead of four lanes in each direction there were now only two. There was less traffic, though, so it didn't matter. Remembering the road map I'd studied before, I knew I was now driving through the San Joaquin Valley. Water had changed California. A number of feature stories I'd researched and written when I was working for the *Eureka Standard* had to do with water. The water that came out of the mountain country up in the northern part of the state was channelled down to irrigate the agricultural breadbasket of the state, mainly the San Joaquin Valley. Once this had all been desert but that had changed. Somewhere in the dark, off to one side, would be a series of canals bringing irrigation water down to water the thousands of acres of cropland.

That meant that on the other side, in daylight, I'd be seeing the continuation of that mountain range I'd driven through earlier. Thinking things like that helped to pass the time.

I'd long since finished the coffee I'd bought at Starbucks and was thinking about finding another cup. One of the benefits of the I-5 freeway was that it wasn't broken up by going through any towns, the highway sped around them. When it was first put in, that fact meant the death of many little such towns. It also meant I'd have to wait until I reached the next truck stop to find a hot cup of coffee.

Funny how a person's mind works. Here I was thinking about making a coffee stop when it dawned on me what Son had found in one of my stories that helped him with the armoured car hold-up. Again I had to laugh. It had to be the story that I wrote where the hero – I couldn't remember the name I'd given him – was riding shotgun on a Wells Fargo stage. The plan Son used had to be the one I created for the bad guys when they held up the stage, taking the strongbox. Oh boy, who would ever read that and turn it around to an armoured car. That had to be it. That damn Son Cardonsky.

CHAPTER THIRTY-SIX

One of the other good things about travelling on the I-5 was the rest stops. Every so often the state transportation department had built places where you could pull off the road to take a break, stretch your legs and make a trip to the bathroom. In many of these, volunteer groups grab the opportunity to sell coffee. The first one I stopped at was just outside of Bakersfield, a place, according to the sign, called Buttonwillow. A cute name, but the coffee was terrible.

It wasn't much past that rest stop that the highway, all four lanes of it, cut through a golf course. No kidding. And it was pretty well lit up, too. Lots of trees and shrubs separated the highway from the fairways, but there they were, on both sides.

The station I'd had died out, simply faded away as I drove south. I loved these modern car radios that came with a button that could seek the next station. The music the radio found wasn't the soft, easy listening kind. I'd left the sophisticated latte-and-croissants part of the state; we were now in Buck Owens country. Buck Owens. Now that brought back memories.

Once upon a time, when Inez and I were at our happiest, we'd make the drive across to Reno, the Biggest Little City in Nevada. Inez loved the dollar slot machine and I liked to spend a few dollars at the blackjack table. It was about four hours to drive each way. We'd get to our hotel at about eight in the evening, we always called ahead for a room at the same place, and after dumping our suitcase we'd head downstairs to check out who was playing in one of the lounges. Thinking about Buck Owens reminded me of the time he and his band were the headliners.

At one point in the evening we found ourselves standing in line for tickets to the next show when a big man in a dark suit, black T-shirt, no tie and a face that reminded me of my first grade teacher, all frowns and hard, cold eyes, pushed me aside.

'Let's make some room here.' His voice sounded like it was coming from the bottom of a barrel.

Instinctively I pushed back. It was like coming up against a Sherman tank only one with a thin coating of wool.

'Hey.' The Sherman tank grunted and grabbed my arm. Visualize a five-fingered clamp.

'That ain't necessary,' a softer, heavily accented voice cut in. My arm was instantly released.

'Man, I'm sorry about that,' the Southern drawl said. 'My boy gets a little excited when we get in crowds. You know how it is.'

I glanced back and there he was. His picture was on posters all over the place; Buck Owens Tonite!!! Where his bodyguard was built like every good bodyguard would be, this guy was just the opposite. Short, round-faced with a big smile, his yellow-blond hair cut in what we used to call a Flat-Top. The Man himself.

'Man, let me make it up to you, his rough housing you and all. Milo,' Owens called over a shoulder without taking his eyes or his toothy smile away from me, 'make sure these good people get right up front, ya hear?'

As I remembered, Inez was pretty excited to be seated at a table up next to the stage. Until about halfway through the show.

'Bernie,' she said, leaning close and whispering in my ear. 'Are you enjoying this? They certainly seem to be awfully loud.'

The song they were playing, as I recall, was 'Act Naturally', the same piece of music that was now playing on the radio. Yes, sir, I was in Buck Owens country. This part of California wasn't classical music country; this was cowboy country, California style.

The Buttonwillow coffee hadn't only tasted like they'd used muddy irrigation water to make it, the brew also had the capacity to go right through me. I made it to the rest stop at Lebec but for a while there it was touch and go.

Lebec isn't on most maps, I figure, because there isn't much there. But it is the end of the straight part of the I-5 freeway. Letting the blood flow through my legs a minute, I took a look at a huge road map hanging off a wall. You know the 'You Are here' kind. Where I happened to be was southern end of the Tejon Pass, the start of the forty-mile stretch through the Tehachapi Mountains, better known as the Grapevine. I can vaguely remember that in the dead of winter the Grapevine can be tough to get over for truckers. Apparently there's lots of snow and wind with the highway having some steep climbs. It was still dark but I didn't think that this time of year there would be any reason to concern myself.

It was easy to tell when I'd reached the end of the Grapevine. One moment all I could see was the highway ahead of me in the headlights, then round a curve and bang! below and for as far as I could see were lights. Streetlights, car lights, advertising lights, miles and miles of lights in square patterns: the street lay-outs of Los Angeles. Scary.

Looking down at this landscape made me feel like I was seeing an alien planet for the first time. I mean the lights go on as far as the eye can see, clear to the horizon. And it's still the best part of an hour before the sun comes up. Doesn't anyone sleep down there?

CHAPTER THIRTY-SEVEN

Dropping down into the valley I spotted one of the big green-and-white state highway signs. This one informed me that I was 121 miles from San Diego. Steve and the kidnap group were only a few miles beyond that.

The sky off to my left was starting to get light as the freeway wound through more miles of modern California life. This was the place that had drawn people from the rest of the nation since the Great Depression. For nearly a hundred years they have come from everywhere, hoping to fulfill their dreams of the 'good life'. Hollywood had to be over that way somewhere and over there were the long lazy beaches and girls with big breasts, shapely tanned legs and long sun-bleached hair. Even as dawn was making me squint my eyes, causing me to cuss because I forgot my sunglasses, I considered the fact that this was the land of year-round sunshine. I was fighting to keep my eyes open.

Keeping up with the growing traffic helped with that, or at least gave me more to think about. All of a sudden I was in bumper-to-bumper strings of cars intermingled with the long-haul truckers. People going to work, I figured, warning myself to stay awake.

Past the worst that Los Angeles had to offer, the view from the interstate turned almost beautiful. On my left the sun was warming the world, out the other side long vistas of Pacific Ocean appeared. I liked catching glimpses of the white crests breaking on the surf and the sun sparkling on the water further out. For about fifty miles my attention was split equally on water and the road.

This was a totally new world for me and had been since I'd left the San Francisco Bay area. All night I'd been driving through parts of the state I'd never seen before and hadn't seen then, and now there was almost more than I could take in. If I wasn't so damn sleepy and was headed for something other than where I was going, I would have to take the time to look it over.

Getting closer to San Diego the pavement and traffic streamed away from the ocean, I-5 had cut back inland and once again I was passing through an endless stream of spitting-image housing developments. Signs warned of a junction coming, I had a choice, continue on I-5 or take another interstate freeway, 805. Somewhere I recalled seeing the word bypass in relation to 805 so I didn't hesitate.

A short time later the end came fast and I almost screwed up. Even with all the big colourful signs I wasn't prepared when 805 rejoined I-5. That's when the whole trip suddenly came to an end. Almost instantly, within a mile or less, instead of the eight lanes of pavement I'd been on, there were too many lanes to count. It was a real can of worms with lanes coming in from God only knew where and a series of overpasses carrying more traffic from both east and west directions. And suddenly I could see that up ahead nothing was moving. All traffic had come to a standstill. Yeah, it was something to see. Back there a few miles traffic had been moving well above the legal speed limit and just ahead hundreds of cars and pickups were standing, frozen in a dozen or so long lines. I had arrived at the US-Mexican border. There must have been warning signs about it back there but I must have passed them in one of those times I'd been sleeping.

But I was saved. Whoever had designed this affair had taken into account fools like me; an off-ramp let me escape. I wasn't alone. I fell into place behind a dirty blue Toyota and took that exit. Figuring the guy ahead would know where he was going, I stayed behind him only to find myself in the biggest supermarket parking lot I'd ever seen. I pulled into a place between the white lines, turned off the ignition and sat for a bit listening to the silence. No motion and no engine noise. If I had a good cup of coffee in my hand I'd think I was in paradise. Instead I called Steve's cell phone.

His greeting wasn't the friendliest.

'Where the hell are you?'

'I don't have a clue. All I know is, I almost ended up in Tijuana. Let me see,' I got out and looked around. 'Hey, according to that big sign over there, I'm in the parking lot at the San Diego Factory Outlet. Know where that is?'

Steve relented with a laugh. 'Yeah, you're just across the freeway from me. Look, find the overpass, it's there, all you have to do is get out of that lot. You won't miss it. It'll take you across the interstate. On this side, when you get to the intersection look over to your right. You'll see the big sign. The Best Western Inn. I'm in room 210, second floor towards the left end. I'll be out at the railing. Our friends haven't opened their door yet. I've been sitting here watching, waiting until you got here.'

'You got a coffee pot?'

'Yeah, come on over. I have a cup ready for you.'

It wasn't quite as easy as he had made it sound; even finding the damn overpass was confusing. Believe me, that parking lot is big. But I eventually figured out how to get out of it and, like he said, the Best Western was there on the opposite corner.

True to his word, he had a cup of coffee to hand to me. It certainly wasn't Starbucks, but it was hot and strong. I stood in the middle of the room while he went to stand by the window, keeping watch.

Noticing that I remained on my feet, Steve got defensive.

'Hey, you can sit down, the place is better than it looks. I mean, there's easy access out to the freeway; you didn't have any trouble finding it, did you?'

'No, not really. But I've been on my butt too long. I'll stand, thank you.'

'All right then. But the rooms aren't bad. Well, mine should've been cleaned before I was given the key, but it's cheaper than one of the big fancy places out overlooking the border.'

'Stop trying to convince me, Steve. I don't care. Hell, we won't be here long enough to let it bother. What's the plan, grab the woman and make the drive back north?'

Steve acted like he hadn't heard me. 'Well, to be honest, I did see a few cockroaches when I first got into the room. Oh, and there's the railroad tracks over there.' He pointed over his shoulder. 'I would guess it's used to bring cars up from one of the assembly plants just over the border. The good news is that there seems to be only one train a night. The bad part is that it's a long train, makes a helluva lot of noise and goes roaring by some time after one in the morning. You'll hear it.'

'Yeah, should have known. The motel is on Rail Street, after all. You should have realized there'd be a train somewhere in the picture. Now, talk to me, do you have anything planned?'

'No, I thought I'd wait until you got here. I figure they booked this place because it was kinda hidden, being off the main drag. I figure they plan on grabbing the ransom money and hot-footing it across the border. You know, disappear down in some ritzy coastal city. I've heard you can live pretty damn good, if you've got a few dollars to spread around.' He stopped talking and leaned forward, closely inspecting what was left of my black eye.

'That's looking good. Some nice shades of green mixed with the black but even that is starting to look more grey than black. It's all quite colour-co-ordinated, especially when seen wrapped around the red of your bloodshot eyeball. Looking good, I'd say.'

I didn't comment on his black eye, which was almost back to normal.

'OK, enough with the sympathy. Let's get on with it. Now, the ransom money is here and the kidnapper is there. Are you saying we should just make the delivery? By the way, are you sure, positively sure the people you've been watching are who we are looking for?'

Smiling, Steve nodded. 'Remember? I told you, she is the woman in the photo I took from Gussling's place all right, and I checked with the front desk. It's them all right. Right down there in room 145. What more can I do?'

I shook my head. 'Look, I'm tired. I've had a long drive and way too much excitement before that. I'm feeling cranky and shouldn't be taking it out on you. What say I catch a couple hours' sack time? It isn't going to matter much if we don't do anything right away, does it? I mean if we go forcing the woman to go back with us, it won't help matters if I fall asleep just this side of Bakersfield, would it?'

'No, Bern, I wasn't going to suggest that. What I was thinking . . . well, I was hoping you'd get here a couple hours ago. But you didn't. What I had in mind was to just bust in on them before the world comes fully awake. One of us could grab the woman and the other could hold off Jardin. I thought if we could get them while they were asleep we could put Mrs Gussling into the back of the Monte Carlo and get the hell out of Dodge. You did fill the gas tank didn't you?'

'Yeah, yeah, back at a truck stop just this side of San Diego.' I finished the coffee and looked longingly at the bed. Shaking my head, I brought my fuzzy mind back to the question. 'So you think that'll take care of it? You think it'll be that easy, that she won't put up a fight?' I shook my head. 'That idea would never work. I still believe she's part of this.'

'Yeah, you're right. But it's the best I could come up with. And I agree. One thing I've seen is that they're too friendly when they're down around the pool. Yeah, she's part of it, all right. But what's she going to do? Yell and cause a ruckus? I doubt it. After all if the local cops are brought in, all we have to do is explain our position. The cops could make a couple phone calls and Jardin goes to jail. Maybe her too, I don't know.'

'Let me think about it. I'm too damn tired to think clearly right now. There's no real rush, is there? The only one who's chomping at the bit, wanting to get things done, is old man Gussling. He can wait. Let me get a couple hours sleep and then we can figure something out.'

CHAPTER THIRTY-EIGHT

Steve let me sleep until about one in the afternoon. I could have used a few more hours but he was worried.

'Your cell phone,' he said, pointing to the instrument. Before letting my head hit the pillow I'd emptied my pockets on to the top of the dresser. It wasn't buzzing now. 'It's been ringing about every ten minutes or so. I didn't want to answer it but whoever it is isn't giving up easily.'

That made sense.

'You know,' I said, climbing off the bed. 'I'll bet it's your friend, the tennis pro. He was expecting me to have the ransom money ready. OK, so what do I tell him?'

Stretching and pulling on my pants, I had to admit that a little sleep made a world of difference. A good cup of coffee and I'd feel alive again.

'When he calls the next time I'll answer it. What'll I tell him?'

'Tell him you've got the money. Let him give you directions on how to make the trade. Think about it, if he's down here and he thinks you and the ransom are up in the Bay area, then whatever he's planning, one of you will have to make the trip. He won't know we know they're down here next to the border and they won't want us to know that. So what do you bet he'll be figuring on catching a flight up north? We let him go through with that. He takes off and we go over and collect Mrs G and drive home. Should be as easy as that.'

'Are they still over there?'

I jerked a thumb over my shoulder as I went into the bathroom. I didn't hear his answer until I came back out after brushing my teeth. Washing my face with cold water, I had taken the time to inspect my eye. The swelling had gone down and the worst of the discolouration had lightened up. I didn't think it looked too bad. A hell of a lot better than a couple days ago.

'Yeah,' Steve had waited until I came back into the main room before answering. 'They came out earlier, right after you fell into bed. Probably went down to the restaurant for coffee. They weren't gone long. He came back carrying a newspaper and she had a grocery sack filled with something. I've been watching but they haven't left their room since. Yesterday it was early afternoon before they hit the pool.'

'OK, so once again, we'll wait for—' my cell buzzed before I could finish.

Smiling at Steve I pushed the talk button.

'This is Bernie Gould.'

'Where in the hell have you been?' It was the kidnapper and he was yelling. I could hear panic in his voice. 'You were supposed to be there yesterday morning at nine waiting for my call. What the hell are you pulling? Have you got the damn ransom money?'

I smiled at Steve. 'Yes, I've got it. Things have finally come together. Now, how do you want this exchange to happen? Let's get this over with and get Mrs Gussling home with her husband. You tell me where and when?'

'I've got it worked out,' he said, calming down. 'You know the Maritime Park right outside Fort Mason?'

'You mean down on the San Francisco waterfront? Where those old square-rigger sailing-ships are tied to the wharf?'

'That's the place. Over on the other side of the museum, where the cable-car turntable is, right there on the corner of Beach and Hyde there is a line of artist's stands. Umbrellas with their art displayed in the shade. You take that briefcase with the ransom money and stand in front of the first one. Hold the briefcase in front of you. A guy'll come along and tell you he's from Argentina. You hand over the briefcase. No problems. You don't follow the guy. After the money is checked, Mrs Gussling will be released. You just wait. I figure it'll take no more than fifteen minutes for the money to be counted. You got all that?'

Slowly as if I was writing it all down, I repeated the directions. If this were all on the level, it might work out. Of course, if the police had been involved things would be different, but this was a simple Argentine kidnapping and, like everyone had been saying, no problem.

'Yeah, I got it. When does all this take place?'

'I want to make it tough on anyone trying to follow the briefcase. It gets dark at about seven thirty or so. You be there by then and after we know the coast is clear someone'll come by for the briefcase. It'll be some time between seven and eight. You just wait where I told you, on that street corner. Right there with the artists.'

'You want me to wait until eight tonight?'

Jardin chuckled. 'You and your friends have made me wait for nearly three days. You can wait until tonight.' He was still laughing as he hung up.

Steve listened as I explained what I'd been told. 'Why in hell would he put it off until tonight?'

'Waiting until the sun goes down would make it harder to follow him. And too, there'll be less street traffic.'

'Yeah, I guess. It'll make it easier for him to get a flight north, too, I suppose. OK, so do we wait until he goes?'

'Uh huh. Why not?' I answered. 'Let's go get a late breakfast. He probably won't leave until after lunch. There's no reason for us to sit around twiddling our thumbs. I'm starved.'

CHAPTER THIRTY-NINE

Neither the hostage nor the hostage-taker had ever seen either of us and wouldn't know us from Adam, so we simply went down to the motel restaurant. Once inside it was impossible to know exactly where in the US we were. There is something to be said about standardization. If one Applebee's is good, does having more than 1,000 or 1,500 of them spread out over the nation make things better? Looking around, reading the oversized menu or even gazing out the window at the traffic on the freeway I saw no proof that we were just a couple miles inside the US of A.

I ordered a big breakfast of hotcakes, eggs over easy and link sausage. Steve left out the stack of hotcakes. Dammit, I'd had a big day yesterday and was hungry. I knew, wherever we were, whether just up the block from a foreign country or in Bullhead City, Arizona, the food on my plate would taste exactly the same. Not knowing what the day would bring, I ate every bit of it.

We hadn't really talked about anything except the kidnapping, hadn't really had the time. Now we did. Over our second cups of coffee I told him about my run in with Hugo and Murphy.

The coffee, I will admit, was pretty good. I was just finishing my story when the waitress refilled our cups for the third or fourth time.

'Bern, you're telling me you murdered two men, hid their bodies in the forests and expect to get away with it?'

'No, I never said that. What I did say was that neither of those two men would likely bother me again. Me or anyone else that Pistilli wants to question. Will I get away with it? You'll notice I didn't tell you in what part of the state forest system I dumped the pair. Not that I don't trust you, but, well, some things just don't need to be said. I figure that police detective, Quincy, will by now have found the Chevy Tahoe, searched the

170

underground drugstore and put Pistilli away. What I'm betting he hasn't found and isn't likely to find are two of Pistilli's gang, namely Hugo and Murphy. Ask yourself, how much time is the San Francisco Organized Crime Strike Force likely to spend looking for them? So do I think I'll get away with it? Without a doubt. And it wasn't murder. It was self-defence.'

For a long moment Steve sat holding his steaming coffee cup and stared at me.

'You know, I don't think I ever really knew you. Makes me wonder just what kind of Clark Kent reporter-type you are. All those times when we've repoed someone's car or truck, I always had the feeling I had to protect you, make sure you were never in harm's way. Shit, I carried a gun for how many years? Never pulled it and only fired it out on the range twice a year as qualification. And here you are, not only knowing a lot about silencers and automatic pistols but also how to dispose of bodies.'

'Actually,' I couldn't help acting like a smartass, 'it was a suppressor on the revolver, not a silencer.' That only caused him to frown more.

Not getting the reaction I expected, I quickly went on. 'Well, to tell the truth, it was the research I've had to do for my novels. To make things sound right I have to know what impact a small calibre like the .22 would have. You know what I mean?'

'I guess.' I hadn't made my friend and partner feel very good by telling him about my run in with Pistilli's men.

Waving off the ever-helpful waitress with her coffee pot, I let it go. 'Look, don't you think we ought to get back to the room. It might be that Jardin plans on taking an early plane. If that were to happen, maybe we could get out of here this afternoon.'

He hadn't left yet. When we walked back we had to pass by the pool. We were just in time to watch Mrs Gussling dive off the diving board. Steve nudged me, lifting his chin towards a man in a tight black swimming suit, lying back in a yellow banana chair watching the woman.

I didn't blame him. Mrs Gussling was long-legged and the bottom of her swim suit rode high up on her thighs, making her legs look even longer. I liked the bikini she had on and didn't push Steve to walk faster. We stopped halfway up the stairs to the second floor to watch her pull herself out of the water.

Too far away to hear what she said, we were close enough to enjoy what we saw.

171

Most of the rest of the afternoon, when I wasn't dozing on one of the beds in the room Steve had taken, we watched and waited. Through a crack in the drapes he watched the pair sun and swim while I caught up on my sleep. My sleep wasn't the nice, deep kind. Telling him all about Murphy and Hugo had got me thinking about it, picturing it all far too vividly for sweet dreams. Until now I had simply pushed it back somewhere in a dark corner of my mind but lying there was like watching a movie, like I was watching it all happen to someone else. I came wide awake when he prodded me.

'They're back in their room now, Bern. I didn't want to bother you, but they came up about an hour ago, changed out of their swim suits and went down to the restaurant. I figured they were going for an early supper. They're back.'

'Hmm, OK. What time is it?'

'Going on five. He must plan on going directly to the waterfront when he arrives.'

'OK, so what? We give him a few minutes to drive off and then make our move on the woman?'

'Yeah. Look,' he was pointing, 'there's a taxi just stopped in front of their room.'

Standing there we watched as Jardin, dressed in black Levis and a soft-looking leather jacket came out, closing the motel room door behind him.

'That's good,' Steve said quietly as the taxi pulled round and went out of sight. 'His leaving early means we can get an early start back ourselves. Hurry up, get your shoes on while I pack up what little stuff I've got.'

After checking to make sure we hadn't left anything behind, I unlocked the car long enough for Steve to put his overnight bag in the trunk.

'Is that it?' he said, still whispering and pointing at the dark leather briefcase. 'Is that the ransom money?'

'Yep, all two million dollars of it.'

The briefcase was right where I'd left it, standing upright, still wedged in between the spare tyre and the back wall of the trunk. Steve reached in and placed his hand on the briefcase.

'That's certain to be the closest I'll ever get to two million. We get that back to the insurance company and a good part of it will be ours, Bern. Just think, not only are we getting a short holiday down south but will end up getting pretty damn good pay for doing it. Come on, let's get that woman and get the hell out of here.'

Room 145 looked just like all the others, only the bronzed numerals screwed to the door were different. The drapes on the big picture window were closed and when I put my head close to the door I couldn't hear a thing.

'You sure she's in there?' I whispered.

Steve nodded and reached up to knock.

'What is it?' Her words were muffled. I could barely make out what she'd said.

Steve answered, garbling his words making them sound like gibberish.

'What?' she asked louder. I heard the security chain being taken off and the door opened. 'What do you want?'

She'd barely got the question out when Steve pushed hard against the door, knocking her back against one of the twin beds, her legs falling open. Mrs Gussling was wearing no more than one of the big motel towels and when she fell it dropped away from her body. She had another towel wrapped around her head.

'What the hell are you doing? Who the hell are you guys?' she yelled, not bothering to pull the big towel up around her body. I stepped in and closed the door.

'Now, Mrs Gussling,' Steve said, a big smile on his face, 'we're here to save you from that nasty kidnapper. My name's Steve Gunnison and my partner here is Bernie Gould. We're the contact that your friend Jardin has been dealing with. We were hired by your loving husband.'

'You're what?' she said, still not moving to cover herself, her eyes quickly going from Steve to me. 'I don't know what you're talking about. You'd better get the fuck out of here before I call the manager.'

Not waiting, she rolled over, sitting up and grabbing for the phone. Steve was quicker.

'I can't believe you want someone to come in, do you? Really?'

Steve was holding both her wrists, talking to her in a calm, quiet manner. Letting him do all the work, I let myself enjoy what I was seeing. Her body was perfectly suntanned, the smooth golden brown was unblemished by any lines or white areas.

Glancing at Steve I could see he wasn't shy about looking either.

'Think a little about how you'd explain it all, Mrs Gussling, especially after we call your husband. Now, why don't you wrap that towel around you, sit back and we'll discuss the situation like adults.'

CHAPTER FORTY

Slowly, after he had released her hands, she lifted the towel around herself again, tucking it above her breasts. Sitting up straight, she lifted enough to smooth the material under her hips. Taking her time, she studied Steve and then me, looking us both over from shoe leather to hair line.

'OK, so you're working with my husband. How'd you find me?'

'That wasn't so hard,' Steve said. 'The trail down here to San Ysidro was pretty plain. The whole plan to get a hold of the insurance company's kidnap money was good, but you and your boyfriend made too many errors.'

'Uh huh. And so you and your quiet friend over there just come breaking in. So what happens now?'

'Well, the first thing is for you to get dressed. Then the three of us will take a little drive north. What your husband and the insurance company people do after that is up to them.'

'I see. So you're in for the reward money. How much would that be, I wonder? Ten per cent? Twenty? Why go to that extreme? Especially when I make you a better offer? You do have the ransom money, don't you? Of course you would. Let me see if I've got this right. They gave you the ransom. You somehow figured out where we were and came down here. If you pay out the ransom, you get paid for making the delivery and saving me. I go home with gentle Teddy then later I can join back up with Tony and we take off once again but without the ransom money. But if you were to return both the money and my lovely little ass, then you'd get a bigger reward from the insurance company. Now that's your plan, isn't it?'

Somehow the towel started sliding from where she'd secured it. She stopped it from falling by cupping one hand around a breast, holding the terry cloth tight. Her smile was full and seductive, the kind seen in the movies when the *femme fatale* makes her sexy offer.

Neither Steve nor I said anything. Both of us stood looking down at her, smiling, waiting.

'Now let's think about it. Here we are, just the three of us. And the ransom money. Yes?' Nobody answered. She laughed, not taking her eyes off Steve's face. 'Who would know if you gave me half that two million? I'd go my way and you, with half a million each, could go yours. Go back and tell them, sorry but we got snookered. I'm sure that for five hundred thousand dollars one of you could come up with a good, believable story. Now, isn't that a better deal than just ten or twenty per cent?'

If I had been directing this movie, at that point, having made her offer, I'd have had her lean back and maybe let the towel drop down. Or maybe not. Maybe it'd be a more effective scene to just have her lean back, supported by one arm, the towel held to her breast with the other hand.

Steve broke in on my mental movie.

'I don't think it'd work out. The best thing is for you to get dressed, get your stuff together and we all get in the car. Maybe along the way we can get to know each other, maybe not. But if we don't waste any time now we can have you back with your loving family before midnight.'

'Fuck you, Jack,' she snarled, coming to her feet and holding the towel up to her neck with both hands. The smile was gone. 'What'll you do if I don't do what you want, dress me? I'd like to see that happen.'

That stopped me. What would we do? Luckily we didn't have to come up with an answer. Before either of us could respond, the motel door slammed open and Antonio Jardin stood in the open doorway.

'What the hell. . . ?' Jardin was quick, I'll give him that. It was probably all that tennis he played. We had been so busy with studying Claire Gussling's better attributes we hadn't heard the boyfriend's key in the lock. Or maybe I hadn't shut the door completely. It didn't matter. Before anyone in the room could react, Jardin had a mean-looking little automatic in his hand, pointing at us.

'Who in the hell are you two and what are you doing in my room?'

Normally, I'd have to admit that Jardin was a good-looking young man. With a gun in his hand though, his smile took on an uglier snarling look.

CHAPTER FORTY-ONE

I looked him over and saw he was wearing a tight black T-shirt under his jacket. It matched his equally tight black Levis. I couldn't tell where he'd been carrying the gun and I suppose it didn't really matter. The pistol was small, probably another .22 calibre or maybe what the cops called a Saturday Night Special. Small, it was almost lost in his hand, but that didn't take away from its deadliness.

True to form, Claire Gussling hadn't moved. Still holding the towel like a short dress, she was back to being happy.

'They came for me, darling. Said they were working for my husband. Somehow they discovered where we were and when you left, they came to rescue me. Isn't that a hoot?'

'Came to rescue. . . ?' he said, not finishing his sentence. 'How'd you find us?'

He was standing with his back to the closed door; the pistol wasn't moving. With Steve and me standing so close together it didn't have to.

'That doesn't matter,' Steve answered. I thought he sounded his usual calm self. Thinking about Hugo and Murphy and their guns, I was far from being calm. But then Steve had carried a revolver for quite a few years. Maybe he was more used to being in the company of firearms. I sure as hell wasn't.

'What does matter,' he went on, talking slow as if explaining to a child, 'is that you're in a world of trouble. Kidnapping, even if the hostage goes along with it, is still a major crime, you know.'

'Yeah? And who's got the gun? Shut up and let me think.' Maybe for the first time Jardin saw what Claire was wearing. 'Honey, get dressed. We've got to get out of here.'

'What are we going to do, Tony?'

177

'Get your clothes on. I'll think of something. You two, what did you say your names were?'

The woman hadn't moved. She answered for us. 'Steve something and Bernie Gould, Tony. They're the ones you've been talking to on the phone about the ransom money.'

'Is that right? Come all the way down here to bring it to me, huh? Sweetheart, I told you, go get some clothes on. You two, sit down there on the bed and keep quiet.'

After grabbing a dress and some underwear out of an open suitcase Claire went into the bathroom, shutting the door behind her.

This was the second time in as many days I'd had a gun pointed at me. It wasn't any better than before. It didn't seem to bother Steve at all. Shrugging, he sat down, leaning his back against the headboard. I sat gingerly on the other end. Jardin didn't move away from the door.

'Won't do you any good,' Steve said. 'Bernie, I don't think he'll shoot us. The only thing he can do now is to get the hell out of here, make his escape across the border.' He was talking to me, not even looking at the man. Calm, he chuckled. 'What I'm wondering is, will the little lady go along with that?'

Jardin wasn't impressed. He snorted.

'Fool. You said it, kidnapping is a federal offence. Well, so is murder. And the border is damn close. Once I'm down there nobody'll ever find me.' Jardin stopped. 'What do you mean, she won't go along? Hell, don't you know? This is all her idea.'

I thought it was time to let him in on the truth.

'I hate to be the bearer of bad news,' I cut in from my place at the foot of the bed. 'It may have been her plan but I somehow don't think running for the border without the ransom money is going to set well with Mrs Gussling.'

'Hey, you're the contact guy, the guy on the phone. I recognize your voice.' The gun was pointing directly at me now. 'You're the one that's been jacking me around. Damn, you must have been right here when I was telling you where to meet me. Well, lucky for me, my flight was cancelled. I figured I'd come back and set it up again for tomorrow. Walked right in and saved the day. What a lucky break. I should go out and buy a lottery ticket.'

Steve chuckled and waved a hand nonchalantly, 'Now that's a good idea. Take your little water pistol and go buy a ticket.'

The gun shifted and once again was pointing at my partner. 'Don't get funny. And shut up, I got to think.'

'I'd say so,' Steve said calmly, 'and while you're at it, think about this; your lady friend in there was planning on cutting you out.'

'What do you mean, cutting me out?'

It was my turn again.

'Well,' I said, hoping I sounded as calm as Steve, 'when we came in, telling her we were taking her back to San Francisco, she didn't like the idea much. That's when she made us an offer. She suggested that we take half of the two million and go back home. She'd take the rest and disappear. We could simply explain how we'd been had. Who could prove it? At the time it seemed like a good idea to me.'

'Not such a good idea now, though, is it? But if you were going to share the ransom that means you've got it with you. Where is it?'

I didn't know what Steve was planning but I didn't like the way things were going much.

'Now, that would be telling,' I said, still hoping I was as calm as he was. 'Looks to me like it's all we've got to bargain with.'

Claire Gussling came out of the bathroom.

'What have you figured out, Tony?'

She still looked good. Her dress was some kind of soft material that stopped just above her knees, flowing softly around her thighs as she moved. I would have liked it a lot more if there hadn't been a pistol in the room. The gun looked small in the man's hand, the square black barrel barely making it past his bent trigger finger. The hole in the end was small but that didn't matter, when it was pointed in my direction it took on a larger significance.

Tony was keeping us covered but he was looking directly at Claire Gussling.

'They're trying to tell me you wanted to split the ransom money with them and leave me out. Any truth to that?'

'Of course not, Tony,' she said, quickly with a tinge of seduction back in her voice. 'Remember, I was the one who brought this idea to you. If I wanted to go it on my own I wouldn't have done that, would I? No. Look at them. All they're trying to do is get us fighting. You've got the gun. It figures they'd do or say anything to get out of this room without getting hurt, wouldn't it?'

Tony didn't think about it long. 'Yeah. OK, then, let's get this show on the road. Here's how I see it. You two have the ransom money stashed someplace close. That's all we want. You told me that you'd been hired to make the delivery, so make it. Hand the ransom over and go back north. Tell the insurance company anything you want. Hell, tell her old man the same thing. It won't matter to us; we'll be long gone south. This really isn't an actual kidnapping, you know. It's, what'd you call it, honey? It's a South American business deal. Right, honey?'

'Yeah,' she said, stepping between me and Jardin to pick up a package of cigarettes from the little table. She moved so unexpectedly I didn't have a chance to try and jump him. 'Happens all the time down in Argentina. That's why the companies pay out for the insurance, for Christ's sake. So, how about it? You two going to play it smart, give us the cash and go back north? Then you can pick up your pay cheque and nobody gets hurt. How's that sound?'

I glanced over at Steve. He hadn't moved, except to put his hands up behind his head. A thin smile bent his lips.

'So how does it go now?' he asked, his smile getting bigger. 'Bernie and I go get the briefcase and bring it back to you?'

Jardin's laugh was cold. 'You think I'm stupid? No. What we'll do is, your friend here and I will go get the money. Claire, you and Pasquale here will wait for us. We bring it back, count it, maybe give you a couple thousand to cover your expenses and then we go south. You go north. C'mon, Bernie. Is that your name, Bernie?'

I didn't like it but he was holding the little pistol. I definitely didn't want to go anywhere with him. But I did.

'You stay here, honey, keep our friend there company. Bernie and I'll go pick up the ransom, then you and I are gone. Hey, there, friend,' he looked over at Steve, 'you just sit there while the two of us go for a walk. I'll take good care of him so don't go doing anything stupid. Honey, if he does, give out a scream as loud as you can. OK?'

It was obvious that it wasn't OK, but hostage victim or not there wasn't much she could do about it but agree. She nodded and we went out the door, Jardin and his little pistol right behind me.

'Where you got the money stashed?'

I couldn't think of a lie that would change things. 'It's in the car, parked over there.'

'OK, lead the way. But remember, this little peashooter won't make much noise, Nobody'll know you've been shot. Play it straight and you go home with a little bonus. Do something stupid and . . . poof, you're dead and we're gone.'

I kept walking, taking the same gravelled path round the end of the pool that Steve and I had taken earlier in the day, when we'd been enjoying the sight of a kidnap victim in her bikini. The sun had set and none of the other motel guests was using the pool. We were all alone.

'All I'm worried about is your nerves. I certainly don't want any hasty trigger-pulling.'

He chuckled.

As we got to the car I was about to walk back to the trunk when he put his hand on my shoulder, stopping me.

'This it?'

I nodded.

'The money's in there?' He pointed with his free hand towards the back of the car.

'Yeah, in a briefcase.'

'Hmm, you know, this is a good-looking car. Wait a minute, now. We're not in any hurry. Tell me the truth; was there anything to what you were saying back there? Did Claire actually want to split the ransom with the two of you?'

'Yes, we did talk about it, just before you come back. I guess she was leaving her husband and running off with you.'

'Yeah, she said there were good reasons for her to get away. Something about how things between them were different up here from when they were down in Argentina. That's what got us talking about Argentina, and then one day she told me about the kidnap insurance. Boy, talk about a light bulb going off. That was all it took and now look at where we are. Everything is falling apart. How did you find us, anyhow?' he asked, then, before I could answer he waved me off.

'Never mind, it doesn't matter. What'd you do, watch me go out in that cab?'

I nodded.

'Well, I'll tell you what. Come round to the passenger door. You slide across, get behind the wheel. I'll be right behind you. Let's take a little drive. See how this old bus runs, you know?'

181

CHAPTER FORTY-TWO

I liked this less and less all the time. But I did what he said.

Following his directions, with the little pistol now pointed at my side, I drove up over the overpass and into the entrance to the big outlet shopping centre. Was I ever going to get away from people with guns making me their chauffeur?

'Man, that's one helluva store, isn't it?'

I stopped to let a big Buick try to get into a parking spot that was only slightly big enough and didn't answer.

'Drive on around. Let's take a look at what's out back.'

The big sign read 'Las Americas, shopping so close to Mexico you can smell the tequila.' And it turned out to be true. Or almost true. Going round behind the last of the huge concrete box stores, dumpsters were backed up to the back wall in a formation that went on for as far as I could see. On the other side of the narrow access road, strong-looking cyclone fencing at least ten feet tall was topped with rolls of razor wire. On the other side of the fencing was a wide, shallow cement culvert that carried a very thin stream of brackish-looking water. That had to be the Tijuana River. Just over there was Mexico. Somehow, even now with dusk coming on, it looked more desolate on this side.

'Pull over there.' Jardin pointed at a break in the cyclone fence. Had someone tried to get in from the river? A wetback wanting to go shopping? Or was someone trying to escape the stress of too many stores? The thoughts were streaming through my mind. Anything to keep me from worrying that he might be thinking of dumping my body into the dried-up riverbed.

'Turn it off and get out. Slowly. I'll be right behind you. And take the keys. I want to look at the money.'

True to his word, he stayed with me, poking me gently in the back a couple times to let me know he was there.

'I'm thinking,' he said, sounding more like he was talking to himself than to me. 'This is a pretty good-looking car. It'd bring a good price, I get it across the border. That won't be any problem. Just drive it over, a guy heading over to TJ for the evening dog races or maybe to drop in on a couple strip clubs. See the girl and the donkey, you know? Only keep driving. Down to Ensenada, say, then across to the Sea of Cortez, grab the ferry over to Puerto Peñasco. I've been there. A nice little fishing village. Got a good hotel and all. OK,' he poked me again, 'open up the trunk and let's take a look.'

I have to tell you, I was thinking a lot faster than I was moving. Taking my time and fumbling with the lock a little, I tried to delay things. At least until I could think of some way out of this. Nothing was coming. My mind was a jumble.

'C'mon, stop fucking around. Get the damn lid open.'

I slipped the key into the lock, twisted it and the trunk lid popped up.

'That it?' he pointed at the briefcase wedged between the black never-been-used tyre and the back of the trunk.

'Yeah.'

'Well, get it out of there.' He stepped back a little so he could watch.

I'd crammed the leather briefcase in tight and had to move the jack out of the way. I pulled the briefcase free, lifted it out with my right hand and dropped in on the ground. I didn't even look but hoped like hell he'd been watching the money and not me.

It's funny how things happen. I mean, there I was, about to hand two million dollars over to a guy, a guy who was pointing a gun at me and with a handy little hole in the fence over there. There I was trying desperately to come up with a rescue plan and, then, without even thinking, I acted. Dropping the briefcase with my right hand, I swung the tyre-iron with my left, coming around and catching him on the elbow.

'Owww,' he yelped, dropping the gun and grabbing his arm with his other hand.

I was on that little pistol like a snake on a fieldmouse.

Jardin's reflexes were good. Damn good. He had to be in some pain, but I barely got the pistol in my hand before he was on me.

'Give me that, you bastard,' he snarled, holding on to my arm and trying to prise my fingers from around the little gun. Pushing, he knocked the back of my head against the edge of the trunk lid. Pain made my eyes water but I couldn't let go. Oh, God, he was strong. I suppose swinging a tennis racket all day long will do that for you. He was strong enough to bend my wrist up, forcing my hand to open.

I couldn't tell which of us had a finger on the trigger but the gun fired. It was so quiet that for an instant I wasn't even sure it had gone off. His grunt was louder. Then the pressure was off my arm and he relaxed, his body falling as if every muscle had turned to water.

Slowly he collapsed into a bundle at my feet, his legs curled under him, arms falling as part of the tangle. I leaned back against the open trunk, breathing fast and heavy. The little pistol hung from my hand, held only by having my thumb around the short black plastic grip.

Almost *déjà vu*, I thought. Yesterday it was in a well-lighted underground garage and tonight behind the largest outlet shopping centre in Southern California. A series of fluorescent light fixtures ran the length of the building we had parked behind, the plastic shields that covered them defusing the light somewhat but still illuminating the two-car-width paved strip between the building and the fence. The night sky had gone from deep blue to near black without my noticing. Out there was black, in here as light as if the sun was directly overhead.

Slowly my breathing settled down and I came out of my fog. I couldn't stand here like a dolt, waiting for some other fool to come driving around back. Not while I was holding a gun with a dead body settling in at my feet, anyhow.

My first thought was to toss the pistol over into the river. Hell, there was that hole in the fence. It was big enough for a body to pass through. Why not get rid of Jardin that way, too? Think, I ordered myself, why not?

Because sooner or later he'd be found was why not. And then sooner or later he'd be identified and traced back to Claire Gussling. That would just naturally bring Steve and me into the frame. There had to be a better way. Think.

CHAPTER FORTY-THREE

First, get the body out of sight. Grabbing a hold of his shirt collar was when I discovered I still had a hold of the little gun. I wouldn't need it again. Using a greasy rag from the trunk to wipe it down, I walked over and threw it as far out into the dry riverbed as I could. I didn't even hear it hit. I didn't think it'd be there long.

Jardin may have had good, no better than good, reflexes but as a dead man he was a load and a half. Not yet stiffening, lifting his body into the trunk of the Monte Carlo took both hands and my knee. But once inside he fitted nicely. I took the briefcase up front with me. He didn't need to have it close by.

Driving on around the series of buildings, I took my time going through the various sections of the parking lot back to the overpass. I still hadn't thought about what to do with Jardin but my mind was working on it. By the time I got back to the Best Western Inn I had it figured out.

Like many of the Best Western Inn chain of motels, this one was a series of long rectangular buildings, each two storeys tall. The rooms faced on to the central courtyard/parking lot with the swimming pool at the far end from the manager's office. I had noticed earlier that, behind the buildings, additional parking was available for semi-trucks and RVs. That's where I headed.

Most of one end of the back lot was filled with trucks, all with long trailers behind them, all lined up in a row. Some had their refrigeration units running. I could hear the monotonous drone of the little motors sounding like a hive of huge bumblebees. Those folks paying for the rooms at that end of the building must be going crazy.

Spread out over the rest of the lot were a couple dozen Greyhound bus-sized motor-homes. These, I suspected, were tourists wanting to keep

185

their luxury homes on wheels secure while visiting across the border. Or maybe they just wanted to take a real long hot shower. Hard to say.

A line of scrubby-looking trees separated the parking lot from the railroad tracks on the other side. From what I could tell, backing up to the leafy dark-green border, they were either short bushy trees or tall bushy bushes. Obviously they had been chosen for their ability to block out the view on the other side. Just right for what I had in mind.

After parking I stood at the back of the Monte Carlo for a long moment or two, wanting to make sure I was alone. Well, alone, that is, if you didn't count Jardin. I figured it was still early, probably no later than 7.30 or so, but it was about as dark as it was going to get. Out front lights from the nearby freeway, the motel and other businesses made it almost as light as day. That only made things back here seem darker.

Not wanting to wait any longer, I opened the trunk and swore when the light came on. I hadn't noticed it before.

'Ah, well, hell,' I mumbled and, taking one last glance around, grabbed Jardin's wrists in one hand and a knee with the other. Lifting in one swift jerk, I had his body out and on the ground in a somewhat smooth movement. He hadn't gotten any lighter and having one leg drag behind didn't help matters. But he was out of there. Letting him drop, I closed the lid and stood up, stretching my back muscles and breathing heavily like I'd just run up a flight of stairs. Boy, was I out of shape. Standing there I took another long look around. Nobody came running over to see what was going on, yelling and waking up the world.

I was about to bend down to pick the body up when lights flared down at the far corner of the motel building. A semi-truck came slowly round the building, its bright lights outlining everything. I'd already ducked out of sight and watched as the driver took his rig down to join the others. Once again I had to make the effort to bring my heartbeat under control.

When things returned to darkness, I half-dragged and half-carried the body through an opening in the bushes, stopping on the other side to rest again. Standing with my back to the brush, I looked out over the railroad tracks. Out here the light coming from somewhere, maybe the stars overhead or maybe overflow from the commercial areas, was dim. A dirt road ran along the way between me and the tracks, the dust thick in the double ruts. On the other side I could see that one set of tracks was dark and the other silvery ribbons going away in both directions. The dark set was more than likely rusty and not used.

To my right, back towards the border, the tracks disappeared a short distance away. Looking the other way I could see the silver ribbons running off towards downtown San Diego in a straight-as-a-ruler line. That suited me perfectly. A freight train loaded down with Fords and Chevys that had been assembled by low-paid Mexican labour would be picking up steam as it came around the corner, heading for who knows where.

It was a little lighter away from the motel and I could see what I was doing as I picked Jardin's body up. Moving as quickly as I could, I stepped across the dirt road and up on to the mound that carried the rusty set of tracks. I kept going. On the far side I carefully laid the body down, placing Jardin's chest across the far rail, his head and shoulders lying in between the shiny rails, his legs pointing out towards the open brush land.

Steve had mentioned that the train came through during the early hours. My thought was that the engineer would be on the body before he saw it, even if he had his head out the window and was watching to make sure the track was still there. Which I doubted he'd be doing. How long has it been since you've waved to a train driver as the train went by?

Anyhow, what was left after that would be strawberry jam. It was doubtful that any investigation would turn up the bullet or even the wound. Most assuredly, the railroad officials would want to believe it was simply an illegal Mexican, probably drunk, who had lain down and got run over. They wouldn't want a big investigation and that would be the end of it. Steve Gunnison, Bernard Gould and the Gusslings wouldn't even come into the picture.

OK, back to the others before it got too late.

CHAPTER FORTY-FOUR

'Where's Tony?' was the greeting Claire Gussling gave me when Steve opened the door to room 145 at my knock.

I had come straight to the room after parking in the space allotted to Steve's room. Until I walked through the door, I hadn't given any thought to the possibility that Jardin's blood might be on me. Apparently there wasn't any.

'He's gone,' I said.

'Hey, what happened to you?' Steve had been standing next to the bathroom door like maybe he'd just come out. Stepping up to me, he pushed his hand against my chin, turning my head. 'You've got a scalp cut. What the hell happened?'

Mrs Gussling wasn't going to be put off. 'Where is Tony? What have you done with him?' She was close to screaming.

I wasn't sure what to say. Every time I've ever lied, it's come back to bite me. Lying isn't all that easy, you know. The closest I could come up with was simply that her Tony was gone. Damn it; don't ask me where to, either. Probably hell, if there is such a place.

'Look, he's been hit,' Steve said, pointing to the back of my head and saving the day. 'I'll bet that damn fool took one look at the money and slugged you. Is that right?'

Now that made it easier. 'Yeah. He made me drive him over to the parking lot in that huge shopping centre. Over across the freeway. He had me park behind the buildings, out of sight. When I handed him the briefcase, well, he went very quiet. I wasn't quite quick enough. He slammed the back of my head. It kind of made me blank out a little. When I came out of it, he was gone.'

'Gone?' She was going to want to know every little thing. 'Gone where? Where would he have gone to?'

'I don't know. To tell the truth, I wonder why he didn't take the Monte Carlo. I mean he did say something about it. Taking the car I mean.'

'I don't understand. Why would he take the car?'

I shook my head and, to make things more plausible, I set down gingerly on the foot of the bed. 'He'd been talking while we drove across that overpass. Telling me about a road out of Ensenada over to a ferry that'd take him to someplace, a fishing village he knew about. Said there was a good hotel, almost a resort over there. I can't remember the name of the place.'

'Puerto Peñasco,' Claire Gussling said, her voice now hard and cold. 'That's where he's from. It's a little resort town on the Sea of Cortez. We'd planned to take that ferry and then from there we'd get a plane to fly us over to the east coast, Cancun, maybe. Or Belize. We hadn't decided. Damn him. He's taken the money and left me here.'

I thought for a moment she was going to start crying. Her chin trembled a little, but that may have been from anger.

Steve pulled out one of the room's chairs and sat down. I don't know how long the three of us sat there, thinking about how Tony Jardin had double-crossed the poor kidnap victim. Well, I wasn't thinking of that, but I suppose they were.

'So that's that,' Steve said, placing his hands on his knees and standing up. 'There's nothing we can do about it now. I figure Jardin took the easy way, losing himself in the crowd of early-evening shoppers and then simply walking across the border. There's no problem going in that direction. Once he got into downtown Tijuana, well, he's long gone.'

I liked his scenario. It fitted the facts, as he knew them. I didn't say a word.

'OK. We can't sit around here. Mrs Gussling, if you'll get your clothes and stuff together, we'll hit the road. How long did it take you to drive down, Bern?'

I didn't think he wanted to give the woman time to think.

'About eight hours.'

'OK, tell you what. We'll split it. I'll drive for the first half and you take the second half. Make it easy on both of us. We should be in San Francisco by, what would you say, four in the morning?'

'Yeah, about that. Before breakfast, anyhow.'

'I don't want to go back,' Claire said quietly. 'There's nothing for me back there. Don't you understand?'

'Hey, we can't just leave you here,' Steve said. 'Anyhow, you do have things there. A husband, for one and, well, your life.'

I took a different approach. 'Think about it, Mrs Gussling. You might not want to go back to your husband or to your home in Saratoga, but Steve's right, you can't stay here. What have you got, a couple credit cards? Don't you think your husband'll cancel them when we tell him you didn't want to come back? What'll you do then? Go back with us. Get a good lawyer. Do the things there you can't do down here. Think about it.'

She did. Nodding slowly, she thought long and hard. Eventually without saying a thing, she got up and started packing.

'Hey,' I cut in, 'I'll go bring the car round. I left it . . . well, never mind, I'll go get it and meet you out front.'

Steve headed for the door. 'I'll get my gear. It won't take me long and I'll meet you here. Say five minutes?'

'Yeah.'

I had to get that briefcase out of the front seat.

Hurrying and trying to think of where to hide it, I almost panicked. The only place was the trunk. Opening it, I saw there might be room back behind the spare tyre if I stood it upright. If nobody looked too closely they'd never see it. When Steve came back I had it hidden as good as I could.

'Here,' he said tossing his overnight case in alongside mine. 'You worked her round pretty slick. How'd you know she'd go for it?'

'Something Jardin said. Anyway, she was leaving her old man so she couldn't be all that happy with her marriage, could she? I'd say she'll go back and start divorce proceedings and try to take him for all he's worth.'

'And you and I go back and get our ten per cent. Oh, well, that's better than a poke in the eye with a sharp stick,' he said resignedly.

CHAPTER FORTY-FIVE

On the road, with me alone in the back seat, I thought I'd have a lot of time to think. Up front, Steve and Claire weren't talking much and the radio was turned so low all I could hear was a faint melodic hum.

I had a lot to think about, too. In the space of a very few days I had been the cause of three men being dead. Over the years as a reporter I'd covered a number of deaths; at least three were murder cases and the rest accidents of one kind or another. Writing fictional crime stories, as I had been trying to do, I'd researched and drafted a number of killings. Death wasn't exactly something I thought about a lot, except fictionally, but then this wasn't just death I was worrying about. In the wrong minds, it could be counted as murder. At least, two of them could, anyway. I might get away with arguing self-defence with Jardin.

But wasn't I in grave danger up at the casino's basement? Wouldn't the deaths of Murphy and that big lug, Hugo, be construed by a sharp defence attorney as self-defence?

The fact remained, however, I had killed men. Three times I had killed.

I wanted to give this a lot of thought, get it settled in my mind once and for all. It didn't work. Within twenty miles of freeway boredom I fell asleep. Obviously it really didn't worry me much.

'OK, Bern,' Steve said, shaking me awake.

I fought it for an instant, trying to hold on to the dream I'd been having. Like a thick fog running headlong into the bright morning sun, whatever it had been faded away.

'All right, I'm up. Where are we?'

'One of those rest stops. We're a couple hundred miles out side LA.

From what that last road sign said, we're about halfway. It's well after midnight. You were sleeping so good I let you go on snoring but now I'm having trouble keeping my eyes open. C'mon, there's hot coffee over there. It'll wake you up and you can take over the wheel. Our lovely little lady passenger is all curled up getting her share of beauty sleep.'

Steve was right, the coffee being sold at the little espresso stand was strong enough to wake up the dead. That reminded me of Jardin. Sipping the hot brew, I stood by the front fender coming fully awake and silently cursing myself for that train of thought. I almost laughed at that; wake up the dead and then train of thought. It was almost one o'clock in the morning. I wondered if the train had left the auto factory yet.

Shaking my head at the early-morning thoughts, I got behind the wheel and pulled back on to the road. Steve was already spread out on the back seat as much as he could and was snoring softly. Before closing the car door, in the brief illumination given off by the dome light I saw that Claire had pushed the seat back as far as it would go which gave her legs room to stretch. Asleep, her skirt had ridden up about mid-thigh. She wasn't wearing hose and didn't need it. In the short-lived flash of light I saw that her legs were not only perfectly formed but made me think of milk chocolate. I'd been too long without getting close to a woman.

Now I had a couple of things not to think about, her legs and Jardin. Keeping my eyes on the highway and I tried to channel my thoughts into other streams. Like wondering how things would go when we dropped the lovely Mrs Gussling off at her house there in Saratoga. Should we go directly there? It'd be early. If we were halfway to the Bay area we would be getting in long before the morning paper was delivered. But where else could we take her? Find an all-night coffee shop and sit and wait for daylight? Not likely.

'I'm awake,' she said softly.

I glanced over and in the light coming from the dashboard saw her bring the back of her bucket seat to a more upright position. Stretching, she yawned, then shivered and settled back, curling her legs under her. Women can do that but I'd never seen a man sit that way. Nice knees.

'Good morning,' I said, bringing my eyes back to the two lanes of pavement stretching out ahead in the headlights.

'What time is it?'

The Monte Carlo's digital clock, right below the AM/FM radio, glowed a soft pale green.

'Ten past one,' I said, pointing to it.

'Gawd, I feel like I've been sleeping in a box, my neck and shoulders are all aching. Where are we?'

'I just took over. Been sleeping in the back seat. Steve says we're about halfway between LA and the Bay area. I figure we'll be another three hours on the road.'

'Hmm,' I saw her nod in the weak dashlights.

Nothing more was said for a while. I had decided not to think any more about Jardin, Gussling or what we'd be doing next. Remembering the glimpse of her legs and how my mind had fastened on them, brought my mind around to Inez.

I had kept myself busy after she left and even if the possibility of finding female company had reared its head, I don't think I'd have taken advantage of it. The feeling of relief that came when she wasn't there was too good to want to change. Until the place was empty I hadn't realized how guilty I'd been feeling, sitting at the keyboard, more wrapped up with my fictional people than with her. Damn, what kind of fool was I anyway?

I really enjoyed writing my stories. It'd be better to have them all published, to have someone else read them and enjoy them, but there was a good feeling from just creating them. It was, I suppose, the fun of living another person's life. Or seeing things develop in someone else's world, even if I had created that world. I smiled to myself wondering if all writers were really voyeurs at heart.

CHAPTER FORTY-SIX

Claire, still staring out into the mostly dark scenery, cut into my thoughts.

'We had to leave BA, you know. The company forced us to come back to the States.' Being careful to keep the bottom of her skirt around her knees, she turned in the bucket seat to face me.

'BA being Buenos Aires?' I asked.

'Yes, good old Buenos Aires. It's a huge place, you know. The city itself is about the same size as LA but, just like Los Angeles, there are a couple dozen suburbs surrounding it. Take all those people living in the basin and you've got more than twelve million people. We lived in a gated barrio called Villa Luro. Nice big houses with lots of lawns and lots of nice Mestizo men and boys to keep them mowed. It was a good life.'

'But you came back to California?'

'We had no choice. That's what I've been thinking about, what to do now that Tony took off with the money. We were going to . . . well, that doesn't matter any more. What matters is what I am going to do.'

'Steve found out you met Tony at the Saratoga tennis club.' I wanted to keep her talking, both to help me stay awake but also hoping for an answer to the question of what to do when we got to Saratoga.

'I heard him talking to one of the other instructors. He is a very attractive man and he spoke a kind of Spanish that is very like that spoken in Argentina. A lot of different . . . umm . . . I guess dialects are spoken in Mexico and the rest of South America. It was fun, talking to him in a kind of Spanish that none of those old frogs understood.'

'Frogs?'

Claire laughed, a nice soft laugh that made me want to keep hearing it. 'Yeah, you know, all those other women in their dazzling white tennis shorts and blouses, sitting around the courts watching the men play, looking like frogs sitting around a frog pond.'

'And you joined them.'

'No, I pissed them off by taking Tony from them. He was mine from that first day. It wasn't long before I got the idea of the ransom. That would give me enough money to get clean, get a long way away from Teddy. God, how I hate that man. That's what I've been thinking about, how to get away from Theodore Gussling with enough money to make a new life.'

'Are you talking about a divorce? He's been pretty adamant about getting you safely back from the kidnappers, you know. He gave us the feeling that he really cares.'

Her laugh this time was even softer in the darkness.

'Oh, he cares all right. You see, it all ties in with why we had to come back to California. The company, the all-mighty makers of slot machines, Havershack Industries, was worried about the rumours they'd been hearing, worried about the company image. They brought their hotshot vice-president for sales and training back so they could fire him. Couldn't have him out there on the loose, could they? No sir, he might get caught and what would that do to the very upstanding image of the company? Bring him back, threaten him and then quietly get rid of him. Take the name of Gussling off the masthead. Erase it from all the letterheads. I wish they would go ahead and erase him.'

'I don't understand what you're talking about.'

'No, there's no reason you should, is there? Well, I'll tell you. Maybe then you'll see why I have to get away from him. He's sick, you know. I mean really sick. In the head. That's why I have to get away from him. Now, before he drags me down, too. It was all right, when we were in Argentina. I could keep control of things pretty well down there. Anyway, there are so many of those little brown-skinned *vagabundas*, homeless girls. Hundreds of them. Oh, hell, probably thousands. That's what he likes, you know.'

All of a sudden I wasn't so comfortable with her laugh.

'I don't think I'm getting the picture,' was all I could come up with.

'You ought to hear him when he's excited, sexually excited. It's like there are two of him, one all animated, all keyed-up and the other, I don't know, it's like the other guy is standing off watching, or something.'

'You can see this other guy?'

'No. But I could hear him. At first it was kinda fun. When we were making love Teddy would do things and the other voice would tell him other things to do. Sometimes, in the early years, I'd tell him what I wanted.' She laughed softly. 'It was funny. Almost like there were three of us in the room at the same time.'

'In the early years you said. What changed?'

'I don't know. After a while he didn't pay so much attention to me as he had before. Then when we were sent to BA, well, things really changed. For both of us. That was OK, too. I mean we had a marriage that was comfortable for both of us. He could do his dirty little things and I was free to enjoy what I enjoyed.'

Her voice had a sense of good times remembered. It made me wonder what she enjoyed.

'The only rule was,' she went on after a few miles, 'we didn't bring any part of it home. Well, he did. All those girls he'd hire to clean and cook and every other duty as assigned. For months he thought I was blind, deaf and dumb. But I wasn't. Me and my little digital camera got it all. Boy, those Japanese do know how to make those little cameras that can take nice clear photos, don't they? When I showed him some of the photos I had him by his raging balls.'

'Did these girls complain?'

'No. You have to understand, there are people coming into the city all the time, immigrants from Peru or Bolivia.' Now she sounded like a lecturing professor. 'They come into Argentina just like the Mexicans are flooding into California, looking for a good life. But just like here, the good life isn't just waiting around for them to have. So here are these girls, wanting and dreaming. Poor little things. So willing when someone shows them a little gentleness, a little love. It's true,' she said, the softness disappearing, 'I enjoyed my share, but I never brought them into our home. Not once.'

'And he didn't know what you were doing?'

'He didn't care. And while he was simply having his way with them, I didn't really care either. I thought if anyone found out why there was such a turnover in the girls coming to work for us, well, it was none of their business. The world of sex down there, with all these young girls and boys, none of whom have the slightest chance to make a good living unless they use their bodies, is different from the way we see it up here.' She paused a little before going on, 'or maybe it really isn't. Maybe North Americans just know how to hide it better.'

I wanted to get away from the sex part and back to her disgust with her husband. 'Was it the photos you were taking that did it? Did someone in the company find out?'

'No. I've still got the photos. At least some of them, the ones I like, the ones that bring back good memories for me. No, it was when someone did notice the number of girls that came once or twice and then were never seen again. That's when I figured out what he was doing and I got scared. Someone must have told the head office because it wasn't long after the girls started disappearing that he was told to complete whatever programmes he was involved with and close down his office. No real explanation, just that business had fallen off and we were to come back to the home headquarters. He knows he's being forced out of his position. The company is being cagey about it, but it's clear; he is history and the sooner the better.'

'And this leaves you, where?'

'That's what I'm trying to figure out. If I file for divorce now, under California law I would get half of everything. There's the house, that monstrosity we bought four years ago. It should be worth quite a bit, and then there's his retirement plus any separation pay-out he may be given. That could be enough. But I've been thinking about a way I could get it all. That's why I'm telling you this. I may need your help.'

CHAPTER FORTY-SEVEN

'You and your buddy back there, you're some kind of private detectives, aren't you? Well that's what I need, a go-between. Someone who has contacts with the San Francisco police. You're perfect for the job.'

'Nope, you got the wrong people. Steve and I are just a couple guys hired to deliver a briefcase of ransom money. It all started as a favour for a banking friend of Steve's. The insurance company went along with it because they didn't want the police involved. They saw no reason to let anyone else know about the kidnap insurance coverage. All we're into it for is a pretty good payday.'

'You're not licensed? How come the insurance company handed the ransom over to you, then?'

Keeping my attention to the nighttime truck traffic, I smiled. In the gloom of the dashlights I doubt if she saw it.

'The banker friend and the insurance company got together and worked out a bonding agreement. If we take off with the money, nobody loses anything except us. We'll be hunted down for a sizable reward. No, I don't think we can help you with whatever you're thinking of doing.'

She was so quiet for so long I had to glance over to see if she was still awake. Steve was still cutting firewood in the back and Claire Gussling was staring ahead at the highway.

'OK,' she said after a while, 'tell me this, do you know anyone on the San Francisco police force?'

I hesitated before answering, trying to decide which answer to give. What would I be getting into if I said yes, a certain detective named Quincy? Or what opportunity would I be passing up if I lied?

'Yeah, fact is, I do. Special Detective Quincy. He's part of the force's

Major Crimes Section. What kind of story are you thinking about sharing with him?'

'I'm not. You are. I'll tell you and you tell him. If there's some kind of reward, then you keep it. If not, then' – she paused a beat then, dropping her voice and putting a lot of bedroom into it, completed the sentence – 'well, we can work something out.'

Once again she had shifted around until she was half-turned towards me. Even in the dimness of the light from the speedometer I could see how the skirt of her dress had inched up. She had parted her legs far enough so the darkness above her thighs was shown. Like a schoolboy peeking up the teacher's skirt I felt a blush coming on.

'What,' I said, again trying for calm, 'exactly am I telling this officer? And if I'm going to continue operating this car at,' glancing down at the speed indicator, 'twenty miles over the limit, you'd better tug the bottom of that dress down.'

She chuckled and pulled it down to just above her knees.

'I'll tell you, but only if you promise to let me file divorce papers with an attorney first.'

I gave that some thought. 'Does this have anything to do with what went on in Argentina?'

'Yes. Everything to do with that.'

'Then whatever you tell me, the law here won't be able to act on it very fast. I imagine it'll take some time. They'll have to contact the police down there – hell, maybe even the embassy, I don't know. And you'll have to have some pretty strong proof to make all that happen.' I stopped and thought about it a little.

'From what you said a while back, this has to do with those young homeless girls, doesn't it?' I wasn't sure, but I thought she nodded. 'If so, then what will you do to stay out of the picture? The cops down there get digging around, won't they find out about your involvement?'

This time she did laugh. 'I would imagine so. But let me tell you, what I was doing with certain girls wasn't anything like what he was doing. And I can give the police lots of proof. Before and after photos.' Soft laughter sounded behind her words. 'The digital camera I used did a good job of taking shots in murky light. Not picture perfect, but clear enough you can see who is doing what. Now, are you going to help me?'

Once more she dropped a hand to the hem of her dress and drew it slowly up over her thighs.

CHAPTER FORTY-EIGHT

'Hey, we there yet?' Steve called from the back seat. I wondered how long he'd been awake and was glad he was. Having to keep my attention focused on the early morning traffic would be all the harder if a striptease was going on in the next bucket seat.

'Uh, we're another hour from the city,' I said, dropping my eyes to the digital clock. 'Maybe a little less.'

Claire had turned a little in the car seat, stretching her now covered legs as straight as she could.

'So, what is the plan, Stan? When we get closer to the Bay area, I mean. Are we going to drop the Mrs here off at her place there in Saratoga? It's still a couple hours before the sun makes a showing. What do you think, Mrs Gussling?'

When she didn't offer an answer I glanced her way. She was sitting with her gaze fixed down the road, her hands folded in her lap. I decided to make a suggestion.

'How about we let you out at a motel? That way you can get a couple hours sleep and not bust right in. I would guess you might feel better if you called your husband later in the morning and let him know where you are and that you're safe and sound.' And, I didn't add, that way you don't have to face the man until you really want to, say after making a call to your friendly divorce attorney.

'OK,' she said quietly.

Traffic started picking up a little after we left I-5 and got on to the 580. A big well-lit sign announced we were now on the MacArthur Freeway. I wondered if it had been named after the WWII hero, General Douglas MacArthur, but didn't mention it.

'How does this sound,' I asked after a while. 'I can take the San Mateo

Bridge over to the San Francisco peninsula, that's close enough to the international airport for there to be a number of motels. You can get a place to spend the rest of the night. Then sometime in the morning you give me a call and we'll pick you up and take you to your husband.' I hesitated, then added, 'or wherever you'd like to go.'

'Now that sounds good to me,' Steve kicked in, 'and if you don't mind my saying it, Mrs Gussling, it'll probably be a good idea if we check you in with your husband's company. Kinda let everyone know you have been returned.'

'And,' she said, smiling as she turned to look back over her shoulder, 'prove you two did your job so you can get paid.'

'Well, yes, there is that.'

Nothing else was said.

Finding a motel after getting off the bridge was simple; we passed three before reaching the Bayshore Freeway. Claire didn't show a preference so I took the next one I saw, one with what I thought was a grand name, The San Mateo Marriott San Francisco AirportHotel.

The Marriott was a very upscale version of the Best Western in that it looked more like one of those early haciendas owned by the original Californios back when this part of California was owned by Mexico. Back before the Catholic Church sent out the missionaries to 'civilize' the countryside. A huge circular drive set back from the busy street fronted the place. The two-storey building was covered with sparkling white plaster under the traditional curved red tile roof. Huge mature palm trees lined the drive.

Getting her bag out of the trunk, I said, keeping my voice low enough so that Steve, moving to the front, couldn't hear. 'You call me after you get up and after you decide how you want to handle things. If you want me to get in touch with my police friend, I'll need some time to get in touch with him. If you want to simply call your husband, well, let me know. OK with you?'

'Yes. I don't think I'll be calling Teddy. You'll hear from me. Oh, but I don't have your number.'

'C'mon, I'll carry your bag in for you.'

While she checked in, the clerk looking like he was still half asleep, I jotted down my cell number.

'OK,' she said heading back out the door, 'I'll wait for you to call.'

Steve didn't ask any questions until we had gotten close to downtown

San Francisco. Traffic was brisk on the Bayshore and got brisker as we got closer to the downtown area. I chose to stay on the Bayshore until we got close to the downtown district where it would simply run out of steam to become just another two-way city street.

My plan was to take the off ramp on to the Embarcadero, a four-lane street that curved around the waterfront to the entrance to the Golden Gate Bridge. I was damn busy trying to think of a way to get the briefcase out of the trunk without Steve seeing it before we got to my place. I didn't feel like coming up with an explanation, although it probably would have been easier.

Without knowing it, my partner in crime solved the problem.

'All right, Bern. Let me in on it. What're you and the sweet soon-to-be divorced lady planning?'

'Soon to be divorced?'

'You didn't think I was going to sleep through all that and miss out, did you?'

'Sneaky Steve, huh? Anyway, if you heard anything, you heard enough to know that we're not planning anything.'

'I didn't hear it all, but I did catch the words divorce and good attorney bandied about. Anyway, it only makes sense. She was working awfully hard to get away from the old fart.' I heard him chuckle. 'At least she had a new boyfriend and was willing to disappear with the money. That probably didn't change much when Tony the Boy Wonder got the jump on her. So, what's she up to now?'

'She said she didn't want to go out to Saratoga this morning, didn't want to face her husband just yet. I gave her my number and she'll call me later. She's working on something. Something she wouldn't tell me about but that happened back when they were in Argentina. Whatever it is, she thinks it's ammunition to use against Gussling in divorce proceedings. All she asked was if we had any contacts with the San Francisco police department.'

'Which we don't. Oh, wait a minute, how about that cop that came calling after you had your run-in with Pistilli? Are you going to talk to him about this thing, whatever it is?'

'Yeah, I think so. But I want to think about it first.'

'Hmm, look,' he said when I stopped for a light at the corner of Broadway, 'why don't you drop me off at my place and go on over to Sausalito. That'll save me from driving over and then coming back and you can pick me up when little Miss Sunshine calls you. Doesn't that make sense?'

Makes sense, I didn't say out loud, and answers the briefcase problem. I took a left on Broadway and drove up one of the hills that San Francisco is famous for to Gouch Street. His apartment was bigger than mine but still it was only a one-bedroom place. I had little worry that he'd ask me to stay over.

Leaving him standing in front of his apartment building, I drove off, fighting sleep all the way across the bridge to my hovel in Sausalito. No matter how tired I was, I didn't forget to get both my overnight case and the briefcase out of the car. The overnight bag was thrown into a corner of my living-room-bedroom, the briefcase went to the back of the closet.

CHAPTER FORTY-NINE

My last thought before falling asleep was that I should set the alarm clock. There was no way something as small as my cell phone would wake me up. But it did.

I'd left it on the kitchen counter; it and the little microwave took up pretty much all of that level area.

'Yeah,' I snarled. Standing with the phone to the side of my head I looked out the back window to see what kind of day I was missing. Typical San Francisco bay overcast. The low, solid cloud-cover was a washed-out grey. Looking for shadows down on the street I couldn't see any. That meant the sun hadn't burned through very far yet. Probably wasn't more than nine or so. I hadn't looked.

'Mr Gould?' It was Claire. Of course it was, who else would be calling me at this time on a dirty overcast Monday morning?

Monday. The past weekend had been one of the longest in my life.

'Good morning,' I answered, trying to sound a lot more awake and cheerful than I was. 'I gather you're up and ready to fight the battle?'

'Fight the battle? Oh, you mean the divorce. Yes. I've talked to a girlfriend, someone I knew in school. She's gone through four husbands and has done quite well for herself. She recommended someone. I called the man and have an appointment to see him at four this afternoon. Are you still willing to help me?'

'Yes. I'll set something up with my friend from the City's finest. Now, do you want me to come pick you up or have you some other plan for that?'

'If you would come get me, I'd appreciate it. Teddy'll be at the office by now. If you will run me out to Saratoga, I'll pick up a few things.'

'I hope those things are what you want to share with Quincy.'

Her soft laugh was back to sounding evil. 'You better believe it. After talking to Maddie, well, I'm more than ready.'

'OK, let me get a little breakfast and make a couple calls. Are you carrying your cell?'

She gave me the number. While I was pouring milk into a bowl of cereal I punched in Steve's number. The milk was only a day or so past its use-by date and didn't smell exactly right but it was all I had. Steve answered after half a dozen rings. It was clear that I had woken him up.

'Yeah?'

'Good morning, sunshine.' I decided not to be grumpy. 'Hope I'm not disturbing you this fine and lovely morning.'

'Ah, Christ. My mouth tastes like I'd drunk too much musty cheap rum last nght. What time is it?'

'You know, I don't really know. Haven't paid any attention. I called to see if you were up and ready to get things taken care of today. Claire Gussling just called and she's all set. Has an appointment with a divorce attorney and everything.'

'Man, it didn't take her long, did it? OK, what're we going to do? Take her to her husband or to the insurance company, or what?'

'Right now she wants to be picked up and taken out to Saratoga.'

'Whoa up there, partner. I've been doing some thinking on that. Look, you're getting into something with this lady, something that I don't think I want to know about. All I want to do is get my hands on the money we got coming. That's all. So, let's do it this way. We get her to Gussling. The ten per cent is coming from him. Then if you want to do a deal with the lovely Claire, you're on your own. But as your best bud, I gotta warn you. Be damn careful. This woman is a shark. I've met her kind before.'

'I won't argue with you on that. I've got an idea that she's about to hand the police her husband's head on a platter. Once she gives whatever she's holding on her old man to Quincy, I'm out of it. Call it my good deed for the day.'

'OK. But first, let's make sure we get our money.'

My next call was the number on the back of Lieutenant Quincy's business card. He answered right away but didn't sound much happier than Steve had when I woke him up.

'Yeah?'

'Lieutenant Jonathan Quincy?'

'Yeah, what do you want?'

I kept my tone calm and friendly, even putting on a big shit-eating smile just as Steve would. 'This is Bernie Gould. You might recall me as the poor innocent working stiff who accidentally got involved for a brief time with your best friend, Guido Pistilli.'

'Yeah? Innocent? Accident? The jury's still out on that one. And that reminds me, I'll be around to talk to you real soon.'

'How about if we meet this morning? You can buy me a cup of coffee and we can share information.'

'You ready to make a clean breast of what your association with that creep Pistilli was all about? Or do you want to get that fake kidnap story you told me off your chest?'

'Ah, well, maybe a little bit of both or maybe something completely different.'

'OK, I guess I can afford to spend a couple minutes listening. And maybe I'll have something to tell you, too. How about we get together at that so-called restaurant over there in Sausalito? Lou Lou's. I'll be tied up until about two. That suit you?'

'Two this afternoon at Lou Lou's sounds like just what the doctor ordered. See you.'

The taste of the milk-coated cereal wasn't all that good but I was hungry and ate it before getting dressed and driving over to pick up Steve. I thought I'd let him explain to Claire Gussling why we had to go see her husband before I took her out to her house in Saratoga.

CHAPTER FIFTY

When we had dropped her off at the Merriott she'd been wearing the slinky dress that had gone up and down on the night's drive like a window shade. This morning when we pulled up at almost the same place we'd dropped her off she was just coming out of the office. This time she was wearing a full skirt of some kind of heavier material and a matching jacket. Thick ruffles covered the front of her white blouse. Where before she'd been wearing sandals, in the morning sunlight I saw she now had on elegant looking shoes with high heels.

'Maddie brought me some clothes,' she explained as she got into the passenger's side. 'When we talked this morning, I explained that I hadn't a thing to wear, especially when going to face Teddy. She's a real jewel. Do you think I look OK for what is going to happen?'

Steve, I'd noticed, had given her a very thorough looking-over; he smiled and, after closing her door for her, climbed into the back seat.

'You look ready for anything,' he said.

'Where are we going first?'

I waited but Steve didn't answer. 'First stop is to pick up the money your husband is paying for rescuing you.' I had to hold up a hand to stop her from interrupting.

'Yes; that isn't how you said you wanted it to work out, but it's the best way. Neither Steve nor I want any problems from all this and there might be if we simply drop you off at your house.'

She didn't say anything for a bit, then smiled. 'I guess you're right. I'll have to face him sooner or later and this is best for you. OK, and then what?'

'Then we go out to your place. After that, you and I, and Steve if he wants to, will have coffee with a Lieutenant Jonathan Quincy, SFPD.'

Steve cut in. 'That's where you leave me out, old buddy. I'll stop by the bank and deposit my share of the money and see what's on Frank Gorman's list. You think you might want to go back to working with me, Bern?'

'Uh huh. Not right now, Steve. I want to get back to that story I'm working on. See if I can get it going again.'

'OK.' He sat back and started looking out the window.

'So anyway,' I went back to where I was, 'we'll have a meeting with Quincy. You tell him what you want and, well, that's that. I've helped you and that's the end of it.'

'For you,' she laughed, again that little evil sounding laugh. 'For me and my soon to be ex-husband, it'll only be the beginning.'

'OK, then. Steve, you mind if we borrow your car for the afternoon? I'll drop it by later. Maybe you and I can go have a beer or something.'

'OK with me.'

One hates to admit being a coward, but I am. When we got to the offices of Havershack Industries, I stayed back, letting Steve go right behind the well-dressed Mrs Gussling into Gussling's office.

The receptionist sitting behind the big curved desk at Havershack Industries, Inc smiled at seeing Mrs Gussling and picked up a phone. After saying a few words she waved us on. Clarie knew the way.

I moved ahead when we saw the door with Theodore Gussling in gold paint on it and held it for them. I needn't have bothered.

'I'm glad to see you safe, dear,' Gussling said, not getting up from behind his desk to greet his wife. 'I was very worried.'

'Yes, I can imagine. Teddy, please pay these men for the work they did. I have to say, they have done a very fine job.'

Steve and I stood there, not sure what, if anything, we could say. We didn't have to worry. Dear Teddy was already pulling a big cheque book from a desk drawer. Without looking up, he wrote out a cheque signing it with a flourish, and tore it free.

'I think you'll find this is what we agreed on. Gentlemen, I thank you very much for handling this little matter for me. For us.'

Steve took the cheque, looked at it and nodded. I smiled at Claire and we turned to walk out.

'Oh, Mr Gould,' Claire called softly, 'would you mind waiting? I'll only be a moment.'

I nodded.

Oh, boy. That was as cold as it could get. Worse even than when Inez had walked out on me. Women. I could only shake my head.

CHAPTER FIFTY-ONE

After dropping Steve off at the corner of Geary Street and Market, right in front of the massive Bank of California building that housed Frank Gorman's office I drove Claire to Saratoga. We didn't have much to talk about so the trip down and back was silent. She didn't spend much time at the house, I waited in the car.

When she got back in the front bucket seat I noticed she was carrying a large envelope.

'I trust you have enough to entertain the good Lieutenant,' I said, nodding to where the packet rested on her lap. She nodded and unlike on the long drive up from LA, she kept her feet under the dash and her knees together.

'If he really is a good police officer, it should be sufficient. All I can hope is that he moves on the information I'm going to hand him right away. I doubt it'll be long before my soon-to-be-ex is served with the divorce papers.'

'No promises. All I'm going to do is introduce you two and walk away. That's all you asked for.'

'Uh, Bernie,' she softened a little, the first time since I'd picked her up at the Marriott. 'I really would appreciate it if you'd stick around a moment, not just get up and leave. I'll feel better if you're there.'

Well, Quincy did say he had something to talk to me about. I nodded. I'd stick around.

It didn't surprise me when Claire said she'd never been to Lou Lou's Bar and Grill before. She wasn't a Lou Lou's kind of woman. The lunch crowd was beginning to thin out when we walked in and even in Sausalito people were so used to seeing beautifully sexy women that nobody really stared at her. Not really.

We were a few minutes late; traffic across the Golden Gate Bridge was down to a single lane going in our direction, someone was filming a movie scene. The bridge, being one of the most recognizable structures in California, had a history of serving as a backdrop for movies. I remember reading not long ago about the moviemaker who got permission to set up his cameras in order to film a 'day in the life' documentary of the bridge. It pissed the bridge officials off when they learned that what he was really filming was any and all suicides. In the year his cameras were rolling he got nineteen jumpers on film.

Today's moviemaking might have made us a little late but it didn't matter. Lieutenant Jonathan Quincy was reading the morning newspaper when we walked in.

'Hope you weren't waiting long,' I said, holding a chair for Claire and going through the introductions.

It was clear that Fat Henry liked pretty women; he brought menus over to the table himself. Standing a little behind and to the side next to Claire, he was looking down as he dropped the plastic-coated menus on the table. He looked disgusted when he saw there was no cleavage for him to see.

'Let me know when you decide,' he said, already moving away, 'and I'll have one of the girls come take your order.'

Both Quincy and I laughed, Claire didn't understand why but didn't ask. She had other things on her mind and proved it by carefully placing her large envelope on top of the menus and keeping her hand on it.

'Lieutenant, in here are photos of girls being murdered.' She didn't stop after dropping that bombshell. 'The man is my husband, Theodore Gussling. This took place in Buenos Aires and the four girls in the pictures are all *vagabundas*. It's unlikely that anyone will be able to remember who they were. The streets are filled with homeless girls and boys down there in BA. It was when my husband managed the sales office there. I'm sure the police in BA will be interested in solving these murders.'

She pushed the envelope across, then put her hands in her lap, watching Quincy. Without rushing, the police officer picked up the envelope and shook out the photos. From where I was sitting I wasn't able to see clearly what the pictures showed. Quincy could and for a long moment, using a fingernail to move them aside, one by one, he studied them.

'When were these taken, Mrs Gussling?'

'Recently. I took the first set when he brought the girl to our house. That was just after the first of the year. He'd never done that before, bringing his girls to the house. That first time, he didn't expect me to be there. After that time I made sure whenever he showed signs of going out he'd think I was also going to be gone. I'd leave before him and then wait. After he'd left the house, I'd go back and get my camera. He would bring the girls in through the garage and down to the wine cellar. That's where he'd do it, down in the cellar.'

'And you didn't think to help the girls?'

Claire's smile was thin but full of malice. She didn't say anything, just shook her head slowly.

Quincy tried again. 'Why didn't you take these to the police down there? Why wait until now?'

'I eventually let poor Teddy know that I had the photos. My plan was to blackmail him with them but before I could he was ordered back here to the company office. He knows I have them and when I told him this morning that I was seeing a divorce attorney he just about had a heart attack. He knows I'll use them to get everything he's got in the settlement.'

'And that's why you're giving them to me.' It wasn't a question.

Still smiling Claire pushed her chair away from the table and stood up. 'Yes. And I was careful to wipe them clean of fingerprints before placing them in the envelope. If you do what you should, the police down there will be interested, don't you think? That should make my getting everything quite easy, wouldn't you say? That's all I want.'

212

CHAPTER FIFTY-TWO

Claire, holding that smug look on her face, didn't even nod in my direction but got up and walked out just as a waitress came over to take out order.

'Hey, you guys causing that woman trouble?'

'No,' Quincy said, shaking his head. 'Bring us a couple bottles of beer, will you? Thanks.' He went back to studying the photos.

Before she came back with the beer I moved my chair around so I was facing him. Leaning back, I couldn't see anything of the pictures; I didn't want to.

I had drunk about half of my beer before he sighed and carefully shoved the photos back into the envelope.

'OK, Bernie, tell me what you know about this woman.'

I hesitated, trying to decide how much to tell him. He didn't give me a choice.

'Look. This isn't the time to get cute. This woman could be in a lot of trouble. If it turns out these photos are real, by not reporting the murder she becomes as guilty as the man. You don't want to get caught trying to protect her, trust me.'

Taking a deep breath, I nodded. 'That is if it can be proved that they are real. And that the law in Argentina is anything like ours. But I'll tell you what you want to know because it seems to me if he was killing girls down there he might be doing the same thing here. Didn't you say something about a serial killer being at work here in the Bay Area? I seem to recall reading something about it in the papers, a series of rapes and murders?'

Quincy sat staring at me for a long moment before lifting the beer bottle to his lips and drinking. 'Yeah, that crossed my mind, too. These photos,' he tapped the envelope, 'are pretty damn close to similar ones taken at the scene of at least one of the strangulations. For a minute one of them looked a lot like that girl who was found over at Fort Funston, the first one. Now, let's hear it.'

So, over another bottle of beer, I told him everything, from when Steve asked me to help with the ransom to driving back to the city last night. The only thing I left out was the part about Antonio Jardin's accident with the freight train. He didn't need to know that.

Back when I was a working reporter, when I was about to interview someone, I'd always haul out my little journalist notebook and pen and take notes. Later when it came time to write the story, I wouldn't be able to read my pen scratchings but the person I'd been talking to wouldn't know that. The notebook and pen were props. People expected the reporter to take notes; that's what reporters did. Like most journalists, though, I didn't need them. Oh, maybe once in a while to remind me of certain things or to back up the quotes, but all in all my memory of what was said was enough. Quincy didn't take any notes while I talked. I figured his memory was good enough.

'And you guys brought her back and dumped her at her husband's office? Was anything said when she walked in?'

'They were like strangers. He didn't get off his butt. Stayed behind his desk. "Hi, I'm glad to see you back safe and sound. Here, fellas, here's a cheque to go with my thanks." She just stood there with a cold smile on her puss.'

'Yeah, she strikes me that that'd be the case. OK. So I'll go back to the office and start the groundwork. See if we can somehow tie him into our rape/murder cases.'

'Will you be calling the police in Argentina?'

'Naw. I'll turn that over to the district attorney and let his office decide what to do. Likely it'll end up with the photos being sent down there and that'll be all. Let them deal with it. Meanwhile we've got a possible lead that we didn't have before. I guess I can thank you for that.'

I liked that. Having a police officer thank me for something was a new one. Again, back in the olden days of my newspaper servitude the cops were more likely to be yelling at me to keep out of their hair. I liked it this way.

Quincy wasn't through. 'There's one other person I'd like to thank. It's doubtful that I'll ever know who he is, though. It happened while you were off chasing to Tijuana. I got a phone call. An anonymous tip. The guy told me where I could find enough evidence to nail your old friend, Pistilli. Yeah. The caller didn't give out his name or say how he knew to call and ask for me, though.'

'Probably from one of your business cards, don't you think?'

'Yeah, maybe. Anyway the caller asked that I don't spend too much time trying to find him, so I won't. But if I ever did discover his identity I'd have to shake his hand. We'd been after that creep, Pistilli, for a long time and now we got him. He's been arraigned on a whole truckload of charges, most having to do with the sale of illegal drugs. The feds found a whole damn drug warehouse under that casino Pistilli was running.'

He smiled and went on. 'Funny thing, though. You remember those two cretins that did Pistilli's dirty work for him? Sure you do. Arnie Murphy and Hugo Montero? I seem to recall you telling me something about them asking you to visit their boss. Well, anyhow, when we busted Pistilli we thought we'd get those two at the same time. We didn't. They weren't around. Fact is, there hasn't been hide nor hair of them seen in the last three or four days. We know they were involved, we found their wallets and got their prints off the SUV that was sitting in the casino's lot and down in that basement.' He shook his head again. 'It's sure strange, where they could be.'

I didn't think I had anything to offer him on that, either. He did a good job of shaking my hand when we left the place, though.

CHAPTER FIFTY-THREE

The rest of the day I spent back in my hovel of an apartment trying to get something going with the story I'd been working on. It had all been there, back when I'd first thought it through. It only became muddled when I tried to put it down on paper. Or rather on the computer screen. This couldn't be what I'd heard described as writer's block, there was nothing to block. Damn.

The buzzing of my phone saved the day. To make it even better, the little piece of high-tech equipment happened to be lying right there.

'Hello.'

'Hey there, Bernie. It's me, your old buddy, Son Cardonsky. Look, I was hoping to catch you. I'm just passing through and can't stop long. You gonna be around for the next hour or so?'

Son Cardonsky. Well, I guess it could be worse. 'Yeah, I'll be here. Where are you?'

'Oh, just coming across the bridge. Be there in a couple minutes,' he said and hung up.

I sat there, staring at the empty screen, thinking about Son. Wonder if he's heard about Pistilli's problems? Maybe I'll have some good news for the damn fool.

He hadn't.

'No, what about Pistilli?' he asked after coming in, looking around and accepting a cup of coffee. All I had was instant and that was good enough. I certainly didn't want to make things too good for him. What I wanted was for him to go away. 'I've been very careful to stay as far from him and his two sidekicks as I can.'

'I have it on good authority that Pistilli is going away. Multiple drug charges, I'm told.' Seeing his look of disbelief, I explained. 'That's straight from a new friend of mine, a member of the San Francisco police force.' I quickly told him what Quincy had told me about finding a drug warehouse and tying Pistilli to it.

'And how about his hired thugs? They get rounded up, too?'

'No. According to my cop friend, those two have disappeared. He told me because he knew they had been bothering me.'

Son leaned back against the tiny counter. After taking a little sip of the coffee, he'd put the still full cup on the drain board and ignored it. I didn't blame him. It tasted like I imagined liquid cordovan shoepolish would taste. I put my cup next to his, wondering if I'd have to get a dangerous substance removal permit before dumping it down the drain.

'Well,' Son said after thinking about it for a bit, 'I guess if Pistilli's out of the picture, and his two boys are missing in action, then you and I have nothing to worry about. That the way you see it?'

I had to think about that a minute myself. If I agreed he would probably feel safe and I'd be saddled with his friendship for evermore. Or until he screwed up again. And he would. No. I decided to take the easy way out. Of course then he made me feel bad about it.

'Son, I'm not so sure about how safe it is. I mean, according to Lieutenant Quincy, you might have been identified as having something to do with a certain armoured car robbery. If the big boss is gone, it might be that the hired help are looking for some kind of pay-off. Hiding out can get expensive. But then I guess you'd know about that, wouldn't you? So, feel safe? I don't know. Myself, with Pistilli about to face some heavy time in San Quentin, I imagine he won't be a bother to me. But those two, Hugo and Murphy, do they know about you? I seem to remember you saying something about them having a discussion with you about a card game.'

'Damn, I never looked at it like that. You're probably right. It wouldn't do to be seen around town for a while. OK,' he said, taking a long white business-sized envelope out of an inside pocket, 'here. This is the money I told you I was holding for you. Your share.'

I must have looked the question. 'C'mon, Bernie, you know. You earned a share of both the card game and the armoured car. It was your plans, remember? You don't think I'd forget my "angel" do you?'

See what I mean? Now, holding the envelope I felt bad about letting him think there were still bad guys searching for him. Funny thing, though, when he waved as he went out the door, that bad feeling disappeared like the famous San Francisco fog getting burned up by the morning sun.

CHAPTER FIFTY-FOUR

The next morning, that'd be Tuesday, I deposited most of the money Son left me in my new bank account. If I didn't get too extravagant I'd have enough to live on for another month or so without having to go do any jobs with Steve.

I called him to let him know. 'Hey, man. How are you doing? Your friend Gorman have a list for you to work on?'

'Yeah, and I could use your help on a couple of them.'

'Nope, that's what this call is about. I come into a little money and have a new story idea to work on. Come on around in a week or so and I'll read the outline, see what you think.'

'Yeah? Well, don't forget, I've got your half of the kidnap pay-off here. But dammit, Bernie. I'm serious, I could really use your help.'

'Well, give me the rest of the week to get this started. Then, well, maybe.'

'OK. I'll call you sometime over the weekend.'

And that was that. After filling the little refrigerator and laying in a supply of mid-range red wine I went to work. The idea I had was all about what I'd gotten involved in, you know, with Pistilli and Son. My story wouldn't be on that exactly, but on the armoured car hold-up. Instead of rewriting a western drama about a stagecoach robbery, I'd make it an armoured car heist. Throw in a subplot using the casino and Pistilli's drug dealing. Maybe work in the sexual aspects Claire tried to use on me. All that should make a good story.

I got to work.

Nobody bothered me for two whole days. I'll tell you, I was burning up the keyboard. Until someone knocked on my door.

My mind was still on the story as I headed over to see who it was. I stopped before I got there. What if it was Inez? How would I handle that?

Whoever it was knocked again. Heavier, this time. That wouldn't be Inez. It was Lieutenant Quincy.

'Well, how long does it take you to get across the room to answer the door?' he growled and pushed by me.

I didn't respond. Turning around, he took a deep breath, smiled and handed me a bottle of whisky.

'Here, in honour of our celebration I got a bottle of good Scotch. None of that cheap coffee you gave me last time. You do have a couple glasses, don't you?'

That's all I had, two glasses. One of them had been used that morning for my orange juice and the other for my glass of wine with dinner the night before. As I quickly washed them up, I asked what we were celebrating.

'The arrest and imminent conviction of one Theodore Gussling on six counts,' he said proudly. 'We had enough but when we went out to his house we found the black van he'd used. Boy, he hadn't bothered a bit to clean it up. Anyway, this morning he was charged with three counts of first degree murder and three of rape. There're a couple other counts, too. Kidnapping, deprivation of liberty and stuff like that. First degree murder is the best, though. He'll get the needle for sure. And it's all due to your good work.'

I held the glasses while he poured. Putting the bottle on the table next to my laptop, we clicked glasses and drank. It had been a long time since I'd tasted any hard liquor. Wine and a beer now and again was more my speed. This could change that, though.

Taking a small sip, I felt the liquor flow over my tongue and simply fade away like a morning mist. It never got as far as my throat. Delicious. I took another little sip to see if the sensation would repeat itself. It did. Now I was smiling.

'Man, that's good stuff. You sure it's legal?'

Quincy laughed. 'Don't get the habit, old son. This stuff is damn expensive. I doubt you can keep doing enough of the good work helping out the law to afford many bottles of it.'

'Yeah, that's right. You said we were celebrating my good work? How do you figure that?'

'Oh, don't bullshit me, my friend. You were the one who got that crazy wife of his to turn him over. You knew what it was all about. Too bad there's no reward. You could use it to move out of this hovel.'

'Hey, I like it here. Nobody but people like you come bother me.'

'Yeah.' Looking around he nodded. 'But you got to admit, a lot of your good work was just dumb luck.'

'Now you didn't have to say that. Anyway, what part of it do you consider luck?'

'That phony kidnapping that never got reported. If you hadn't been working on that, you wouldn't have got close enough to the sweet innocent Mrs Gussling to have her tip you off about her old man. You got to admit, it was lucky you were in the right place at the right time.'

I was focusing on the Scotch and didn't comment.

'But that's all history now, isn't it. What with all the talking she did, making sure we got enough on her old man, she let slip a lot about that so-called kidnapping. Enough that she got a bad case of foot-in-the-mouth disease. The DA thinks she'll end up at the Tehachapi Woman's Prison. Probably get five to ten for attempted felony insurance fraud.'

Another sip of Scotch slipped across my tongue.

'You and your partner made a few bucks out of that, didn't you?' I nodded. 'And that's what she said her boyfriend got, a few bucks out of the deal. She thinks her tennis pro boyfriend got away with the two million dollars in ransom money and is somewhere down in Mexico spending it. Is that the way you figure it?'

'Hell, I don't know where he is. Burning in hell for all I know. The two million? Well, as far as that's concerned, I do know that for a while there it was a question who was going to get away with being able to double-cross whom first.'

'Whom?'

'Yeah, I was a journalist once upon a time.'

'Ah, God save us all.'

He reached over to pour another finger of the fine liquor in my glass. Sitting there quietly, enjoying the Scotch, I was trying to figure out how to get him out of there.

'Bernie, you really got to get another place to live. Dammit, it's musty-smelling in here. I'll bet you haven't had a window open in days.'

He was right. I hadn't noticed, but now I did.

It turned out to be a good thing, though. We had one more drink from the bottle and he said something about a meeting. He left the bottle.

CHAPTER FIFTY-FIVE

Steve called me on Saturday and we had lunch at Lou Lou's. I hadn't finished the Scotch that Quincy had brought over and I thought long and hard about inviting my partner up for a drink. I didn't.

'Now, Bern, let's talk a little about helping me out. It's a BMW. A flash rig bought by a young wheeler-dealer but not paid for. Hasn't made the last four payments and hasn't responded to any letters from the bank. I could use your help.'

We were in one of the booths, slick vinyl seats, the kind that if they weren't pretty well worn you'd slip right out of, with the Formica table between us. We had each ordered the house special; the hamburger that helped make Lou Lou's famous. Well, one of the reasons, anyhow. They were made with a half pound of ground top sirloin that Fat Henry made into large patties using a secret mix of spices, shredded cheese and bits of jalapeño peppers. Having finished our meal, we were sucking on bottles of beer, trying to put the fire out without losing the good taste of the sandwich.

I sat back thinking about things. The story I was working on was simply flowing. Since starting it I hadn't had any trouble putting out the 2,000 words a day. I mean the words were just gushing. That left me with enough time to spend the afternoons visiting a couple art galleries over in the city. I'd have time to help him out.

There were a couple other things I'd have to make decisions about soon. First there was that briefcase with the two million dollars sitting in the back of my closet. I hadn't bothered to even look at it since tossing it back there. A couple of my shirts had fallen off their hangers and I'd left them there, half covering the worn leather piece of luggage. Sooner or later I'd have to come up with a story to tell Steve. After all, half of that money was his, wasn't it?

Then there was Inez. Should I call her? I laughed silently about that. Man, if I called her and told her I was a published writer and was hot on the next novel, it was a sure bet she'd want to see about our getting back together.

'Ha!' I did laugh out loud. If she knew about the money in the closet, she'd be on me like a suntan.

'What's so funny? Bern, listen. I can't do this BMW thing alone. You gotta help me out?'

I nodded. 'OK. No problem. I'll help.'

Inez and the ransom money would have to wait.